Tina McElroy Ansa

Tina McElroy Ansa's first novel BABY OF THE FAMILY was named a Notable Book of the Year by the *New York Times* for two years running. UGLY WAYS, her second, was a bestseller in America and won the prestigious Blackboard Award for 1995 Book of the Year. Her new novel is THE HAND I FAN WITH, also published by Sceptre. Tina McElroy Ansa lives with her husband on St Simons Island, off the coast of Georgia.

SCEPTRE

Also by Tina McElroy Ansa and available from Sceptre

Baby of the Family
The Hand I Fan With

Ugly
Ways

TINA McELROY ANSA

SCEPTRE

Copyright © 1993 Tina McElroy Ansa

First published in 1993 by Harcourt Brace & Company
First published in the UK in 1996 by Hodder and Stoughton
A division of Hodder Headline PLC
A Sceptre Paperback

10 9 8 7 6 5 4 3 2 1

A CIP catalogue record for this book is   ♦
available from the British Library

ISBN 0 340 67505 5

Printed and bound in Great Britain by
Cox and Wyman Ltd, Reading, Berkshire

Hodder and Stoughton
A division of Hodder Headline PLC
338 Euston Road
London NW1 3BH

For Jonée,
whose love sustains me

Acknowledgments

I am blessed with a family of friends and supporters who contributed to me and my writing of this novel.

I wish to thank my family, especially my sister Marian M. Kerr, for being there for me, my editor Claire Wachtel at Harcourt Brace who listened to me, laughed with me, and understood me; the friends on my island home who have bolstered my strength and been strong for me when I needed them, especially novelist Eugenia Price, author Joyce Blackburn, artist Ana Bel Lee Washington, and Susan Oliver.

I am grateful to Tuck, Ladysmith, and, in particular, Zora, for their invaluable companionship.

And I thank St. Simons Island, which continues to offer me the beauty, peace, and acceptance of home.

Ugly
Ways

∫

CHAPTER 1

"Come get me."

When Betty picked up the receiver of the cream-colored wall phone, the voice on the other end was already speaking. It sounded as if it came from the grave.

"Come get me. Come . . . get . . . me. Come . . . get . . . me," the voice kept repeating slowly, deliberately, as if each word carried some specific meaning.

Betty turned her head away from the phone and massaged her temples.

"Damn," she said to her sister Emily, who was sitting at the rec room bar looking at herself in the mirror through rows of glasses and leafing through a stack of her father's science fiction magazines. Emily fiddled with her thick black shiny bangs awhile and finally pulled them back behind her ears with the rest of her hair, blow-dried straight and even nearly down to her shoulders. "We ain't even had Mudear's funeral yet and the Lovejoy family's already falling apart. It's Annie Ruth."

Emily bit her lower lip and shook her head slowly.

Betty took a deep breath. "Annie Ruth," she said serenely into the receiver. "Annie Ruth, where are you?"

"Come . . . get . . . me" was the only response.

"Sugar, you have to tell me where you are for me to come get you. Now, calm down and stop acting so silly. Tell me where you are. Are you here in town? Are you here in Mulberry?"

There was a long pause. Betty could just imagine her baby sister dramatically brushing her soft thin hair back out of her face with the flat of her free hand, then sighing deeply. Betty could hear her labored breathing over the phone.

"Uh-huh, I'm home," Annie Ruth finally said.

"Okay, you're home. Now, where are you at home? You're not out on the street, are you? What's all that noise? Just be quiet for a minute and let me listen. . . .

"Is that some kind of a PA system? You can't be at the train station, can you? No, not this soon. The airport?"

"Yes," Annie Ruth said.

"The airport?"

"Yes."

Betty sighed. "We're on our way. Stay by the phones. You hear me? Stay right there by the phones."

Emily didn't say a word. She just picked up her sister's car keys, tossed Betty's purse to her, and, grabbing her red-fringed cowboy jacket and Betty's beige light cashmere shawl, headed out the door toward the newly painted double carport.

Betty stopped long enough at the small table by the front door
to scribble a note to their father on a yellow Post-It——"Poppa,
we've gone to get Annie Ruth"——and stick it on the mirror over
the table before following her sister's rounded red-fringed figure
to her own big silver Town Car with the black fabric roof. Her
butt looked like two ripe apples.

"I'll drive your car," Emily said as she slipped behind the steering
wheel into the thick black velour contour seat and threw the coats
in the back.

Even though it was a chilly fall day, Betty rolled down the
window as soon as she got in the car. Her sister pulled out of the
driveway and headed down the narrow suburban street past modern brick houses that all looked the same. Only their parents'
house stood out from the other cookie-cutter ranch-style and split-
level brick and wooden houses that each had the carport on either
the left or the right. Even from the end of the street where Emily
made the turn under an ornate black wrought-iron sign stretched
between two mortar columns that said SHERWOOD FOREST, Betty
could see the big screened porch attached to the back of her parents' house and the grove of trees and lush vegetation growing in
the front and back yards. Next to the manicured lawns and thin
rows of shrubbery surrounding the other houses, her parents' home
looked as if it had been picked up from a tropical plantation and
dropped in place in a different zone.

Opening the car window was the one concession Betty made
to her sister about smoking cigarettes. Even though Emily smoked
enough marijuana to keep a small country's economy going, Betty
knew Emily couldn't stand the smell of cigarette smoke getting in
her hair and clothes.

The brisk wind blowing in Betty's face and tousling her short
permed hair felt good. Emily watched her out of the corner of her

eye as Betty smoothed her hair back into place. Even after it was arranged as before, she continued to run her fingers through it—really just over the top of it because it was hardly long enough for her to get her fingers through. Betty continued raking her square manicured nails—shining with clear gloss, no color—through the ringlets at the nape of her neck as she reached in her purse for her cigarettes and matches and lit up the first cigarette she had had in two hours. The bracing wind and the first lungful of smoke sort of brought her back to herself. Ever since she had gotten the message from Poppa on her answering machine that Mudear had passed during the night, she had felt as if she were drifting in and out of herself, almost dizzy.

As she smoked, she continued to play with the short hair at the nape of her neck.

"Well, it looks like everything is already arranged," Emily said as she drove down the long country road that led to the interstate. She could have driven it with her eyes closed. She had just taken this same route coming down from her home in Atlanta. She sighed a bit, but it was more for changes she saw along the side of the road than for thoughts of her mother's funeral. It seemed housing construction was going up everywhere she looked, uprooting the trees and greenery she loved so much about this part of Mulberry, turning the woods of pines and pin oaks and chinaberry trees into the barren stretches developers called subdivisions and tiny office parks. The smell of the razed pine and cedar trees reminded her of Christmas, not a happy thought. From time to time there would suddenly appear stretches of roadside that looked the way it had when Emily was a child. Broadleaf oaks tucked in so tightly with short squat pines and prospering cypress seedlings and ferns that one would think there wouldn't be enough room for a group of tall Georgia pines to grow there, too. But just as suddenly the thick green clump of trees would disappear, leaving fields of scorched-looking grass.

As recently as five years ago, Emily thought as she scanned the countryside, all of this was rows and rows of corn or beans or just fields for grazing cattle or goats. Along the interstate and state highways around Mulberry there had been peach orchards and pecan groves with homemade signs tacked to trees promising, "Freshly Sheeled Pecans" or "The Meatiest Pecans in Middle Georgia." Seeing the land surrounding her small hometown lying exposed and useless made her feel as violated as she thought the earth must have felt.

"Well," Betty said as she stubbed her half-smoked cigarette out in the already overflowing car ashtray. "Most everything. Poppa has already done a lot. I'm gonna do Mudear's hair and makeup sometime. Poppa said Mudear didn't say anything or leave any instructions on how she wanted services handled specifically."

"I can hardly believe it. That's not like her," Emily said.

Betty didn't reply.

"I would have thought she would have left stacks of written messages and maybe recorded videotapes of her explicit instructions on how she wanted just everything conducted." Emily could almost hear Betty decide not to respond and take her bait. "Yeah, that's not like her at all." Emily pretended to talk casually, keeping her focus on the road.

Betty leaned her head farther out the window a second like a dog in hot weather looking for a refreshing breeze on its tongue. Then, she settled back in her seat.

"I guess you and Poppa made sure it's a closed casket," Emily persisted. "You know how she'd always say, 'Daughters, don't you have a whole lot of strangers and family that don't like me be looking down on me in my casket.' "

Betty sighed again and spoke. "Don't nobody feel like talking about her now, Emily." Then, Betty lit up another cigarette and reached over to punch up a CD to punctuate her statement. As Olitha Adams's voice filled the interior of the car, Emily looked at her sister next to her with her head thrown back on the headrest and accepted that Betty could not be persuaded.

By the time they reached the exit ramp leading to the tiny airport, Betty felt almost herself again and strong enough to deal with Annie Ruth and her theatrics.

As soon as they entered the airport terminal, Betty and Emily saw their younger sister at the end of the short corridor by the airport's only bank of public phones.

"Good God," Emily said. "She's actually sitting in a wheel-chair."

Annie Ruth looked terrible. The dark circles that all the girls in the family had inherited from their father were even more pro-nounced than usual, deeper smudges under Annie Ruth's eyes as if someone with dirty thumbs had wiped away her falling tears. She had obviously applied makeup sometime in the last twelve or so hours, but she hadn't bothered to freshen it lately. Crimson lipstick had left only a rose outline on her full wide lips and dark teal-blue eye shadow was still visible over only one eye.

There was a big scuff on the toe of one of her purple suede high-heeled pumps that made Betty wince because she knew there was no way to repair the damaged spot. Annie Ruth had carelessly thrown her big slouchy suede bag, purple, too, on the floor by the side of the wheelchair.

Her green tweed suit with the short jacket trimmed in amaranth suede at the collar, cuffs, and pockets was a bit wrinkled but so stylish, so good-looking, that both Betty and Emily immediately wondered if there was any way they could fit into it. Even as teenagers, they had never had fights over clothes, or over anything,. for that matter. They loved to wear each other's outfits, intimately digging into each other's closets and drawers for accessories and skirts and jackets to complement their own wardrobes. One of the things they regretted most about living in separate cities was lack of access to each other's clothes.

"I know she sees us," Emily said through clenched teeth as they headed down the nearly deserted airport corridor.

When they reached Annie Ruth, they saw that a skinny blond stewardess stood next to their sister looking panicked and totally unprepared by her experience on the little propeller planes that flew into the Mulberry airstrip for this level of emergency.

"We'll take her," Betty said with a tight smile to the woman, who actually breathed a sigh of relief, pressed a wad of damp air-sickness bags into Betty's hand, and rushed off without saying a word, dragging her luggage cart behind her.

Emily and Betty both squatted down beside Annie Ruth's wheelchair and Betty reached out and smoothed down her sister's wild rufous hair.

Annie Ruth looked as if she had just been pulled thrashing and struggling from the deep end of a pool. She smelled faintly of vomit.

Then, Betty took her hand, squeezed it, and it began.

Outsiders would have called it a game. But it was much too serious and necessary to be called so frivolous a name. It was more of a ritual.

Betty looked into Annie Ruth's face, still streaked with traces of some expensive European makeup, and said, "Once, when I lived in New York that time I ran away, I had an urge for a blind man. Stood outside the Lighthouse for the Blind building all afternoon once 'til I saw one come out that I liked. I bumped into him and pretended it was an accident. We started talking, and I fucked my blind man."

Emily spoke next. "I let a man I worked with stay at my house two nights once because he used the word 'juxtaposition' correctly in a sentence."

Annie Ruth raised the gaze of her brown eyes slowly, tilted her head to one side, she was too weary to play around. She looked from one sister's eyes to the other's and then said, "I fucked a chink once."

Her sisters were speechless. Annie Ruth had won. Emily took one of Annie Ruth's arms and Betty took the other. Then, they gently lifted her from the wheelchair and guided her down the corridor toward the baggage claim and exit.

CHAPTER 2

The three of them headed back under a sign over the corridor that proclaimed, "WELCOME to Mulberry—The Big Little Town in the Heart of Georgia."

Betty, the only one of them who still lived in Mulberry, noticed the people at the airport watching the three of them as they made their way to the baggage claim area. She recognized many of the folks there and knew that in a town the size of Mulberry they all knew who she and her sisters were, too. She motioned for one of the two skycaps to help take Annie Ruth's plum-colored tapestry luggage—five bags in all—off the revolving carousel.

"Where's her Louis Vuitton steamer trunk?" Emily whispered to Betty as she moved to help the skycap.

Betty could feel the commotion they were causing around them as they made their way to the tiny airport parking lot with all the baggage. With so many people looking, Betty thought of what Mudear would say to them when as teenagers they had complained that people seemed to stare at them when they went downtown to shop or to pay the family bills. Mudear would always reply, "Just yell at them, 'Ain't ya'll never seen no crowd of good-looking brown-skinned colored women before?' That'll stop 'em in their tracks."

The sight of the three sisters at the airport—Annie Ruth, a half-madeup, perfumed wreck, still needing to be supported by a sister's firm hand under each arm—all trailed by the skycap, whom Betty knew, too, made even the woman at the Avis rental counter rubberneck around the corner of her booth to get a better look. Betty could already see the tongues wagging. She had always made her living working in beauty shops—the hotbeds of gossip—and she knew from experience that Mulberry had not stopped discussing and dissecting the Lovejoy family since the day Mudear changed.

Years before, it had been Emily, not Annie Ruth, who everyone in town who knew the Lovejoy family felt would be the first one to go crazy. Even some members of the family had thought that Emily would crack first. First, that is, after Mudear. Nearly everyone over the age of forty in Mulberry claimed they knew the date that they said Mudear lost her mind.

"It was one of the coldest winter days we ever had here in Mulberry," women would say, recounting the beginning of Mudear's seclusion. "And she ain't come out of that house since. At least, not during daylight hours. Except to move to that new one in Sherwood Forest. Even then, I don't know nobody who saw her move. And to work in her garden at night. Yeah, at night. Esther always did think she was above the laws of God and man.

"Heck, that woman didn't even come out of the house to go to her own mother's funeral."

Betty would hear the townswomen whisper about her family even as they sat in the specially designed chrome chairs in Lovejoy's 2, her sleek modern beauty shop at the Mulberry Mall, leafing through the latest issues of her magazines and sipping her complimentary coffee, tea, bottled water, and Coke. She would have to talk herself out of leaving the strong-smelling, lye-based straighteners in their hair a few minutes too long, to bald them in retaliation for their talk. She feared a lawsuit when all their hair fell out. But still, she couldn't bring herself to confront the women directly. She had nothing to say in the family's defense. She knew what they said was true. She and her sisters—still little girls—had sat next to Poppa in the hot little church in East Mulberry in front of their grandmother's casket to represent Mudear while Mudear stayed at home looking at T.V. It made Betty mad that Mudear's actions had left her and her sisters so vulnerable, so defenseless, open and raw to the town's gossip. Always had.

So, it was Emily—the middle girl—who everyone in town who knew the family felt would be the next one to lose her mind. There were quite a few citizens of Mulberry who figured it was only a matter of time before all the Lovejoys were seen running up and down the streets of Sherwood Forest half-naked with their hair standing on top of their heads. Some said the whole family had "walking insanity" like other folks had "walking pneumonia." They still went about their daily routines, but as far as people in Mulberry were concerned all the Lovejoys were walking-, talking-, working-, shopping-crazy.

Some townspeople swore you could see it in the way Emily talked . . . through clenched teeth. She also had, even as a child, the habit of unconsciously biting her bottom lip while she thought something over. These habits lent everything she said—even the most mundane statements—an intensity that she rarely wished to express.

Some of her grammar school teachers grew to hate her for her wild eyes and lip biting. "Look at her back there, looking wise and otherwise," Miss Leslie, her second-grade teacher, had muttered to herself at least twice a week for one whole school year.

Emily never went so far as to live up to her mother's epithet of a "raving, ranting maniac." But she came as close to it as she dared and still have enough of an edge to back off. In one of her recurring dreams, Betty saw Emily flitting on the precipice of craziness, an actual ravine. "What an unbelievably insane, foolish thing to do," she remembered saying in her dream. Even awake, when Emily talked, sometimes, Betty could see her just flouncing up to the fanged monster image of craziness and shimmying her shoulders at it. Then, jerking away at the last minute just as insanity reached out its claw for her. She flirted with it.

It was Emily of the 4:00 A.M. long-distance calls. "Now, tell me, Betty, now tell me. Now, if a woman loves a man and she does all she can for him and she tries to make him happy, then, shouldn't that man love her back? Now, tell me, now, isn't that the way it should be?"

Betty would be so sleepy. "Well, Em-Em," Betty would say, trying to speak as if it were noon straight up and she didn't have to rise in a few hours and open up her beauty shop and do some heads. "You know it doesn't always work out that way."

"But if you love him, if he's married or not, it doesn't matter, does it? If you love him and you do all you can for him and you're there for him. Now, tell me, shouldn't that man love you back?"

Betty would even fall into the soft, calm manner of speaking she had used with Emily since childhood, using the pet name for her middle sister, "Em-Em." Her use of it sometimes forced Emily into seeing that she was just talking to her sister Betty, not to her psychiatrist, Dr. Axelton, or to a palm reader or priestess who professed to have all the answers.

It was Emily who drove around her neighborhood in Southwest Atlanta at various hours of the day and night, looking for all the world like a wolf clutching the steering wheel of her red Datsun, her eyes darting dangerously here and there, always in search of something. Atlanta was not so far away. The stories got back to Mulberry.

But it wasn't Emily who went first. It was Annie Ruth. Two years before. Everyone called it a nervous breakdown. Mudear called it a heart attack.

Annie Ruth, an anchor at a television station in Washington, D.C., at the time, checked into an expensive private clinic in Virginia for a rest. Then, when she checked out two weeks later, she took the anchor job at the Los Angeles station that had been trying to hire her for nearly a year.

The word of Annie Ruth's breakdown spread quickly in Mulberry. Mudear went right to work. Over the phone she told Carrie, the one woman she still talked with in town and who still talked with her, "Cut, my baby done gone and had a heart attack. Working in that fast-paced northern city, all that stress and overtime and all that. You know, Carrie, all my girls are working women."

Mudear couldn't help it. She went with the strength. That had been her life's philosophy, at least since her youngest was five, and she much preferred to think of her child falling victim to a heart attack, the disease of the hardworking, rather than letting herself become the plaything of the mind's whim. A nervous breakdown. Mudear couldn't even bring herself to say the words. A nervous breakdown.

It was so weak sounding. A breakdown. "What she got to break down about?" Mudear had asked the walls of her sumptuous bedroom over and over. And then she had badgered her husband when he came home from work in the chalk mines with the same question. "What she got to break down about?"

Even when Betty, considered the strongest of the girls, went through that period when she couldn't stop itching and scratching herself even after she went to the dermatologist and got a soothing lotion that didn't work, she showed up for work every day, helped put on the annual hair and beauty show like always, and made sure dinner was cooked for Mudear and Poppa.

She was only doing what was expected of her. What Mudear expected of her. She could still hear Mudear say, "Save that crazy shit for your own time, now get up off that floor and go on to that cosmetology seminar, like you got some sense."

Taking care of responsibilities, duties, business was always the first priority. If the three girls expected to live out their lives in Mudear's good graces, then they had to produce.

"There's nothing worse than a trifling, slouchy woman. It's okay for a man, what more can you expect? That don't have nothing to do with my girls. Being a trifling man. You know what I expect and you know why I expect it.

"Women who don't care nothing about themselves," Mudear would mutter to herself as she sat by the kitchen window looking out over her yard and overseeing dinner preparation in a flowered housecoat with a flounce at the neckline. "Don't even take baths. Be smelling like the city docks." And her daughters would immediately stop their cleaning or cooking or chopping or washing or frying and begin scrutinizing each other for signs of triflingness, smelling the air around each other. They never felt they could assume that their mother was referring to some event or person far removed from them. They couldn't take that chance.

It was what Betty finally said to Annie Ruth at the airport to get her to walk back to where the car was parked under her own steam.

"Don't be so trifling, Annie Ruth," Betty whispered to her baby sister as Emily showed the skycap the way to the car. "Buck up."

The girls never even considered saying what they all had thought at one time or another when Mudear went into one of her tirades about triflingness: that Mudear was probably the most trifling woman they had ever seen. A woman who spent most of her days lying in her throne of a bed or in a reclining chair or lounging on a chaise longue dressed in pretty nightclothes or a pastel housecoat. Doing nothing with her time but looking at television, directing the running of her household, making sure her girls did all the work to her specifications. Then, if she felt like it, some gardening at night.

She did nothing else. Nothing, that is, but wash out her own drawers each night after everyone else had gone to bed.

CHAPTER 3

When the three Lovejoy sisters walked into the foyer of their parents' split-level house, they were not even aware of it, but they dropped the bags they were carrying and reached for each other, their fingertips barely brushing. All three of them felt the absence within the house, a house that even still smelled faintly like Mudear, like red spicy cinnamon balls. The girls all caught the scent of the fiery candy at the same time and almost looked around for Mudear to appear.

They had been nearly silent on the car trip from the airport. Annie Ruth, back in the bosom of her sisters, had just about regained her composure as she lay across the backseat of the car listening to Sade sing of faith, trust, and love. Pulling herself together was what each of the Lovejoy girls did best. But there in the hall, its bare cream-colored walls reminding them that Mudear hated pictures of any kind on the wall, the living room furniture lived-in and free of what she called "Sherwood Forest plastic," it hit them all that their mother, who had ruled this modern brick split-level ranch house for nearly thirty years, had ruled it in the same way she had commanded their old two-story wooden house in East Mulberry before, was truly dead. They fell into each other's arms weeping and moaning like the surviving village elders at the funeral of a child.

They felt again as they had for a good time after Mudear changed when they were young children. Like survivors of a war. Like Vietnamese boat people, soldiers, young boys turned men on the battlefield, bloodied, gimp-legged, hobbling on to the promise of peacetime. Stepping over the dead bodies, the ones who didn't make it, who didn't survive.

For a long while they didn't even notice that their father was standing there next to them by the door, his long strong arms dangling uselessly at his side, waiting to greet Annie Ruth, his youngest. They were too taken with themselves to notice him. Too taken with their own personal sorrow. They didn't mean to exclude him. They never did. They were just too busy with themselves to think of him.

These girls always did belong to Mudear, he thought. He silently waited his turn.

They were hardly girls. Betty had just turned forty-two, Emily was thirty-eight, and Annie Ruth, the baby, was still thirty-five, although she told people she was thirty-two. A woman with two days' makeup on she had met one night taking a whore's bath in the sink of an L.A. nightclub ladies' room had instructed Annie Ruth with a wink, "You look young, hon. Play younger."

The sisters, still dressed in their outerwear, smelling of de-

signer perfume and cigarette smoke, wept in the hallway until
their sobs faded into moans and then trailed off into muffled hic-
cups. It wasn't that they mourned for Mudear as much as they
feared the absence of her, the lacuna they knew her absence would
leave in their lives.

Their father stood to the side watching the whole scene of his
daughters' weeping like an atheist watching a Passion play. At one
time he, too, had worshiped at the altar of Mudear, weeping, bow-
ing, pleasing. First, out of awe. Then, out of competition. Then,
out of fear, he worshiped.

"Betty Jean?" he finally said softly to his eldest daughter. She
turned wiping the tears dripping from her high cheekbones.

Betty heaved a sigh and said, "We okay, Poppa. It was just
coming in the house and knowing she's not here. That's all. We
okay. You want something to eat?" and she began taking off her
shawl as she headed for the kitchen.

While Emily struggled to push the luggage out of the en-
tranceway, Annie Ruth turned to her father.

"Hi, Poppa," she said and walked over to get her hello hug.
He hugged the way many men did: stiffly, like a stick figure inside
his long-sleeved plaid shirt and worn brown work pants with his
arms and body at angles to her. He didn't embrace her. Rather,
he let her lean against him, let her brush her cheek against his as
he patted her on the back sharply two times.

Annie Ruth steeled herself for the brush of his beard stubble
against her cheek, but she was not at all prepared for the doughy
feel of his face. Her father's face felt to Annie Ruth like her grandfather's had the few times they had visited him in the country
when she was a child. Poppa can't be that old, she thought.

Their father was just sixty-eight, a year away from retirement at the kaolin mines outside of town where he had worked since he was nineteen. He still had the slowly weakening strong slim body of a man who had spent his youth and most of his middle years digging and hauling chunks and boulders of the soft white stone. He had always taken pride in the way he looked—his tall strong body, his large head, his big feet, his slender hands—being careful not to take on a paunch and soft sagging breasts when the company was hit with a class action discrimination suit and he moved from laborer to lower management. He almost welcomed the sweat-producing work that Mudear had delegated to him in her garden for keeping him in some kind of shape.

"A man never know when he gon' be called on to take care of himself," he'd mutter to himself as he struggled—sweaty and out of breath—to dig a hole at the edge of Mudear's garden big enough to accommodate another of her new nearly full-sized trees.

The kitchen looked to all of them as it always did. Clean, scrupulously clean. Mudear, even though she didn't use it, wouldn't stand for anything other than a strictly clean kitchen.

"A person can tell what kind of woman you are by checking to see how clean you keep around the burners on your stove" was one of Mudear's favorite dictums.

The kitchen was a smaller room than would have been expected in a house the size of theirs, with three bedrooms. But Mudear had insisted on taking some of the space planned for the kitchen and putting it into the screened porch *she* planned. The first time she had shown some interest in the construction of the new structure was when she had discovered that her husband planned for the kitchen to be one of the largest rooms in the house. "You know good and well I don't spend no time in no kitchen," she had told Poppa.

Their father hardly touched the vegetables and cornbread the girls fixed for him, even though Betty had made a special swing by the new enclosed farmers' market out by the Mulberry Mall to buy his favorites—okra and rutabagas. The four of them sat around the dining room table in near silence looking down at their plates and trying to think of something to say to each other that didn't involve Mudear. But Mudear's presence, as always, was too strong.

"You know we holding off the funeral 'til them relatives of Mudear's up north can get off work and get down here," Poppa said to the table in general.

The girls just made agreeing sounds over their plates.

"All those folks do up there is work. They ought to have plenty money."

Again, the girls just agreed. "Uh-uh," they said.

"So, I was thinking, I wanted all you girls to be here before I said anything." He paused as if getting up his nerve.

" 'Bout what, Poppa?" Betty asked.

"I was thinking we should just move that funeral service, it's not like it's gonna be in a church or anything, just a memorial service in the Parkinson Funeral Home chapel, just move it up to tomorrow or the day after. Shoot, I don't know what I'm holding this funeral out for. I was thinking 'bout it and it just don't make no sense not to go ahead and put your mother in the ground instead of leaving her out there at Parkinson Funeral Home waiting for some unreliable no-good northern Negroes to go hat in hand to some northern white folks to ask for a couple of days off so they can go back 'down south' to bury some backwards country relative.

"It just don't make no sense. All this waiting and not knowing when those folks gonna really show up. If they can't get away from their jobs, they'll just wait 'til the last minute and call with some big high-flown excuse.

"I was just thinking, just move this funeral on up. All this waiting is just too hard on the family, on you girls especially."

Then, Poppa was silent. He had said that all in a rush. He felt like a young boy, the young awkward "Shag" that he had been, saying his Easter speech in front of his old bare-board country church's congregation, nervous, uncertain, afraid of overstepping his bounds. His suggestion was more than the girls had heard him say unsolicited and at one time in years. Annie Ruth didn't think she had ever heard him say so much. The girls just cut their eyes at each other.

"If that's what you want, Poppa, that's what we'll do," Betty said. "Why don't you go on up to bed and try to get some rest. You look wore out."

And he did, the other girls noticed with surprise.

"You're not eating anything, anyway."

Her father just nodded, almost with relief, and sort of patted the tabletop near his plate before pulling his long frame wearily up from his chair and heading out of the dining room for the stairs.

The patting gesture reminded the girls of something they hadn't seen for a long time but couldn't quite put their finger on. It made them feel helpless watching him leave with a slow unsteady gait.

Betty wanted to leave the dishes on the table for a little while, but Emily jumped up as soon as they heard their father's bedroom door close and began running soapy dishwater in the sink.

She smiled and shrugged as she cleared the dishes from in front of her sisters. "Force of habit," she said, scraping the uneaten food into the tall plastic trash can by the door and silently slipping the plates into the sudsy water before placing them in the dish-washer.

By the time the three women had finished the few dishes and pans, Betty was nearly pacing the floor.

"I can't stand this one more minute," she said. "I need a cigarette."

As badly as she wanted a cigarette, the idea of smoking *inside* Mudear's house never crossed her mind. As always, she felt like a little girl sneaking a smoke of rabbit tobacco or an unfiltered Camel pilfered from her grandfather's pack left in the breast pocket of his sweaty farmer's shirt.

"Annie Ruth, fix us something to drink. I got to go out on the porch for a smoke," Betty said as she rummaged through her purse for her pack of Benson & Hedges Menthol Lights and headed out the sliding glass door that connected the screened porch to the back of the house.

Annie Ruth settled on bourbon and ginger ale because that was all that was in the house except for some Scotch. None of them could abide the smell of Scotch. Even though Mudear did not drink, the bottle was hers. At some time, Mudear had heard from Carrie, her only friend in town, that people thought she stayed in the house all day drinking, that the reason no one ever saw her emerge was because she was in there drunk. Immediately, Mudear had stopped drinking any alcohol, even the fancy wine and champagne that the girls sometimes sent for presents.

"Ya'll know I don't give a damn what people say about me, but I be damn if I'll give 'em ammunition to wag they tongues."

Even Betty, who had promised herself three months before that she would stop racing toward that drink at the end of the day and who drank only Evian water with a twist when she went out, had the bourbon. It was what their father drank and kept on the bar in the rec room.

Without conferring, Annie Ruth decided to use the good small old-fashioned glasses, the frosted ones that Mudear had never let them use. She tried to pretend it was no big deal to use them, but her hands shook slightly as she took them out of the glass breakfront and placed them on the bar. For a moment, she feared she would be swept with another wave of nausea.

When she saw Emily watching her quivering hands, she smiled and said, "I guess I'm not as steady yet as I thought." And her sister stood behind her a few seconds and massaged the muscles in the back of her neck with her still-damp hands.

Annie Ruth remembered as a girl standing in front of the cabinet gazing at the glasses the way a child looks at a snow-filled paperweight globe. She believed for years that it was indeed freezing inside the breakfront as she believed it was inside the paperweight. But she was always too frightened of getting caught to open up the cabinet and investigate. Or even to press her fingers to the glass.

She poured them all a drink but made hers mostly ginger ale. She wanted one of her sisters to notice and then again she didn't think she could talk about her pregnancy yet with either of her sisters after what had happened on the plane. She was still working on not throwing her head back and screaming.

Betty stood in a far corner of the screened porch, her crossed arms tucked under her breasts, her body appearing to lean against air in what her sisters called her "Betty pose" ("You got to learn to lean on just about anything you can in this life, even air," Mudear would say, gazing at her oldest daughter). Her broad shoulders were like her sisters'. Their mother called them "Lovejoy shoulders, like men's." Only on Betty they seemed gargantuan. She had to take the shoulder pads out of all her dresses and jackets before she wore them to keep from looking grotesque.

She looked out over the field of waning wildflowers at the edges of the garden in back and took deep drags on her cigarette. The Benson & Hedges Menthol Light felt like a cool sprinkler in her throat and she smoked it all the way down to the filter. Then, she started to put it out in the dirt in one of Mudear's many potted ferns but stopped herself and instead slipped upstairs into the bathroom and flushed the butt down the toilet.

Coming back through the house on her way to the porch, she rubbed her arms through her beige cashmere sweater and decided to collect a thin blanket from an upstairs bedroom and two afghans from the den couch. When she handed an afghan to each of her sisters as they stepped onto the porch, she got a whiff of Mudear's talcum powder rising from the fuzzy yarn. She kept the blanket for herself.

Emily, absentmindedly drying her already dry hands on the breast pockets of her western shirt, sat on the flowered cushion at the far end of the porch sofa and tucked her legs under her. Betty saw her spread her afghan over her lap so no one could see how big her thighs looked splayed against her calves through her fringed jeans.

For most of their lives, Emily had been the slimmest of the girls, petite, a size seven since she hit puberty. But now, in her late thirties, she had started to put on some weight which she at first couldn't see. Then, when she did see it, she became embarrassed by the extra pounds and her inability to lose them. For the first time in her life she had to think about what she ate and how she looked in certain styles. She hated it.

The youthful fashion styles she had always chosen and shown off to perfection now looked a little ridiculous, a bit *jeune fille,* on her expanded figure.

Especially since, as Annie Ruth had pointed out to Betty on the phone one night, she refused to "move her big ass on up one more size and give those skinny clothes to someone who can use 'em before they all go out of style."

"Someone like you, Annie Ruth?" Betty had suggested with a laugh.

"Well, at least I can still get my butt comfortably into *some* size eights."

"Yeah, the expensive ones, right?" Betty had pointed out.

"Well, whether she gives those pretty things to me or not, she better start thinking about getting her body snatched before it's too late," Annie Ruth said knowingly.

"Snatched?" Betty asked with a laugh.

"Yeah, snatched," her sister said. "You know how you snatch your hair back into a ponytail. Well, that's what our sister girl-friend needs to do with her body—with diet and mostly exercise: snatch it back to the size it was, before her body forgets what it was like to be that size."

Betty smiled. "Emily said she can't believe *she's* got to actually go to exercise classes."

Annie Ruth had chuckled like Mudear and said, "Tell her, 'Keep living, daughter.'"

Annie Ruth, still weary from the ordeal of her journey across the country, gave Betty her drink, plopped down on the other end of the sofa, curled up there, and just threw her afghan around her shoulders. Annie Ruth acted as if she felt she had nothing to hide with her body.

All her life she had been called "fine." She had the big legs, ass, and breasts that black men of the sixties and early seventies loved. And they had lavished praise on her for it. When she walked down city streets, even in the North, men felt perfectly justified in shouting at her, "Brick house!" (She assumed that white men felt the same but just didn't have the vocabulary or the nerve to say anything.) Before men's comments on the street had started turning ugly, sometime in the middle seventies, she had enjoyed the attention even though she had resented the implication that she was big and solid enough to be compared to a brick shithouse.

It wasn't that she was hefty, she just had curves that made folks want to run their hands along them the way a farmer in the field fondles a huge ripe warm watermelon.

If she didn't watch it, she felt her rounded butt and big firm breasts could have overtaken her hourglass figure and made her chunky. But there was little chance of that. She was always on some diet or another. Even if television didn't put ten extra pounds on your ass. And she had been known to stick her finger down her throat after she had slipped and enjoyed too much bread and olive oil with her lobster ravioli, salad, and blue cheese dressing.

Now that men seemed to be more influenced by magazine ads and music videos rather than by their own instincts and chose skinnier and skinnier women over their more voluptuous sisters, Annie Ruth watched her diet even more and worked out at her gym at Marina del Rey five days a week instead of her former three, making sure her body stayed "snatched."

Betty looked at her younger sisters wrapped up in their afghans and smiled as she settled in a rocking chair catercorner to them by a stretch of screening, with the blanket thrown over her knees. It comforted her that whenever they all went somewhere together people always commented, "Ya'll must be sisters." Even though their coloring and sizes varied, from Annie Ruth's light brown to Emily's dark, they did look like different versions of the same woman at different stages of her life.

All her life, Mudear had called Betty "big-boned"—"Betty is big-boned, let her pick that box up"—but she wasn't really big-boned. She was just about Emily's size only taller than the other two girls. But as with most things, she couldn't shake Mudear's image of her. In high school, Betty would scrutinize the wrists and hands of her female classmates to compare hers with theirs. Once, she had even unconsciously slipped her fingers around her own wrist and then around the wrist of the girl sitting next to her in the biology lab. The gesture had startled her lab mate so that she dropped the whole frog, the pins, and the wax-filled pan to the floor, splattering both girls with formaldehyde. It seemed that Betty had no hope of attaining the ability to see herself objectively. Mudear's image of her always overwhelmed her own self-image.

Seeing her sisters sitting on the porch snuggled in their afghans made her want to pull them both into her lap and hold them there.

Even the birthday cards that Betty bought for her sisters let them know that under it all she still saw them as little girls. Along with the cards that featured flowers—grown-up flowers like birds of paradise and calla lilies and pale fringed tulips—on the front, she couldn't help sending them a few "For my sis" cards that had drawings of teddy bears and bunnies and little black dolls holding hands, too. She knew her strongest feelings for them were maternal and her sisterly feelings ran a good strong second.

They looked the way they had some thirty years before when

they would all huddle on the floor beside their beds wrapped in their blankets and wait for the fight to be over. Or later, when they squatted in the same spot at the old house and listened to Betty's stories of how it had been before the change.

I'm the only one of us who knows what it's like to really have a mother. To play outside with the other children in the neighborhood 'til we got motley with grit and dirt and mud and to be called in by our mother to take a bath at dusk, a mother who allowed us to walk barefoot all evening so we had to wash our feet again before bedtime. Betty would remind herself of this each evening before settling down to telling her sisters how it was before Mudear changed. She felt like Ishmael, the last one left to tell the story. She took her responsibility seriously.

There was no ashtray in the house, Betty knew that, so she had brought a piece of aluminum foil out from the kitchen. And while Annie Ruth and Emily snuggled down in their seats, getting closer and closer, rubbing their arms and cheeks against the wool and yarn of their wraps smelling faintly of talc, she fashioned a little ashtray out of the foil. It looked like the handiwork of a child's summer crafts class. She even molded little indentations in the side like a real ashtray to rest the butt.

"You don't get extra points for neatness," Annie Ruth said finally with a smile.

They all three laughed softly. It was the first thing Annie Ruth had said since she landed in Mulberry that sounded like her old self. She could always make her sisters laugh. When the three of them usually got together or talked on the phone, they laughed as much as they gossiped, using a familiar verbal shorthand to cut to the laugh. But this time they just chuckled and settled back into solemnity. Betty continued to fiddle with the thing absentmindedly after lighting up her cigarette.

"God, I wish I had a joint," Emily said as she watched Betty flick cigarette ashes into the foil tray.

"A joint? It's bad enough I'm smoking a cigarette in Mudear's house." Betty stopped herself just before saying, "She'd probably turn over in her grave if she knew. . . ." But her pause left a space in their talk hanging on the chill night air as if she had actually voiced it.

They sat enjoying the silence for a while until the sound of a male katydid pierced the night air and they all looked in the direction of Mudear's garden. They almost expected to see Mudear roaming around her garden in the near darkness as she had done nearly every fair night during the spring, summer, fall, and part of the mild winter almost their entire lives.

Her late-night gardening had produced prodigious results. The last of the late profusion of white blooms danced a bit throughout the garden in the wind like spirits. In the falling darkness, the girls could still make out the white trumpet blossoms on the old-fashioned petunia bushes that came up year after year and lasted way into the fall. Even the delicate sprays of alyssum and the fragile blossom of the ginger lily wafted fragrance onto the porch.

When Emily sneezed two times, her sisters automatically looked out the screen porch in search of the hummingbird. For as long as any of them could remember, Emily had been allergic to hummingbirds, sneezing uncontrollably when one or more of the tiny birds were hovering nearby. Mudear always said she was just putting on. But her sisters knew the allergy was real. And though they felt sorry for Emily's allergic affliction, they couldn't help but become excited at the idea of seeing the usually shy creatures flutter around their sister as if she were a red hummingbird feeder.

But Emily set them straight. "Just the end of a cold," she said with a sniff. And they all settled back in their seats disappointed, even though they knew it was too late in the season for a ruby-throated hummingbird to be still flying around middle Georgia. They wrapped themselves in their blankets again and in the silence surrounding them. When another breeze stirred up the smell of cinnamon balls in a cut-glass dish on the table, they gave in to their feelings.

"She could be so mean," Emily said.

"God, Em-Em, not now," Betty said as she began rocking wearily.

"She could be so goddamn mean and heartless." Emily had wanted to say it coldly and matter-of-factly. But her voice broke a bit at the end. And the sound broke the hearts of the other women.

Annie Ruth, who had been waiting for somebody to open the way down that familiar road, jumped in eagerly.

"Mudear, now, she the kinda 'ho that would sit and help you make the most beautiful white strapless gown for the prom."

"Annie Ruth, don't start," Betty almost pleaded.

"You remember, Betty, that pretty white raw silk sheath with the killer split up the back that you made for me," Annie Ruth continued.

Emily took over then.

"And then she help you get dressed for the big night. Zip you up and let you borrow her pearls, her own personal pearls, and you know how she feel 'bout her 'pursnel' things." Annie Ruth took over again. "Tell one of us to dust your shoulders with powder with glitter in it."

"Shit, Annie Ruth, she dead. Let it go."

"Then, she pat you on the back and gently . . ."

"Annie Ruth, dammit, don't nobody feel like doing this tonight."

"Why should tonight be any different?" Emily put in.

"Then, she pat you lightly on the shoulder with those beautiful slender hands of hers, hands that ain't seen the bottom of a sink of dishes in years, and then usher you downstairs to your date. And whisper in your ear, 'Now, don't come on your period in that pretty white dress.' "

They were silent——Betty with her head thrown back, rocking, Annie Ruth and Emily with their chins resting on their knees—— remembering that night and others.

"She's all we ever talk about really. Do you realize that?" Annie Ruth asked the darkened porch. "We start out with our jobs and then men and then clothes and then books we've read, then bills, but we always end up talking about Mudear."

She felt better just saying it out loud.

The other sisters knew they couldn't dispute that. It was the truth. And the porch fell silent again.

"Anybody want a refill?" Annie Ruth jumped up too quickly and the light-headedness made her sway a bit before she caught hold of the back of a chair.

"What for? You haven't finished your first drink yet," Betty pointed out, narrowing her eyes to see Annie Ruth better. She thought she saw her sway.

"I'm not really drinking tonight," Annie Ruth said and made her eyes scan the darkness outside over her sister's head.

"Oh, shit, Annie Ruth," Betty said as she swung her legs down from her seat and planted her wide feet soundly on the porch floor. "How late are you?"

"Late? What you talking 'bout, Betty?"

Betty took a deep drag, put out the cigarette, and lit up another. "Em-Em, are we going to have to spend our entire lives explaining things to you?"

Betty sounded a bit exasperated at her sister's innocence, but she had long ago accepted the fact that Emily had a harder time than the other two accepting things. Emily understood how things were in life, Mudear had seen to that, but she just sometimes refused to accept them. Even more than Annie Ruth, the baby, who hadn't seen as much as Emily had.

Annie Ruth just got up, collected everyone's glasses, and went back in toward the kitchen.

As she made her way through the rec room, she heard Emily saying, "All of us got this far without having no babies. She can't be pregnant now. Now that Mudear's dead and all."

Annie Ruth spun around in the rec room and came back to the porch door.

"Mudear didn't have nothing to do with this," Annie Ruth said tightly. "For once, this is something that Mudear didn't have no hand in."

She turned and went back toward the kitchen to fill the glasses with ice.

"That's a matter of opinion," Betty said. Although Emily couldn't see her in the dark, she knew that her sister's eyes were low and hooded like Mudear's when she was making a point.

CHAPTER 4

Look at them, stretched out there on my screened porch smoking cigarettes and drinking my husband's liquor. Even talking about smoking that marijuana like some kind of damn black girl hippies. And me laying up here in Parkinson Funeral Home with this ugly-assed navy-blue dress on. Talking about me like I ain't in my grave yet. Hell, I ain't in my grave yet. It just goes to show you what they gonna be like when I really am buried and gone.

Trifling! Trifling women! After all I did to raise them right. Well, alright. Maybe I didn't do a lot to raise them, not after the baby was five or so, but I did raise them. I did see to it that they were raised. And raised right. Even if they did have to half raise themselves.

Taught them how to carry themselves. How to keep that part of themselves that was just for themselves to themselves so nobody could take it and walk on it. Tried my best to make them free. As free as I could teach them to be and still be free myself.

How many times did I tell Emily, my middle girl, to pull up that chin, tie up that chin. Look to the stars, I would tell them. Look to the stars. Don't let the whole town see you walking with your head down, like you got something to be ashamed of.

Lord knows this damn little-assed town did try to make them think that. That they had something to be ashamed of. Me mostly. Umph. It's funny really. The one thing in life that they could always look to with pride, a mother who set an example of being her own woman, was the thing that everyone wanted them to be ashamed of.

Well, one thing I can say for them, I don't think they were ever ashamed of me, or embarrassed by me. Never once.

It sure is nice and quiet in here. The Parkinsons always did run a nice establishment. I had forgotten how lovely this old building is. Nice and quiet. Just the way the house used to be at night when I liked it best. Course, 'cause I got my beauty sleep much of the day, I could enjoy the night the way most people couldn't.

In the summer, it was too hot during the day to even think about stirring before four or five o'clock in the afternoon. By the time it got dark, I would have had a good long bath and taken care of myself, hair and stuff. And I would have gotten myself something to eat and looked at a little television. The girls or Ernest would have come home by dark and done whatever I needed doing. And I would have had a little company if I felt like it.

Usually, there would be enough time for a little nap in the evening before I went out to do my gardening. That way I'd be nice and refreshed for my work. What with taking my own time and stopping to rest and admire my work and coming into the house for coffee and to eat something, before you know it, there'd be streaks of color in the sky. And I'd come in and look at movies on videocassettes or early-morning television. Then, lay back down before the girls get up for school.

And in the winter, it was too depressing getting up earlier than afternoon. Seeing the sunlight outside and knowing it wouldn't even be strong enough to warm you if you was to walk out in it. Then, before you know it, the day would start to fade and it would be nighttime. But that didn't do any good because it would be too cold to do any gardening.

But then, in the summertime, it would take so long to get dark enough for me to go outside and get my work done. Oh, well, like the old folks say, "If it ain't one thing, it's three."

I don't seem to be able to feel the daylight on my skin in here the way I used to, but I am adaptable. Shore am gonna miss my plants, though, my flowers the most, I think. I just planted vegetables that made pretty plants. Collards as big as a small child line the walk to the back door. There's a tangle of mint and lavender by a old painted swing, that has mixed and mated so much that their flowers are variegated shades of purple and lavender and it makes your mouth water to brush by it. My patches of old elephant ears were so big and velvety, almost khaki, they held two and three cups of water when it rained.

In the full burst of spring and early summer, the place was a paradise.

Besides my separate rose garden, I had bushes scattered all through the garden. Delicate ones, big showy ones, trailing, climbing, grown in hedges and bushes and over trellises. Tea to cabbage.

I did so love to dig in the dirt. I was just a born gardener. I could taste the soil and tell whether it was acid or alkaline. When I woke up with dirt under my fingernails, it was some of the happiest moments for me.

My garden is a beautiful thing. This time of year I have as many flowers growing almost as in May. Still got begonias and butterfly weed and cannas blooming along with dahlia, big wide dahlias, and delphiniums and Stokes' asters and chrysanthemums. None of the herbs seem to know it's close to winter yet and with some kind of herb planted at every crossway, turn, or corner of the garden, it's a pleasure just to walk through and brush by 'em.

I guess my garden is the thing I'm most proud of.

Other than seeing my girls do so well, of course.

I also taught them how to be ladies. How to do the things that women need to know how to do in this world. How to sew and clean and take care of a house. Make a beautiful centerpiece out of whatever was growing in the nearest yard or field. Even as a little thing, the baby Annie Ruth could step outdoors and come back in with an armful of fall leaves and branches and make a right nice arrangement. I taught 'em that.

They took care of that house a whole lot better than I ever did or ever wanted to. And when things needed taking care of personally, Betty could handle those white bastards down at the gas company or those hinkty folks at Davison's Department Store as well as lots of grown women. Finally even told that old cracker who used to sit in the lobby entrance from store opening to closing to kiss her black ass when she called her names once too often. I was proud of her for that. I probably told her so.

I even taught them to take care of themselves. Many's the time I'd make sure they bought Ivory liquid or Palmolive liquid so when Emily washed dishes she didn't ruin those pretty hands of hers.

She does have the prettiest hands. And it was me, nobody else, who taught those three girls how to take care of what they've been given.

How many girls their age know so much about moisturizing their skin as they do? I never let 'em use soap on their faces and made sure there was always some Pond's cold cream in the house. How many other mothers can say the same?

I never was one for lying. At least, I never was after things changed, so I'd tell them right out what their best attributes were and what failings they didn't even need to waste their time on trying to improve.

I didn't coddle 'em and cuddle 'em to death the way some mothers do. I pushed 'em out there to find out what they was best in. That's how you learn things, by getting on out there and living. They found their strengths by the best way anybody could: by living them.

From the looks of this here dress they bought to bury me in—went out to the mall and bought it out at Rubinstein's, too, know they paid good money for it, the price tag is probably around here somewhere—you can tell they holds a grudge for something though. What in God's name would possess them to go out and spend good money on this navy-blue monstrosity—and they know navy blue is not my color, they know how pretty I look in pastels—when I had all those beautiful bed jackets at home. Hell, some of my old stuff might be a bit outdated, since I ain't had any need for street clothes in a number of years, but even it look better than this shit. They ought to be ashamed. Knowing how those girls love beautiful clothes, I can't believe they weren't trying to say something by picking this thing for me to lie in for all eternity. Them girls got ugly ways about 'em sometimes.

Well, at least it ain't cheap. I never could wear cheap clothes.

You know, some people can wear cheap clothes and look right nice in 'em. I never could. If I ever put on anything cheap, it would stand away from my body like paper-doll clothes and just scream, "Cheap! Cheap! Cheap!" My girls couldn't either, wear anything cheap. When they was teenagers, they'd try to imitate they little friends and go down to Lerner's or one of them shops and get some outfit or other. It would be cute in the bag, but as soon as they put it on, it would start screaming, "Cheap! Cheap! Cheap!" and they'd have to give it to one of their cheap-clothes-wearing friends.

Knowing Annie Ruth, she gonna go through my bed jackets and personal things before the funeral to see what she can take back to that Los Angeles, maybe my pink satin quilted bed jacket, to wear with some tight jeans or expensive evening dress.

I can hear her now. "Oh, yes, this was my Mudear's. I just had to have something of hers." Little witch.

God, them girls got ugly ways about 'em sometimes. They must get them from their father's people.

You would think them girls were mad at me for something.

Just like them to be mad at me for something I don't even know. Just like with the damn telephone. They knew good and damn well that I didn't answer the phone unless I felt like it. Never did anything else but that in their memory. But wouldn't they get pissed off with me when they came home from school or one of those little piece of jobs they messed around with and I was nice enough to tell them that the phone had been ringing off the hook all day.

"Hope wasn't nobody expecting no calls," I'd tell them, nice like, too. Then, they would get fighting mad. Well, not really "fighting" mad because then they'd be mad enough to fight they

ma and don't none of us play that. I guess I got that to be thankful
for, too.

Just the other day I was looking at some talk show, coulda
been Ophrah, that was talking about these children. Call them
Fragile X. They all looked a certain way, long faces and big ears,
and they all had the tendency to fight their mothers. I know it
wasn't funny, but I had to laugh. Of course, Ernest didn't see the
humor of it when I shared it with him later that night. But he's
just about lost all his sense of humor over the years.

I have always tried very hard not to judge my girls too harshly.
For one thing, everybody ain't me. I learned that years ago.

For another, they were too young to remember how it was
before. To remember it and appreciate how much better things
were after that cold, no-heat-and-no-lights-in-that-freezing-assed-
house day when I was able to be what I am. A woman in my own
shoes. And they don't hardly remember their daddy any other way
than his meek, quiety self he is now.

I guess you can't completely blame the girls because they don't
know what their Mudear has done for them. Practically all their
lives—to show them a good example.

Wait a minute! What did she just say? "Mudear, now, she the
kinda 'ho . . ." What the hell kind of thing is that to say about
me, their own Mudear. Have they lost their minds or did they
actually find some of that marijuana they wanted?

They ought to know that dope make you crazy!

CHAPTER 5

When Annie Ruth came back onto the porch, she still felt a bit shaky, but she carried the drinks on a silver tray.

"You sure are getting bold," Betty said as she took her drink off the server Annie Ruth proffered. "First, you pour liquor in Mudear's special cabinet glasses. Now, you serving drinks off her silver tray."

"If we don't use this stuff at some time it's going to revert to ore," Annie Ruth said. "I can still see what terrible shape poor Emily's hands were in after all those Saturdays of sitting in the dining room polishing all this silver and silverware and then putting it back in the breakfront and the blue velvet box for storage 'til it tarnished again."

"I wonder why Mudear never let us use any of it. As much as

she loved pretty things," Emily said as she took her drink from the tray. She was trying not to pounce on Annie Ruth's news, because while her younger sister was inside Betty had made her promise to take it easy.

Betty swirled the ice in her drink a couple of times and waited to see if Annie Ruth was going to say anything. When she didn't, Betty said, " 'Cause they were some of her wedding and anniversary gifts, that's why."

Even Emily didn't need any further explanation.

All the girls knew how Mudear felt about men, husbands especially. When Emily had gotten married to Ron, Mudear had refused to get out of bed to see the bridal party all dressed for the ceremony. Furthermore, she had strictly commanded the rest of the family not to even let Emily into her bedroom dressed in "all that white lacy shit, like she a virgin or something."

"She already done been married once. That ought to be enough for any woman. Lord, I done raised a fool!"

Emily had tried to make excuses for Mudear's absence to Ron's family who had driven down to Mulberry for the ceremony. She had told them that Mudear was in bed with double pneumonia, under strict doctor's orders not to even think about moving for at least three more weeks.

"Poor thing," Emily told Ron's mother. "She can't even lift her head off the pillow."

But Mudear blew that when she yelled out her bedroom window as the bridal party pulled away from the house.

"He'll lead you a dog's life!" Mudear had shrieked in a loud healthy voice. "Remember, I'm the one who told you. He'll lead you a dog's life."

Unfortunately, Mudear had been right. But it didn't lessen the pain the memory of the wedding day experience had left with all the Lovejoy girls.

Each of them wished, whether it was true or not, that Mudear had not raised them with the motto "A man don't give a damn about you."

Annie Ruth placed the silver tray carefully on the table by the sofa and sat down with her own drink. It was just a tall glass of ginger ale and ice. Now that her sisters knew she was pregnant, there didn't seem to be any reason to pretend to sip a cocktail.

"Well, sugar, what you gonna do?" Betty asked gently.

"Do?" Annie Ruth asked, stalling for time. She had begun to bite the pale polish off her thumbnail.

"Exactly. What are you gonna do? You can't be too far along with that little waist of yours."

"Oh, I got lots of time," Annie Ruth said. She tried to sound casual, but she never could lie to her sisters. Not even about something unimportant.

"Then, how come you're not drinking any liquor?" Betty asked, noticing her sister's tall glass of soda.

Annie Ruth just took another swig of ginger ale and swallowed hard.

"Annie Ruth, you can't be thinking of keeping it," Emily said. "You can't actually be thinking of being a mother."

"I didn't actually say I was going to keep it," Annie Ruth said, meaning to speak in a strong assured voice. But she was beginning to feel the waves of anxiety that she had experienced on the plane ride from Los Angeles. She tried to take small gulps of air and blow out through her mouth a few times the way her masseuse had taught her to help overcome anxiety attacks without medication.

"No offense, sugar, but do you know who the father is?" Betty leaned forward and asked.

Annie Ruth sighed.

"Well," she said after a while, "I was pretty sure it was Raphael's. But when I told him, he got pretty ugly. He said, 'No way, beetch.' You know he's Dominican, he talks with an accent. He said, 'No way. You've fucked half of Los Angeles County and now you say *I'm* the father? No way.'"

She stopped to take another sip of soda. Her mouth was so dry.

"So now, it's Delbert's baby."

"What difference does it make whose it is?" Emily screamed as she jumped up from the sofa, knocking over her drink. "You're talking like it makes some difference, like you plan to have the child."

Emily was standing over Annie Ruth biting her bottom lip with that wolfish look in her eyes.

"I know your company insurance must cover the cost of the operation," she said.

Annie Ruth felt trapped by her sister's reaction to the news of her pregnancy and was finding it harder and harder to breathe. She took a few more deep breaths to try to control the quaking feeling in the pit of her stomach.

"I don't know, Emily," she said. "I haven't looked into all of that yet."

"What do you mean, you haven't looked into it yet? What are you waiting for, girl? You are acting like you plan to keep the child."

"Calm down, Em-Em," Betty said solemnly. "This ain't you we talking about. It's Annie Ruth."

Emily spun around to face Betty. "What's that supposed to mean?"

"I'm just saying we know Annie Ruth's not in the best shape she could be in. And maybe now might not be the best time to be screaming at her."

Emily was suddenly chastened, silent.

And Betty continued, "And I was just telling you to keep your voice down. Your voice carries on this night air. And Poppa's right upstairs."

Emily bit her bottom lip, bobbed her head silently, and sat back on her corner of the sofa.

It looked as if Emily were finished for a while, but then she said softly, "But, Betty, you know, we promised."

Her sisters pretended not to have heard.

"Annie Ruth, maybe we better leave this for a little later," Betty said. "Anyway, you look tired. I know I am, if you aren't. You want to come home and stay with me tonight? Naw, don't nobody feel like carrying all your stuff back to my house. I know you don't. Why don't you go on up to bed here and get some rest. Emily's going to stay with me. We'll see you in the morning."

Just the sound of Betty's voice directing the rest of the evening for them made Annie Ruth feel she might just make it through the week.

She rose from the couch and headed for the inside door. Then, she paused, turned, and went over to Emily, who sat with her head down dabbing at the spilled drink. She reached down, hugged her sister, and whispered in her ear, "Once, I burned another black woman's audition tape and letter that I found on the news producer's desk."

Emily reached up and hugged her baby sister back, held her for a while, then let her go.

CHAPTER 6

Poppa could hear the girls talking downstairs on the side porch through his bedroom window upstairs—opened just a crack the way Mudear wanted it. He couldn't make out exactly what they were saying, but the rhythm of their conversation, the patterns of their voices were so familiar that he could almost guess what the whole conversation was going to sound like. First, Annie Ruth would speak, then Betty, then Annie Ruth again, then Emily. All of them taking their turns as if the conversation were scripted and rehearsed.

He marveled at how all of them got to talk. Each taking a turn, each getting in what she wanted to say. When they were younger, he would sit with them and their mother at the dining room table—Mudear at one end, him at the other, Betty on one side by herself with her back to the kitchen, and the other two girls on the other side—and be in awe at the tenor and pace of the conversation. Questions sprang from Mudear. The girls' answers flew back across the table effortlessly. Many evenings, it left him dizzy, almost nauseated as if he were suffering motion sickness or air sickness.

He was grateful at least that they weren't flouncing all around the house tonight. He couldn't stand all the quick unexpected movement that the women produced. It got so, when the girls were teenagers, there seemed to be so much of their activity in the house, he would have to get up from his chair in the living room sometimes and go stand out in the street to get away from it.

"Their mother gets them to do that just to get on my nerves," he would mutter to himself as Mudear yelled from upstairs for one of them to run fetch something for her. "Run get me this thing. Run get me that." He knew that eventually he would grow to hate the sound of her voice. Then, it was just her orders and the activity she generated around her that he had hated. She had died before he grew to hate *her* completely.

The easy conversations, the comfortable camaraderie Mudear and the girls seemed to share, it was never that way with him when they were in the house. It seemed that the girls had never been that way with him. Of course, there had been a time, long ago, it seemed, when his voice was the only one that mattered in the house, when he spoke with a big voice. That was when they were *his* little girls and she was *his* wife.

But then suddenly, it seemed, at the dinner table, on the porch, in the living room, during commercials on the television, he had to fight for a space in the conversation. As if his voice didn't matter. No one fell silent when he began to speak. No one stopped to hear what he had to say.

It finally wasn't worth the fight. He never won anyway.

The four women in the house had overwhelmed him. At first, he had thought it was just his wife who took over his household. But as he began carefully to notice the patterns of the house, he realized it was not just she but everything with a vagina in the house who seemed to want to rule. He had even thought briefly of calling for help. The police? His lodge brothers? Somebody. Sometimes, at work or while he ate dinner or in the middle of the night, he had just wanted to yell, "Womens taking over my house!" at the top of his lungs.

But he knew he couldn't do that. If he had shown any of those signs of weakness, of the panic he had felt for some time, they would trample him, engulf him, overtake him completely.

If only he had had a son, a boy, a manchild to stand staunchly with him, to take up his part sometime. Or even if one of his girls had stood up for him. Just once if one of them had said, "I think Poppa is right, Mudear." Even the thought of it made him shake his head. The outlandishness of the thought. The very idea that someone in that house would stand up to Mudear.

He had no idea that each of his girls had had just that intention at one time or another. Not just as little girls or teenagers but also as grown women living in their own houses. They had all dreamed of it. Of standing up for their father, of being, if only briefly, daddy's little girl, daddy's child.

But the same words resounded in all their heads at the very thought. All their lives they had heard Mudear say, "It's getting so in this house I can't say nothing 'out somebody going running back to *him* with it. Are you *my* child or are you *his,* make up your mind!"

Or intimately, she would ask each of them separately, call them up to her bedroom while Poppa was at work. "If me and your poppa was to get a divorce, who would you go with? You can't run with the hares and hunt with the hounds in this life. Choose." What a question, they noted to each other later in life, to put to a little girl, a child. Choose! It was just like Mudear to put the burden on someone else.

"Mudear." It was the only thing she had stood firm on, insisted on early in their marriage. "That's what I called my mother and that's what I want my children to call me. It's short for 'Mother dear.' No, baby, don't say 'Maa-maa,' say 'Mu-*dear,*' 'Mu-*dear,*' " she would instruct each of the girls from age one on until each said it with just the same lilting inflection on the *dear* that the originator used. At the time, Poppa had thought it was so sweet the way the little girls said it.

It was even what he called her now. Mudear. And for a moment he had to stop and think to remember what her given name was. Esther. Such a beautiful name. Esther. Beautiful. Like she had been at one time. Maybe she still was. She certainly thought of herself that way.

When he first met her, she had reminded him of the sparklers on a stick that children ran with on the Fourth of July. She had actually seemed to send off sparks. She had a firm little body and a laugh like a moving picture star, he thought.

But he stopped himself. He couldn't allow himself to think she was beautiful. Even dead. If he did, then all would be lost.

God! he thought as he sat on the side of the wide bed with his head in his long slim hands. It was so hard to stay strong.

Especially when you were doing something against your will, it was so hard.

"*Mens* needs to talk," he had heard a fellow worker say one day to a bunch of his buddies, effectively banishing a big old pushy woman from their circle at the bar. "Mens needs to talk." The fellowship of men, that was what he needed. He had that fellowship at work. And he had found it when he stopped downtown at The Place to take a little drink before heading home white and chalky from working in the kaolin mines among the other hard-working folks who frequented the popular bar and grill.

But when he needed that fellowship most, at home with his wife and daughters, it wasn't there. Here at home was where he most needed that camaraderie. Didn't they understand that, like the man said, mens needs to talk?

He hadn't given up right away. He had held sway over his home, his wife, his children, his household, his territory for too long to give up that tyranny, that position, that authority right away.

When he had first felt his control slipping away, he had gathered his men friends around him. A few times, he had invited one or two of his friends over. One, a man who fixed televisions, he asked over on the pretext that the TV needed repairing. "Stop by and take a look at my TV, man, and we can have a little drink, too, while you there."

But the friend had had more than a little drink sitting at the kitchen table with Poppa. He had had quite a few, seeming to want to drink the full fifth of Old Forester dry before he left. Then, in his drunken stupor, he had gotten up and, turning the wrong way, had wandered into the living room mistaking it for the bathroom, unzipped his pants, and peed on one of the low side tables next to the sofa. Annie Ruth, still almost a baby then, had discovered it and gone running to her mother yelling, "Tee-tee! Tee-tee!" His friend had been banished from the house by the women.

Any time Ernest dared to mention a friend or coworker in Mudear's hearing, she would say, "I hope he ain't gonna come into my house and pee on the floor."

It was enough to keep him from ever again venturing into the realm of male bonding. He was in this alone.

Ernest looked down at his hands hanging between his legs and shook his head sadly at their condition. At one time, he had taken such pride in his hands. Even though he was now a supervisor near retirement at the mines and rarely had to even pick up a chunk of chalk, his hands still showed the signs of his years in the pits. The white powdery chalk still showed up starkly around and under his nails against his dark brown fingers.

Even though it was one of the first things she stopped doing after the change, Ernest could still picture Mudear seated on a small stool by his chair in the living room, her knees scrunched up to her still firm breasts, one of his hands lounging carelessly in hers. His other hand resting in a small bowl of soapy Lux liquid water on the arm of his chair.

For quite a long time, he relished the memory of that vision, Mudear manicuring his nails. He loved to remember her doing his nails. The filing, clipping, soaking, painting them with clear nail polish. She was so good at it, like everything she tried her hand at, doing his nails. The final step—buffing them to a pink healthy glow—was his favorite. As she zipped the soft pink padded in- strument back and forth across his nails, her whole body shimmied to the rhythm of the buffer. It was almost as good as sex.

At first, after she refused to ever as long as she lived and stayed black ever sit on that stool—whatever happened to that wicker stool, he wondered—and serve him like some slave or something, he tried to do his own nails.

The only reason he did that was some of the guys at the downtown bar noticed what sad shape his nails were falling into around all that soft chalk at work. "Wife ain't taking care a' her job like she supposed to, huh, Ernest?" one of the guys asked two Saturdays in a row while he and his friends lounged over a couple of quarts of cold Pabst Blue Ribbon at The Place downtown.

Ernest had almost balled his fists up in shame. Damn her, he thought. Damn her, damn her. When he came in from work, she had the nerve to be sitting up there in bed polishing her own nails a creamy shell pink. Like she the Queen of Sheba, he had thought. That night he had dreamed that he drove both of his balled-up fists into her smug regal face and made her, *made her,* do his nails again. Made her do 'em right there in bed where she was painting hers.

But when he had awakened the next morning, he had looked over at his wife sleeping peacefully beside him with her muddy garden shoes still on and remembered immediately that he could no longer *make* Mudear do anything he wanted her to do. And he felt like weeping in frustration. Instead, he got up, steeled his back, and went downstairs to the breakfast Betty had made for the family.

He didn't know why he could never completely and finally hate her. Now that she was dead, he had to admit that he even admired some things about her after the change. Near morning, when she climbed back into their bed following her midnight wanderings and began immediately to snore softly, he would lie in the wide king-sized bed beside her and think, She really free. She don't have to get up at any set time in the morning. One of the girls will serve her a light breakfast in bed if that's what she wants. Or if she wakes up hungry, really ravenous like some hungry wild animal, she can stroll downstairs and one of 'em ul fix her pancakes and bacon with lots of butter and Alaga syrup and milk.

He stood and began undressing for bed.

And if the milk and pancakes tear up her stomach, that was okay 'cause she would be at home and could go to the bathroom, her own lavender bathroom, whenever she wanted. And stay in there as long as she liked.

I guess I'm gonna have to die to be that free myself, he thought with a resigned sigh.

Poppa didn't know what he was going to do now that Mudear was dead and, he assumed, out of his life. He didn't think he was ever going to be able to really get her out of his life. He didn't even know if that was what he really wanted . . . Mudear out of his life. Perhaps, now that she was truly gone, he would be able to find someone else, maybe somebody like his drinking buddy Patrice, someone who was not so heartless, so evil, so lacking in what he called a little human kindness.

Sometimes he feared that Mudear either was not human or didn't possess any kind of kindness and living with her all these years, forty-five altogether, had somehow contaminated him. And he feared even more that his girls, Mudear's daughters, would turn out the same way. He shivered slightly as if someone had walked across his grave at the very thought.

When he heard the sound of automobile doors closing, he went over to the side window of the bedroom and saw his two oldest daughters get in their cars. After Emily pulled off in her little red car, he stood there watching Betty sitting in hers parked in the driveway. As he watched, he smiled at the trail of cigarette smoke drifting out her car window. Betty was the only one of his girls who smoked like he did. Mudear had been a heavy smoker at one time, smoked Kool filters. Used to smoke in bed, too. But she told him one night when he came in from work late that she had heard on a medical talk show that smoking gave you wrinkles, so she stopped immediately. It seemed to him that Mudear could do anything she wanted to when she put her mind to it.

And, of course, when Mudear stopped smoking, all smoking in the house had to cease.

Looking down at Betty's cigarette smoke, he felt ashamed that he took pride in the fact that one of his girls smoked like him. As if sucking on these cancer sticks is something to be proud of, he thought. But he couldn't help it. There was so little he could claim in his own children.

CHAPTER 7

Betty sat in her car for a few minutes smoking a cigarette and looking out over the garden and the field of wildflowers around her parents' house before starting the engine. The moon, nearly full, shone through a break in the clouds and flooded the field with a soft white light that made the colors of the late-blooming wild-flowers—goldenrod and blue sage and some black-eyed susans—stand out as in an eerie night painting. And the white blooming flowers and plants of the formal white garden her mother had grown especially to stand out at night—the moonflowers, the stalks of ginger lily spreading in waves against the house, the caladiums and hostas with their pale green and white stripes, the climbing peace roses and the iceberg roses grown as standards—looked like spirits dancing in the autumn wind. The town marveled that Mudear's plants kept blooming so profusely and so late in the season.

Some folks said she had bodies buried back there.

If Mudear were to come back, that's where she would come, Betty thought. She was like some strange exotic mixed-up plant herself.

During the day lounging around in her freshly laundered gowns and robes and pajamas giving off noxious fumes like carbon dioxide as she made everyone's life miserable in the house. Then, at night blossoming and exuding oxygen, coming to life and giving off life in her garden outside. She was like a strange jungle plant that had reversed the natural order of the plant world. Betty had even seen her stoop down and take a bit of her garden dirt in her mouth one night.

Betty could see her mother now as she had seen her innumerable nights wandering around in the field of flowers in her nightclothes, barefoot in the summertime and heavy boots in cooler weather, as if gardening were the most natural thing in the world to be doing in the middle of the night.

For Mudear it was. She had possessed night vision. Extraordinary night vision, as far as Betty could tell. Her night vision extended to seeing at dusk and all the shadings in between when most folks with night vision said it was more difficult to see. Even more unusual, Mudear could not only see in pitch dark as most blessed with the sight could, but she could see just as clearly as day. Mudear could not only make out shapes and figures in the dark, she could see the ants crawling over her vines, the aphids on her roses, the blossoms on her eggplant, the drooping falls on her beard iris. She could see to turn her compost pile and where she left the garden fork she needed for the job leaning against the side of the aluminum storehouse.

She had had Poppa find an old stone park bench with flowers and vines chiseled into its legs, sides, and back and set it down in the middle of where one of the paths of her garden crossed the other. When she was a teenager, Betty would get up to go to the bathroom in the middle of the night and stop to gaze out the window at Mudear sitting on one of her benches brushing the side of her thigh lazily with a huge sprig of lavender and be so mesmerized by her mother's movements that she would forget to go back to bed and would fall asleep at the windowsill.

But Mudear had a knack for doing the strangest things and making them appear, at least for the moment, perfectly natural. Betty thought it was part of her charm, part of her beauty. Not that Mudear could be called a traditional beauty. She was nothing special really, just a little brown-skinned woman past middle age. She was never as pretty as any of her daughters, but she had a way about her, a confidence, a sureness in the way she moved, in the way she squatted down in the dirt next to a plant with real tenderness, a tenderness she never showed her family, that was downright seductive. And she could throw back her little pea head and laugh with such a robustness and a sense of abandon and irony that her daughters learned to talk about people in Mulberry and on television and in the news with a cutting wickedness just to hear her roar.

Mudear's actions just seemed normal. Betty didn't notice right away, for instance, that Mudear never came out of the house like her little classmates' mothers did until her teachers at school began making sly comments in class about mothers who didn't seem to care enough about their daughters to make the effort to show up at parent-teacher meetings. At first, Betty didn't realize they were referring to Mudear. But when the comments became so pointed that she couldn't misinterpret or overlook them, she began to watch her mother in the way that Mudear had quietly taught her to watch other people, then come home and tell her what the girl had observed.

Mudear always talked to her girls as if they were already women. They had conversations, never just silly meaningless small talk. They all understood that Mudear didn't take time for such trivialities as chitchat.

They had never, even before the change, had conversations about school, dates, homework, skinned knees, and such, but rather about feelings and impressions and conjectures and opinions. When they talked of their grade school, it was a discussion of their friends and teachers and other people and their families and their clothes and their personal habits and their personal histories.

If a teacher were cranky with the students, the girls would tell Mudear about it as they cleaned the house when they came home from school. Then, they would discuss the possibilities of the source of her displeasure. Finally, Mudear would make the call.

"Mrs. Johnson's husband probably had hell in him last night and got drunk. Ya'll said she drinks, too, huh? Maybe he didn't pay some bill. I'd be mad, too." Or, "Didn't you tell me Mrs. Johnson's brother and wife just moved in with them with a new baby? Probably kept them all up last night."

Then, on to the next topic.

They would come home offering up their news, perceptions, observations like royal honey for the queen bee. It was what was expected of them. Their ears perked up like little cats' ears when they overheard something outside the house that they thought might pique her interest. Sometimes, her girls brought her the outside world without even realizing it. If Mudear let them visit a friend's house, when they returned they reported to Mudear.

The conversation would begin with a few comments on what

was done, what was seen, what was eaten and then it would slide easily into an examination of the adults and the intricacies of the household: gained weight, lost weight, new clothes, new anything, music playing, other visitors, nervous habits, mother and father touch, speak, fight. Were your little friends unusually quiet today? she would ask.

Anything that would add texture, perspective, feeling to the picture the girls painted for Mudear. Mudear would keep these images in order but overlapping like a plate drawing in a biology book of the human body and all its organs that has many overlays. With all the transparent colored pages in place, the picture took on a three-dimensional appearance that left the girls amazed that Mudear instinctively knew so much without leaving the house.

It added to their mythical image of her.

They never voiced their awareness that Mudear would have no connection with her community if they didn't bring the world to her.

Betty's thoughts seemed to drift out the car window like the cigarette smoke that trailed from her nostrils. She thought again about going back in the house to try and convince Annie Ruth to come stay with her and Emily at her house for the night. But she knew that the three of them could not stay under one roof that night. With the day she had had and the one that loomed ahead, she wouldn't have the strength to keep Emily from interrogating Annie Ruth about her plans. She felt Annie Ruth couldn't take it. Even though her sister looked a lot better now, Betty couldn't stop picturing her as she had been at the airport.

Then, all of a sudden she remembered Matthew, her first boy-friend in high school. Thinking about her sisters always put her in mind of her men. She smiled to herself thinking how he had asked her the first time they met, "You ever been shanghaied?" then proceeded to do it. Taking her to one of the new houses under construction in Sherwood Forest after all the workmen had left for the day, giving her a boost through one of the windows, spreading a tarpaulin splattered with rose-colored paint on the bare floor for them.

If he showed up right now, she thought, I bet he would make love to me. No matter if he's married and got children and a house somewhere with a big mortgage on it that he needs his wife's income to pay for. Right now, he would want to love me.

She took it for granted that he would feel the same way about her that she felt about him. Because he was the first.

Just the smell of sawdust still made her horny.

I wonder if Cinque came by the shop today, she wondered as the thought of being horny made her mind immediately flit to her sculptured, broad-shouldered lover, Cinque. "It's not like he's eighteen or under the legal age or anything," she had told her sisters over and over about the shy local boy who had turned nineteen shortly after Betty hired him to do some quick handyman work in her beauty shop in East Mulberry. Now, she told her sisters primly as if she were doing good works for the church, she was trying to help him get into college. "He's really a very good poet, too," she insisted.

Emily and Annie Ruth had just laughed at their big sister's embarrassment over Cinque. They thought it was great and kept feeding her suggestions to try with him and then come back and share the details with them.

Following Annie Ruth's advice, Betty had one night tied Cinque to the big brass bed in her bedroom.

"Miss Lovejoy," he had gasped. "You gonna make me scream."

"Baby, I think that's the point," she had said, as breathless as he. "This is my house. We are alone. Yell all you want."

When she came back to herself, sitting there in Mudear's driveway looking out over her field of flowers, she nearly blushed and became flustered, putting out her cigarette hurriedly and avoiding her own gaze in the rearview mirror. It seemed Mudear crept into her thoughts at the most unexpected and inopportune times. Like now, she thought as she put the car in reverse, backed out to the empty street, and sped out of Sherwood Forest.

But she knew from talking with her sisters that Mudear did that with all of her girls. It seemed the kind of mother they had touched them all the way through their lives. Not just when they lived with her, not just when they spent time visiting her, but all through their lives. Mudear seeped into their lives and heads as easily as she had used them to go out into the world for her when they were children and she decided not to leave the house.

Betty knew that people in town had all manner of theories concerning Mudear and why she stayed in the house. Over the years, a mythology had grown up around her as if she were some mighty goddess like Oshun out of an ancient legend.

Some in Mulberry thought that Mudear was scared to leave the house. In recent years they had even been able to put a name to it: agoraphobia. As if Mudear were afraid of anything. Some *just knew* that her parents' situation was like that of Mr. Raymond and Miss Edna who lived in a small tin shack in East Mulberry. Mr. Raymond, who had had both his legs amputated because of sugar years before and who moved around in a beat-up wheelchair, kept his wife trapped in the house. As a child, Betty had heard two women ahead of her in the checkout line at the Colonial grocery store say as much about Mudear.

"Poor thing, Esther Lovejoy is just like Miss Edna. She a captive in that house. And Mr. Raymond, he beat Miss Edna, too."

"Well, hell if I'd let a man in a wheelchair beat my ass when I got two good legs and he ain't got none!"

"That what make it so sad. Miss Edna must stand there and *be* beat."

"Well, Esther probably getting her ass whipped in that house, too. That man only allow the girls to leave for school and errands. Yeah, Esther a captive in that house."

The woman paying at the cash register kept clearing her throat and batting her eyes in Betty's direction. But the women speaking wouldn't turn around and see that one of the subjects of their gossip was standing right behind them and just kept talking.

It had taught Betty a valuable lesson for someone who lived in a small town. After that, she never talked about anyone in her beauty shop or anywhere in public without looking over her shoulder first to make sure somebody's relative or friend wasn't listening nearby.

Some folks in town spread the rumor that Mudear had some horrible facial disfigurement that caused her to set herself apart from the world, ashamed of the way she looked. That one amused Betty the most because she knew that Mudear thought she was the prettiest thing going. And that her flawless brown complexion was a matter of inordinate pride with her. But the thing that amazed Betty was when she discovered that Mudear had somehow heard all these rumors, probably from her friend Carrie, and that none of them disturbed the self-contained woman. She even laughed at some of the rumors. Since the change, Mudear didn't give a damn what people thought of her.

Betty envied her for that. Over the years, she had grown to envy Mudear many things.

She certainly knew how to "delegate" work at least if not authority. She was the original "delegator." She delegated heavy garden chores and errands requiring a car to Poppa and most everything else to her eldest daughter.

I can just hear her now, Betty thought. Whatever comes up, Betty will handle it.

Let Betty do it. Let Betty do it. Let Betty pick that up, she big-boned. Let Betty show you how to iron a long sleeve. Let Betty . . .

Shit! Betty thought. *Let her?*

When she pulled out of her parents' driveway, a light rain had begun to fall. She started to stop by her beauty shop in their old neighborhood in East Mulberry on her way home but thought, I don't have the strength to play boss tonight. And she headed home instead, knowing that her two assistant managers would have taken care of both businesses knowing there was a death in the family.

By the time she reached her own house at the top of Pleasant Hill, the light drizzle had grown to a drenching downpour. And Betty noted that Emily's red Datsun wasn't anywhere around. Even though Emily had left Mudear's house at least half an hour before her, Betty tried not to worry as she pulled into the long driveway and parked in the garage next to her big restored stone colonial house and let herself in the old maid's entrance.

CHAPTER 8

Each time Emily was in town after a heavy and long rainfall, she went down to the overpass of the Spring Street bridge over the Ocawatchee River to see if the river was deep enough now to jump in and drown. She was a teenager when she first actually considered the act, but the riverbed always seemed to be muddy red or nearly dry, with hardly enough water rushing over it to come up to her chin. Her father, who loved to fish, said he remembered when the waters of the Ocawatchee regularly overflowed its banks, flooding the houses at the foot of Pleasant Hill, sending chickens and cats and dogs to higher ground. And the fat dark mullet could almost be caught with your hands on the banks. But Emily found that hard to believe.

From the relative protection of the overpass, she had been watching regularly since she was a teenager and had never seen any such phenomenon.

Just like Mudear said, "Don't pay no attention to nothing Poppa say. Poppa'll say anything," she'd think.

But she couldn't stop herself from checking. Checking was something she did all the time. She told herself that she did it to keep some kind of control in her own life. Otherwise, she felt like a child riding a new two-wheel bike down a hill without holding onto the handlebars.

When she came to a doorway wider than one door, she had to count with her foot five times before entering. It amazed her that no one seemed to notice her compulsive actions, as much as she carried them out during the day. But in the government building where she worked as an archivist, among her acquaintances, at her favorite gym where she had just started going to take care of the extra weight she had put on recently, no one pointed out her compulsions. Mudear was the only one who ever said, "Girl, what in the hell are you doing tapping your foot five times on the doorjamb? I have raised a fool." It never dawned on Emily that she had been doing these routines so long, touching a curl in the front of her hair five times, brushing down the hairs of her right eyebrow five times before checking a file, that they seemed part of her makeup, not some alien neurotic compulsions. Just how Emily was.

This evening, just as it had begun to rain again, Emily had headed instinctively for the banks of the Ocawatchee River when she left Mudear's house. It was where she liked to be when she had something to figure out as well as when she considered suicide. And now, with the news of Annie Ruth's pregnancy—a pregnancy that her younger sister had the nerve to think of letting go to completion—on top of Mudear's death, Emily knew she really had something to ponder.

She had only been pregnant once as far as she knew and that pregnancy and her reaction to it had helped to end her second marriage. She never was any good at lying so when her husband, Ron, had asked her if she had really fallen down the steps of their garden apartment or if she had had an abortion, she had told him the truth.

After that, no matter what she said to him, his reply was the same: "You flushed *my* baby down the toilet stool."

When she had told her parents her marriage was over, Mudear had said to her, "It's no surprise to me."

Besides the fact that Mudear thought Ron was crazy, she had been told by Annie Ruth that when he had come to the house the first time for dinner—Mudear, of course, didn't come downstairs for the meal—he had stirred his iced tea with his fork. He had simply slipped it in his mouth to wipe off the few grains of long-grained rice and brown fried-chicken gravy, stuck it in the tall glass of tea, and stirred. Mudear was not forgiving.

"Daughter, if you marry some man who don't know how to use a simple eating utensil right," Mudear had told Emily at the time, "then you a bigger fool than I been saying all these years."

Mudear never fully forgave Emily for marrying Ron. Emily didn't think she really cared whether or not one of her girls married what mothers in Sherwood Forest called a "professional man." But she had overheard Mudear's only friend, Carrie, whom she called "Cut," bragging to her over the telephone about a niece of hers marrying a "pharmacy" from Xavier University. And Emily had always felt in her heart that Mudear might have been a bit more generous if Ron had not worked fixing cars for a living, whether or not he knew how to use a knife and fork.

But his table manners were not the problem for Emily in their marriage. Ron, they all discovered too late to save Emily, was as crazy as his wife.

"He can't seem to let it go," Emily had told her sisters on one of their regular telephone conference calls of Ron's experience in Vietnam. When he began wearing camouflage fatigues to his job as a mechanic, no one paid much attention. But when Emily finally told Betty and Annie Ruth that he was wearing the things day and night, even to bed, she knew she was really in trouble. And so was he.

"I got to wash the dishes every night, not just scrape and stack 'em. He can't stand the smell of rotting anything. He says it reminds him of death and of rotting flesh. And the sound of the dishwasher reminds him of the whir of Huey helicopters twirling overhead to spray him with red-hot tracers. So, I got my hands back in dishwater just like when we were girls."

"Bless her heart," Annie Ruth told Betty on the phone later, "I guess it's like the s' inks say, we do all marry our mothers."

Mudear had ins .ed that Emily do the dishes for the household the whole time the girls were growing up. Emily's long slender model's hands slipped in and out of the soapy Lux suds with grudging efficiency as Mudear held forth from her perch on the sofa. "Now, Emily can't do a damn thing with those pretty hands of hers. Couldn't make a decent centerpiece for the Last Supper if she had the chance and the Garden of Eden to work with. But those long skinny hands sure are pretty, look like something out of a Jergens lotion magazine ad."

Emily, sitting on the banks of the turbid Ocawatchee, could

see Ron in front of her now. Could almost smell the scent of his body fresh out of a shower with Lifebuoy deodorant soap and a hint of his musk clinging to his hairs.

Perhaps another kind of woman could have dealt with Ron and his memories of war, could have even helped him, gone through it with him, been there for him when he screamed at night from his Mekong Delta dreams. But his troubles seemed to just mirror hers too closely. Post-traumatic stress syndrome was what they both suffered from. One would have thought they were made for each other. Instead, they were both so deep in their own distress, in their own misery, that they merely canceled each other out. The war he still fought was too much like the one Emily had to fight with her own demons.

When she tried to help, it only seemed to make matters worse for Ron, confused him. Even as she tried to soothe him, held his hard sweaty body, cried with him, she was really crying for herself and for her sisters and for the destruction that family warfare had wreaked on all of them.

When Ron reluctantly agreed to go to a V.A. counselor for a while and his nightmares suddenly subsided, Emily would still wake in the middle of the night sweating and heaving as if *she* had had a nightmare. And then, to find Ron, her husband, sleeping the sleep of the innocent next to her shaking body would nearly send her into a rage.

I can almost understand why Mudear always said she was surprised more men aren't found murdered in their beds, she would think. Then, she would wish immediately that she hadn't recalled Mudear's words because they always made her remember that each time her mother said them when Emily was young, Emily had a hard time sleeping through the night. Staying awake 'til dawn, waiting to hear the sound of her father's footfall in the hall on his way to the bathroom so she would know that he had made it through the night. That Mudear had not in fact acted on her implied threat against her father. Hacked him to death with a butcher knife, splashed kerosene around his bed linens and set them on fire.

Poor Poppa, she thought now. What he gonna do without Mudear?

Emily shifted her butt uncomfortably on the rocky ground of the riverbank. She had been sitting in a relatively dry spot under the bridge protected from the misty rain. And after rummaging through the back of her car among overdue library books and hair spray from Betty's shop, she had found a plastic garbage bag to spread on the hard wet ground to protect the seat of her favorite jeans. But she still had to unzip the tight pants in order to breathe and sit comfortably.

Once when she came to sit under the bridge in foul weather, she had discovered a makeshift shelter of cardboard boxes left there by some homeless person. That time, fresh from Betty's beauty shop and distraught over the bitter ending of a quickie relationship, she had really planned to kill herself. But the thought of a homeless person in the tiny town of Mulberry kept intruding on her deadly thoughts. And instead of killing herself, she had left her lined leather gloves there with a twenty-dollar bill tucked inside.

All the way back to Atlanta, she had kept saying to herself, A homeless person in Mulberry. A homeless person in Mulberry.

She didn't dare say it, even to herself, but she had thought, it could be Ron. The last time she had seen him, a year or so before, he was walking near the river wearing his old camouflage jacket and dirty jeans with his red toolbox on his shoulder. She had made an illegal U-turn to avoid passing him even though she yearned to ask him what he was doing in Mulberry. She could tell by the way his camouflage jacket hung on his shoulders, a bit too large for him, that he was shooting bad.

It was nearly pitch dark by now, but Emily was confident that Betty wouldn't worry about her when she didn't go directly to her sister's house at the top of Pleasant Hill. Emily thought Betty was used to her wanderings around town when she came home to visit. Although she felt the town hadn't been kind to her, with its gossip and harsh judgments, Emily still loved Mulberry like an old friend. Other than her sisters, she felt her hometown was all she had. The only thing that anchored her to the world was her identity in Mulberry, even if it was as "the craziest Lovejoy sister." She knew all the back streets, even the ones that no longer existed, the ones changed by the construction of the interstate through the middle of Pleasant Hill. The community had complained that the plans were drawn up just to disrupt the black neighborhood. But the highway didn't bother Emily even though it left parts of the community with dead-end streets that overlooked kudzu-covered trees and the expressway instead of more houses. She kept in her mind just how the town had looked when she was a child and walked everywhere, even downtown, by herself.

There was little Emily didn't know about Mulberry. Her job as an archivist gave her easy access to all kinds of material. She had not only mulled over countless old documents—plantation logs, census records, deeds, birth certificates—and ancient newspapers at the state archives in Atlanta and in the local Mulberry libraries to learn the history of the place. And as a senior researcher for the state of Georgia, she had more access to files and archives than most.

She had also made it her business to know the daily and current shape of the town. In Mulberry even in the nineties, Emily thought, people still seemed to know more of the intricacies of other people's intimacies than in any other little town she knew of. Things you would think no one but the parties involved would know. That's how people gossiped in Mulberry. "And he reached over his plate of liver and onions, picked up a dull dinner knife, and threatened to stab her to death with it if she said one more word to him about that garbage disposal."

Listening as she got her hair done to the talk in Betty's first beauty shop, Lovejoy's 1, the one she opened in East Mulberry, Emily would wonder to herself sometimes, now how does she know what they were eating and just what he said? But it was never questioned. The other women would nod their wet and curlered heads in affirmation, slap their copies of *Essence, Lear's, Ebony, Mirabella, American Visions,* or *Vogue* against their thighs, and go on to the next topic.

Emily clung to everything that reminded her of the Mulberry she remembered or thought she remembered as a child.

As a child and a teenager, she never imagined that she would ever feel tenderly toward a town, a community that pegged her and her family crazy, that gossiped about them, that even scorned them when party lists and invitations to be local debutantes were sent out. Not in a million years did she think she would care about Mulberry. But as Mudear always reminded them, "Keep living, daughters."

Emily even chose Lovejoy's 1 to have her hair done each week because it reminded her of old times. The beauty shop was still housed in the original building that Betty, when she was in her mid-twenties, renovated for the first shop she opened. There, she built up a large and loyal following with older women who still preferred to have their hair straightened with a hot comb. She eventually moved them into the era of straightening perms and got their daughters' and granddaughters' business to boot. Eventually, the smell of burning hair in the air was replaced with the stench of straightening chemical perms. But in an antique display case at the front of the shop by the receptionist's desk, Betty still kept examples of the original tools of her trade: the iron hot comb with the charred black wooden handle, three sizes of the long slim iron hot curlers that hairdressers spun around at their axes to cool off, the open gas burner used to heat up the utensils, and the small improved steel heating "oven" that followed.

Scattered among the pressing and curling tools in the case were photographs, eight-by-ten glossies, of the glamorous black women of the forties and fifties—Dorothy Dandridge, Dinah Washington, Lena Horne, Billie Holiday—who had used just these kinds of utensils to keep their coifs in control. The whole shop— though outfitted with every modern convenience—looked like one that these famous women might have stopped in to get their hair done if they had been traveling the "chitlin' circuit" in the South back in another decade.

Betty had even set up an antique barbershop chair with red leather upholstry and brass studs in the middle of the shop and used it herself when she worked on some old special customer, a former teacher or a friend of Mudear's before the change.

Lovejoy's 2, on the other hand, looked as if it could have been transplanted from some tony address on West Fifty-seventh Street in New York City and set down at the far end of the Mulberry Mall. While Lovejoy's 1 was all wood and plaster, Lovejoy's 2 was all glass, chrome, and tall wide mirrors reflecting the track lights spotlighting every chair. The floor was Italian marble, a bitch to keep clean, Betty's cleaning crew discovered, but the customers seemed to think it added to the ambience they sought as they got their hair washed, clipped and colored, chemically straightened, waved, frozen and permed. New customers had to make appointments weeks in advance.

Emily drove down to Mulberry nearly every weekend to get her hair done or perm touched up at Betty's shop. Afterward, she would go see Mudear for a short visit. But even with a new hairdo to buoy Emily's spirits, she always left Mudear's feeling so lonely that the rest of the week she hated herself for going. If Mudear were looking at television or repairing a garden tool on the screen porch, she wouldn't even acknowledge Emily's presence except to ask her to sweep the kitchen floor or to make her a frothy banana–orange juice drink in the blender one of her daughters had bought for her.

Most Saturdays, Mudear didn't seem to notice when Emily left.

It wasn't Mudear that she longed for so much as it was Mulberry. In Atlanta, she missed the small-town feeling of knowing people's business and knowing who was related to whom, who had gone to school with whose brother. But she never even considered moving back to her hometown. Not as long as Mudear was living there, and it was hard to think of Mulberry without Mudear. And it was impossible for her to think of Mudear not living. She was grateful for the protection the hundred and fifty or so miles to Atlanta gave her.

But truly, it was always the loneliness, the wide gap she felt at the pit of her stomach, that made her feel so disconnected. I don't have anyone to care about me, except for my sisters, she would think as she drove back to her empty disheveled apartment each week.

She was alone and lonely. And that was a terrible way of being. It was and had always been what was driving her crazy. All of her good news, her good fortune seemed to fall flat because there was no one outside her sisters in her life to whom it made any difference. No one to share it with.

At least, Betty had had Mudear for a few years before the change. And Annie Ruth had always got so babied and was so cute that everything was an easy slide for her. But me, I ain't never had nothing . . . nothing but my sisters. Lord, if it hadn't been for them, what would I have done? But she knew what she would have done. She would have actually jumped off the Spring Street bridge over the Ocawatchee River, no matter whether the riverbed was bone dry or flush with running muddy water.

CHAPTER 9

I been thinking 'bout Emily or one of them saying, "Mudear, she the kind of 'ho."

From what them girls been talking about, sleeping with this one and sleeping with that one, having babies for they don't know who, sleeping with teenaged boys, them girls been fucking everything in shoe leather. Seem like every man they meet must have a wart on his thing. So, strictly speaking, I ain't the one who's a 'ho. It seems I'm the only woman who lived in that house in Sherwood Forest who's only been with just one man, my husband, my whole life. Heck, I ain't let Ernest even touch me in years. Come to think of it, he hasn't even tried. I guess for us to be hooking up like that, even for relief, seem kinda foolish, all things considered.

But then again, you got to ask yourself, what's a 'ho, anyway?

Whether you stupid enough to sleep with lots of men or whether you sleep with just one is supposed to decide what kind of person you are? If you spread your legs and your mouth, too, it seems from what I see on those X-rated videotapes Ernest bring home sometimes—how any woman could put a man's dick into her mouth I do not know, but then, like I say, I only been with one man in my life, only seen one real dick in my life, so, what do I know about that particular subject? But if you do spread your legs, it don't seem to me to be grounds for calling somebody an ugly name like 'ho. Maybe fool, but not 'ho.

Now, me myself, I never did sleep around the way these girls seem to be making a career out of, but that don't mean nothing just 'cause I didn't do it. Like I say, everybody ain't me.

Lots of times when I'm eating a light meal during the afternoon, I switch on the television to BET "Rap City" or "Yo! MTV Raps" and listen to the songs while I'm eating. And I kinda liked that rap, you know, what they call the energy of it. And I'd be sitting there eating and bobbing my head to the music 'til one day I really started paying attention to the words and I started picking out all the "bitches" and the " 'hos" mixed in among the lyrics. And it made me right mad.

Who them young boys think they are talking 'bout us women like that? And then, it got so that some of the little girls singing in them rap groups are saying the same thing. They got us calling our own selves " 'hos" and "bitches."

I started to send a letter to those young boys in those rap groups—and some of them ain't so young, either—and ask them what they know about a 'ho and what's a 'ho to them anyway. I meant to get Betty or one of them to write it for me.

To let those rapper boys tell it, they be the kind of woman my generation called a "whore." But then, "whore" is just some word made up by men to put women in their place. And ain't it just like a man to put you in your place about something that he wanted from you in the first place.

Now that I think about it, it's what Ernest used to have the nerve to call me when he used to come home 'bout drunk and put us out. He'd call me those names, not because he thought I was actually screwing around on him but because for him that was the worst thing he could think of to say to me. He thought it was the most hurtful thing a man could say to a woman. Call her a whore or a slut.

It's like all the other names men have given what they call "bad" women. Names like "skank" and "cunt"—calling us by our female parts, calling us out of our names for being women. Ugly-sounding names, names that make us sound like we smell. And they all do it. Just the other night, I saw that actor I like so much, Robert De Niro, in one of those Martin Scorchy or whatever his name is movies, call some woman a "skank." Real offhandedly, like it didn't matter to call somebody that. Just hearing it gave me the all-overs. Like he or any man got the right to just offhandedly label somebody with something as ugly-sounding as "skank" or " 'ho."

Even Arsenio said the other night in his monologue "skank 'ho" right there on television. I was shocked. They didn't even bleep it.

It's just like with those young boys who rap, they 'un put it to music, for God's sake. Now, not all of them rapper boys be calling women 'hos and bitches. But I figure if one is doing it, it's one too many.

And if these rapper boys want to "express" their lives like they say they do in their music, then, why don't they talk about men like they talk about women? But then it dawned on me that there ain't no male word for 'ho. So, I guess they wouldn't appreciate being called a 'ho, either.

How those black boys feel if we started calling them "dick"? Like:

> Dick walks in the room and goes for my money.
> This kinda thing make me feel kinda funny.

Or what if we always refer to them as those "gold-digging dicks"?

I never did use the word "whore" that much anyway, but it made me want to stop using it altogether.

But I have to admit I still looked at those rap videos on television.

I guess, besides my garden, I'm gonna miss my cable television the most. I never was much of a reader. Ernest and the girls always had their heads in some book or another. I never much cared for reading. But I did love television.

Course, before, Ernest wouldn't buy no television. Had us cooped up in that house just entertaining ourselves. But then I threatened to buy a television myself with my own money—course I was lying. I didn't have no money, but he didn't know that. But after I put him in his place by paying that electric and gas bill that time, he couldn't chance it. So, he shot out of there and got us a television right quick. Hee-hee.

Back then, we could only get that one Mulberry channel that went off the air around dark and on cloudy days sometimes we could get a fuzzy picture of one Atlanta station. It had so much snow on the screen you couldn't hardly make out whether it was a man, woman, or animal moving around in the picture. Sometimes, I'd make Ernest go up on the roof and fiddle with the antenna. But it was better than listening to Ernest and the radio.

After I told him that about buying the television myself, I'd hear him in another part of the house all the time sneaking 'round looking for my money. He just knew I had a stash somewhere in that house and he was determined to find it. Hee-hee-hee. I'd just lay in my comfortable bed, I think it was the double bed then, and listen to him rummage through drawers and closets and cabinets pretending he was looking for a clean shirt or a can of milk or something. He just knew I had money somewhere.

But he just didn't understand that after I got his ass that one time when I did have a few dollars — thank you, Lord Jesus — and he didn't, that I didn't have no use for no money no more. After that I got everything I wanted without having to spend a dime. Hee-hee.

Come to think of it, I don't know when I have had any actual money in my hands. Right now I can't even remember whose picture is on a twenty-dollar bill.

Lord, can't things change? Like I tell my girls, "Keep living, daughters."

I can remember when I felt like running away to another country if I could scrape together twenty dollars or more. Now, I spend that much on a special trowel for the garden from one of those fancy mail-order places that Betty and 'em send me catalogs for. At least, I did before I died. Well, Lord.

Ernest just didn't understand that I was the type of person who knew both how to abound and how to abase.

CHAPTER 10

Back alone in her old bedroom down the hall from Mudear and Poppa's room, Annie Ruth unfolded and unpacked her large carry-on travel bag, the lightweight leather one Delbert had given her the previous Christmas. The card had been signed, "For my little globe-trotter." She had not recognized the handwriting. She had figured it wasn't his secretary's at the record company because she didn't like Annie Ruth and the woman would never have picked the expensive gift wrapping that the bag came in. Probably a clerk in a store, which meant that Delbert had bought the gift over the phone and had it gift wrapped and sent to him. Annie Ruth had just shrugged. Just shows you how little Delbert knows me, she had thought. I hate to travel. Mudear had made it impossible for any of her girls to truly float through life acting as if they didn't understand what was really going on in just about any situation. "Like a white girl," Annie Ruth said. Mudear had trained them specifically to understand all the signs of any situation: the half-spoken word, the gesture, the cough, the dropped gaze, the shaky voice, the unfamiliar handwriting.

On a regular visit back home, both of her sisters would have been lying across the single bed watching her take new clothes out of her bag. "What ya got pretty?" they'd ask her, eyeing the closed bags greedily. Normally, they enjoyed this clothes-showing ritual as much as they loved getting something from a sister's wardrobe to keep. It was usually like a small free-for-all fashion show whenever the girls got together. Seldom did any of them wait for the bag's owner to remove all the clothes from the suitcase. If Emily or Betty saw some material or color in Annie Ruth's bag that caught her eye, she would dip into the bag like a child discovering a glittery bauble in the bushes in the yard and pull it out. And if they were at Mudear's house and Mudear happened to be interested, they would have to haul all the bags and clothes down to her room for a second show.

This night, Annie Ruth was thankful they weren't there. As a rule, there was no place on earth that she felt safer and happier than in her sisters' circle of love and familiarity. They always knew just what she needed. On the ride home from the airport, Betty and Emily had let her stretch out on the backseat for a while with just the music playing. But not for long.

After a few miles, Betty had smoothed her hair down in back, switched off Sade singing on the CD player, turned around, and said over the black velvet headrest, "Okay, sit up, Annie Ruth." It was an order, but Annie Ruth had just rubbed her face deeper into the plush seats and groaned. She didn't think she had ever felt so nauseated in her life.

"Come on, girl, lift up your head and face the world," Betty coaxed sternly. "Come on, Annie Ruth."

Annie Ruth spoke directly into the seat. "This is the only place on the face of this earth where anybody calls me Annie Ruth."

"Well, when you get back to the Coast, you can become Ruth again. But you home now, girl."

Annie Ruth still didn't sit up or lift up her head, but she did turn her face out of the backseat cushion and toward the window. It was the first time she noticed the light rain beginning to fall.

"Umph, it's raining," she said, noting the bright fall sunshine bouncing off the raindrops on the window.

"Yeah," Emily said, turning on the windshield wipers. "Raining with the sun out. 'Devil must be beating his wife over the head with a frying pan.'"

Emily couldn't help but shudder a little at the saying because when they were younger and someone in their house repeated the old saying, Mudear would always say the same thing: "Humph, if the devil's wife had any sense, she'd set his bed on fire while he sleeping."

Annie Ruth caught her sister's reaction out of the corner of her eye and, remembering how often Emily had been terrorized by some "innocent" statement from Mudear's mouth, she sat up and reached for the back of her sister's neck and gently rubbed it. Just seeing Emily's smile in the rearview mirror made Annie Ruth feel a little stronger and less nauseated. And she took a deep breath and reached in her big suede purse for her cosmetics bag to put on some mauve lipstick with a little orange over it to tone down the pink the way her makeup woman at work had shown her.

Just being with Betty and Emily had made her feel better. But the whole time that she had sat on the porch with her sisters nursing her weak bourbon and ginger ale, Annie Ruth had had to fight the impulse to tell them about the cats.

It was bad enough that they knew about her pregnancy without adding hallucinations to the mix. I guess they're hallucinations, she thought. Of course, they are. They're not real. Of course not.

The only thing that had kept her from blurting out that she saw cats lurking just about everywhere was the words of a psychiatrist. Not even her psychiatrist, a TV psychiatrist. She had heard the woman two days before on the early-morning talk show on the L.A. television station where she was evening anchor. Dressed in a calming authoritative dress and jacket and a large nondescript beaded necklace, the psychiatrist had given a few emergency tips to keep in mind until the doctor came, so to speak.

It seemed that lately there had been a number of cases of anxiety attacks among women living in large urban areas that occurred on the weekends or late at night when mental health people could not be readily reached for help. As a service to these folks, the morning show was asking this photogenic therapist who specialized in such cases to share some of her wisdom with the television audience, many of whom, it had been discovered through demographics, were single women, the likeliest sufferers.

The one hint that had stuck in Annie Ruth's mind—she was only half listening to the report as she lay in bed reading the morning paper—was the one she felt, on reflection, was the one she truly needed. Namely: don't go around telling everybody just how crazy you are. Keep your neurosis to yourself until you can share it with a qualified mental health professional.

The doctor announced at the end of her segment that she was

writing a book to be published the next spring on the subject. Annie Ruth made a note in her leather time organizer to buy it as soon as it hit the stores.

The psychiatrist's advice was the only thing that had kept her from telling everyone on Flight 754 all the way from Los Angeles to Atlanta, and then her fellow passengers on the smaller prop Flight 1117 from Atlanta to Mulberry, about the strange sights she saw walking up and down the aisles.

The cat sightings had begun a couple of weeks before when Betty intimated over the phone that Mudear didn't seem herself, that she had a terrible cough she couldn't seem to shake. Annie Ruth had tried for a number of days to pretend that she did not see what she thought she saw. But she couldn't. First, it was the big yellow tabby she thought she caught sight of in the makeup room. She had yelled, but the little fur ball had scampered off by the time someone came to see it . . . and to see about her.

Then, while she was on the air reading the evening news a few days before Mudear died, she felt something soft brush up against her ankle and she screamed right into camera 2, "There's a cat under my desk!"

No one reacted for a while because the director, a tall hunky gay blond California boy, felt pulled in two directions. On the one hand, he knew he had to switch cameras and get his popular evening anchorwoman off the air. He had been watching her all week peeking around corners, looking over her shoulder, checking in drawers, and he knew she was not quite right. Besides, he had heard from a friend of his from her previous station about her two-week "rest" at the clinic outside of D.C. On the other hand, he couldn't resist pondering what a nervous breakdown on the air would do for his news show's ratings. Hell, he had seen *Network*.

The cats made Annie Ruth think of all the stories she had heard all her life from her family about cats and what suspicious, sneaky, vicious, filthy creatures they were. When the girls were small, they would sit on the floor between two of their beds in the old house. And in the darkened room, illuminated only by the cream-colored dinner candle Emily kept in a shoebox along with matches and things under her bed, Betty would tell them about the time the cat tried to kill Annie Ruth in her crib.

"I was about seven or eight," Betty would begin the story, "and they had just brought you home from the hospital, Annie Ruth, not too long before. We didn't ever have any pets around the house, but about the time you came home, a big old gray cat started hanging around the house. Somebody must have been feeding it because it hung around and hung around 'til I looked for him every morning when I went to school.

"Then, one day I came home from school and that cat was inside on the back porch. He must have walked in with somebody, and he was in the corner staying out of the way. I didn't say anything 'cause I kind of liked him. Then, it was the next day. I had just come in when I heard Mudear upstairs let out a scream and I ran upstairs. I didn't know what had happened to her. And when I ran into Mudear's room where they kept Annie Ruth's crib, I saw something that, like Mudear say, made my blood run cold. That big old gray cat was up over your crib, Annie Ruth, with one of his paws just dangling down to where you were laying. Mudear was standing there with this scary look on her face. She said the first thing she thought about was stories she had heard as a girl about cats suffocating babies in their sleep while they try to be sucking the babies' milk out of their throats. I don't know. That's what Mudear said.

"So, Mudear let out another scream and grabbed for that cat with all her strength and it jumped right out of her reach to the windowsill and tried to get out a hole in the screen no bigger than my thumb. I don't know how he planned to squeeze through a little old hole that little. But it didn't matter 'cause Mudear went after him again and grabbed hold of him by his skin and threw him so hard against the wall he bounced off and fell on the floor just like he was dead. But he wasn't because I could see his stomach moving up and down.

"And then, Mudear and me ran over to your crib . . . I don't know where you were, Emily. You were just a little girl, maybe you were sleeping. Anyway, we ran over to your crib, Annie Ruth, and Mudear said she nearly passed out when she saw your rich red blood on the collar of your little white shirt. That cat took a swipe at Annie Ruth with his old long sharp claws and nearly ripped her throat open!

"Well, it wasn't exactly ripped open, but it was bad. They had to call the doctor, and he said if that cat scratch had been an inch over to the left it would have severed Annie Ruth's jugular vein. Uh-huh, Emily, an important one."

"What happened to that cat, Betty?"

"What you think happened? Mudear killed that cat."

Remembering the story, Annie Ruth thought, it's a damn shame the best you can say about your mother is that she killed a cat for you once.

Anyway, she hadn't seen a cat since she landed in Mulberry.

The last one sighted had been on the plane when she had gotten on and found her seat number. Perched on the back of the seat was a gray cat with a white bib. Annie Ruth let out a little gasp and threw her purple suede purse as hard as she could at the cat. All the contents of the bag came tumbling out, but the cat jumped down soundlessly and ran to the rear of the plane toward the coach seating. And that was the last she saw of the feline. The man sitting next to her didn't say a word and tried to avert his eyes from her during the entire flight.

Now that she was home with her sisters and could think more clearly, it didn't surprise Annie Ruth that it was cats that she saw. More than any other animal, she hated cats. It was her family's fault. Not only was she brought up on Betty's story about her early encounter with a cat. She had grown up hearing the most vile stories and tales about cats.

Now that she thought about it, Mudear had always used the image of cats to describe her most horrendous thoughts. When Betty had gone through that phase that time and couldn't stop scratching herself, and then, she couldn't seem to get it together and go on with her life after her divorce and moved back in with Poppa and Mudear for a while, Betty told her that Mudear had talked about cats all the time. Mudear would exclaim from her bed from time to time in exasperation, "Shit, craziness is hanging around this damn house like a hungry cat smelling fish!"

It was just what poor Betty had needed to hear in her state, Annie Ruth thought as she took a black cotton knit cat suit out of her bag, folded it over once, and laid it on the back of the dressing table chair.

I can wear that tomorrow when we go to the funeral home, she thought as she moved to another bag to get her short high-heeled black boots. In a third bag, she found a smaller quilted bag, opened it, and took out a beaded blue, yellow, and red necklace from South Africa, a gift from the anthropology professor at UCLA she had dated.

One of the few truly boring black men she had ever met, she thought, and started to chuckle at the thought of the distinguished-looking professor who lived a varied and interesting life but who seemed incapable of communicating any of that on a date. But she stopped laughing when she was suddenly swept with such a wave of nausea that she had to sit down at the dressing table and hold her head between her legs to keep from throwing up all over the baby-blue shag carpet.

For a while she thought she was going to have to run to the bathroom all the way at the end of the hall and throw up, but the feeling left as suddenly as it had come on. That was the way it had been happening for the past couple of weeks. Her morning sickness came around all times of the day. And nothing—eating soda crackers, drinking ginger ale, abstaining from food—nothing seemed to help.

She stood up slowly, took a couple of deep breaths, and patted her stomach.

"It's gonna be okay," she said out loud.

Now, she commanded herself not to get up and check under the bed for a feline visitor even though she thought she heard a faint rustling under the dust ruffle around the bottom of the bed.

If I don't give in to it, she thought, it won't be there. As she threw back the covers, she noticed the clean sheets on the bed had a slightly musty odor. Mudear must have been sicker for longer than we knew to allow sheets to smell like this in her house, she thought as she fluffed up the pillows and flapped the sheets of the familiar bed.

Then, she was immediately sorry that she had invoked Mudear's name. Now, I'll never get to sleep. And she knew she would need every little bit of strength she had to face Mudear in her casket the next morning.

It didn't matter, because before she could take off her new silk robe and lay her head down, a flood of nausea swept over her again, forcing her to jump up and run to the bathroom next door, the lavender one, Mudear's own personal bathroom.

CHAPTER 11

I t's funny that Annie Ruth should be seeing cats everywhere. There's always been something about cats and the women in this family.

When I was just a little girl, the strangest thing happened to me that had to do with a cat. That's when we had the house in Greenwood Bottom way out Broadway. I wasn't any more than about seven or eight and my mother, I called her Mudear, too, had sent me to the store four streets over from my house to get a nickel's worth of fatback meat to go in some turnip greens. It was in the summertime and my mother always had a big garden. She grew collards and turnips winter and summer. That's where I get my love for gardening from. Back then, most everyone had a little vegetable garden where they grew beans and greens and tomatoes and such for their family.

Anyway, she sent me to the store. It was run by two Italian brothers. The only other white business in that area was Joe's Saloon that was run by Jews. And just before I got to the store, I thought I saw this little boy who was a friend of my brother's running 'round the side of a house. I called out his name, but by the time I did, he had disappeared 'round the back of the house. So, I went 'round there to see what he was doing. But when I rounded the corner, he wasn't nowhere in sight. So, I went up the back steps—in those days, you didn't have no fear about going up on somebody's porch. Not like now where I see all kinds of things on the TV about missing and murdered children and little children running the streets all times of the day and night 'out anybody knowing where they at. But when I ran up the steps, I tripped on something and fell and nearly broke my neck. If I hadn't grabbed onto the porch post, I would 'a taken a bad fall. When I looked around to see what had tripped me up, I was surprised to see a cat laying on the steps just as fat and sassy as anything. It was a sleek black cat with white paws and a little white vest. I don't know where it came from unless it came from under the house 'cause I didn't see it at first. But it was laying there just licking itself and acting as if it had paid that month's rent on the porch.

I'd never been around cats much, but this was such a pretty cat, I sat down on the steps and watched it lick and bathe itself. And before I knew it, I was stroking the cat's soft black fur and listening to it purr and growl down in its stomach. It felt so good to rub the cat, and it must have felt just as good to that cat because it stood up and stretched its long black body one time and slowly walked around me where I was sitting on the top of the porch. Then, it laid back down in the same exact spot and turned on its back for me to rub its black and white stomach. And when I did, it just curled up its pretty white paws and extended its long milky clear nails and seemed to curl them up, too.

Its fur was so soft and the sounds it was making was so smooth and soothing that I forgot I was on an errand for my Mudear, and I almost dozed off just sitting there in the hot summer sun. It was about the prettiest cat I think I'd ever seen. The whole time I was stroking its fur I was talking to it. I'd never had no pet of my own.

"You sure are pretty," I said to the cat. "You belong to anybody? I wonder what Mudear say if I bring you home. She so softhearted, I bet she let me keep you. What you think she say?"

And then I giggled 'cause it sound like the cat almost meowed a answer to my question. I'd heard about cats purring and all, but I'd never held one close and heard it myself. It just made me giggle to hear the purrs and rolls and clicks the cat was making. It was so entertaining and soothing that it was a while before I realized that this cat wasn't just making random cat noises. It was doing something more. It was purring a little tune, a song with notes and a rhythm.

Well, I tell you, my eyes flew open and I sat up straight then. I couldn't believe my ears at first. So, I leaned forward to hear better. I always was a brave little child. Didn't much scare me. But what I heard coming out of that cat's mouth made me jump up so fast I bumped my head on the post of the porch.

As clear as day, I heard the cat purring a little melody and singing the words to the song.

> Your mammy don't wear no drawers
> I saw her when she pulled them off.
> She sold 'em to Santy Claus.

> *Don't she know it's 'gainst the law.*
> *To wear them dirty drawers.*

I didn't know whether to laugh or scream. I hadn't ever spent much time around animals, cats especially, but I knew enough to know cats and dogs don't talk, let alone sing. But still, I had to believe my own ears. This cat was singing. It was singing like a gravelly whiskey-voiced old woman. She was singing it right, too, just the way it should be sung, with the beat on the last word of each line.

> *Your mammy don't wear no* drawers
> *I saw her when she pulled them* off.
> *She sold 'em to Santy* Claus.
> *Don't she know it's 'gainst the* law.
> *To wear them dirty* drawers.

I knew how the song was supposed to be sung—coming down hard on the last word of every line—because I had heard a woman and a group of men singing it outside Joe's Saloon right there in my neighborhood. They were probably drunk out there singing, but I didn't know nothing about being drunk then.

I just stood there frozen to the spot I was standing in, watching that singing cat who now wasn't saying a word. Then, the animal stood up and stretched herself again—I guessed it was a girl cat by its voice and because when it turned over on its back for me to rub its stomach I could see her titties. I called 'em buttons. She stretched to her full length, pushing her front paws out on the cracked wooden porch, waving her shiny black tail back and forth, then dragging her hind legs behind her so her whole body was laying flat against the floor like a mouse slipping under a closed door. She stopped for a moment as still as the little statues of Jesus the Italian brothers kept near the cash register of their store. Then, she came to life again and began slowly licking her shoulder down to the front of her paw. She rolled her marble cat eyes up to stare me right in the face. I still hadn't moved. She had this real lazy look on her face and her face looked just like a little teacup. Then, she start walking toward me again.

Lord, it was like it was yesterday.

The cat's haunches rose and her body looked like it disappeared between her shoulder blades. She was looking right into my face again and I could hardly believe it, but the cat's eyes turned from pale yellow to green to glowing orange to fiery red right before my eyes.

I may not have known much about cats, but I knew this wasn't no ordinary cat and this cat meant me some harm. I turned to run and got all twisted up in my feet. To look at me now you wouldn't know I used to be real clumsy. But my feet got all tangled, and I fell down them steps. Hard, too. I tumbled down those steps and landed in the yard with a thud. I was sure I had broke some bones, but all I could see was that red-eyed black and white cat coming at me.

I just let out a scream, jumped up, and ran all the way back home just sure that devil cat was on my tail. Mudear just laughed when I told her about it. And she promised that she wouldn't let no cat get me. Then, she told me to go on out to play and just forget about that old cat.

I went out, but I didn't wander far for a while and I sure didn't forget about that singing cat. I can almost hear it now.

La-la-la-la-la-la-la.
Uh-um-uh-uh-uh-uh-uh.

CHAPTER 12

Ernest bent slowly and picked up his boxer shorts and rolled them together in a ball with his T-shirt that he threw in the natural wicker laundry hamper at the far end of the room. He turned out the overhead light and went to his side of the bed. He sat down gingerly and stretched his long frame out carefully on the edge of the king-sized bed so as not to disturb it. Then, he remembered that his wife was not lounging across the other side, taking up more than three-fourths of the wide mattress. In the dark, he reached his hand out a bit and touched the empty side of the cool cotton sheet decorated with a fall motif of leaves and grapes and fruits of the harvest just to make sure she wasn't still lying there, her arms flailed out at her sides, her legs seemingly akimbo to her body, snoring lightly with her dark full lips parted. "The sleep of the innocent," she called it.

Without her, the bed seemed enormous to Ernest. Over the years, their marriage bed had gotten bigger and bigger, he thought, remembering the slender cot they shared as newlyweds in a rented room, then the twin bed somebody in her family gave them. Then, the double bed of the first bedroom furniture he ever bought, made of thin plywood and painted with a cheap stain. It was right after Mudear changed that they moved up to a queen-sized bed, good sturdy furniture. Then, Esther took up so much of that with her careless sleeping that he finally bought their first king-sized bed, then the present bed with a fabric canopy that the girls bought. They had shared that bed until the paramedics came and took her to the hospital.

He was still having trouble believing that Mudear had become sick, much less died. Although he had imagined killing her numerous times, he had never envisioned her actually being dead, especially being *killed* by something as ordinary as pneumonia. It seemed that one night he had trouble sleeping because of her sudden hacking cough and a few nights later—nights she had spent in bed rather than roaming around the house and yard—she had had trouble breathing and was carted off by the paramedics to die in the Mulberry Medical Center. She hated the fact that it was not called a hospital. "What you gonna tell people? 'She in the *Medical Center'?*"

Hell, she was strong as a mule. Never really had a sick day in her life. Had that perfect eyesight and all her teeth, God knows she got her rest and nutrition, didn't know the meaning of stress and tension. The way she pampered herself youda thought we was rich as cream. She shoulda lived forever.

Resting the side of his head on his bare arm on the pillow, he felt his thick salt-and-pepper hair growing long and beginning to curl over the frayed top of his sweat-lined pajama collar. Women still liked to play in his thick shaggy hair. Women he didn't even know would come up behind him as he sat on a bar stool at The Place and stick their fingers in his hair and twirl it around while they struck up a conversation.

"Shag" was his nickname from childhood. He could still hear it ringing again sometimes the way it had in the fields and lanes on the outskirts of Mulberry when he was a boy growing up in the country. Mudear had even called him that for a second when they first got married. It was, he thought for the first time, her pet name for him. But it had been so long since Mudear had a pet name for anything, let alone him, that it was hard to remember if he liked her calling him that or not.

But I was so full of myself then, he thought, so sure about how things should be, so sure about always being right, that I guess I was . . . He stopped thinking for a while, struck by the weight of what he was about to say to himself.

I guess, he thought slowly, I guess I was like Mudear.

He had tried over the years to discern why he was the kind of man he was when he and Mudear had gotten married, when the girls were little and still able to love their daddy. For so long, he had found it impossible not to place all the blame for his behavior on the capable, culpable Mudear. How could he do anything else but blame her?

If she hadn't been such a heartless bitch, he reasoned. If she hadn't turned the girls—his own children—against him. If she hadn't burned the okra every day. If she didn't always have to have her say. If she hadn't taken so long with the stew meat that time. If she hadn't had to clip articles out of the newspaper to prove he was wrong about something.

Sure, he had slapped her a few times after they were married a couple of years. But that was how things was then, he thought. Then, a man controlled his household, his wife, his family. Wasn't even no big to-do about it. Just a couple of taps really just to shut her up and let her know who was who and what was what. Most mens did that every now and then at that time, he thought. That's how it was then, it was a way to rule your house. You said something and your woman did it. If she didn't, you showed her that she better. People understood that then.

But he had finally, over the years, accepted that the more that Mudear had done for him, the more he figured she should do for him. And the more he feared all the things she knew how to do.

Maybe it was seeing her so capable, so able to take care of everything that was thrown her way. She never seemed to buckle, but rather to steel herself and go forward. He had to admit, it had scared him. He remembered his twenty-year-old mind trying to take all of Esther in, even before the change, and being overwhelmed by this woman he had married.

He knew that he was the first man she ever knew, ever to touch her in her private places. But she came to lovemaking that first time as if she had been made for it. She wasn't shy or modest about her body. She reveled in her strong little body—short big legs, a miniature hourglass figure—and the first time she saw him naked she had reveled in his, too. His was the first penis she felt and really looked at in the light. He could tell by the bemused, inquisitive expression she had on her face as if she were discovering maleness . . . in him. He let her examine him, but he didn't like it. It was too much for him.

He still remembered lying in their little newlywed bed while Mudear knelt by the bedside table lamp moving her face closer and closer to his penis, scanning him with her mouth hanging slightly open. Then, she lifted his dick up with her finger and gently blew on the underside.

Even in his arousal, Ernest thought in panic, "Good God, she's gonna touch my johnson with her mouth!" And he rolled out of bed away from her and stood glowering down at her upturned smiling face. He stood there silently, his feet astride, his hands in fists hanging at his sides. He found he had no words to express his outrage at her behavior. So, finally, he stormed off to their bathroom, his turgid penis bobbing in front of him as he walked.

Even the way she walked around their first rented room with no clothes on as if it were the most natural thing for a newly married woman to do. Like she had been doing it all her life. It made him uncomfortable.

He would watch awhile, then throw her her old cotton robe he would find rolled up in a ball among their damp and sweaty bed linens to cover herself and she'd just catch it, a good solid catch, too, laugh, and throw it back at him with her naked self.

She never did have no shame, he thought.

His mind was spinning so fast going over and over his life with Mudear that he just about gave up on getting any sleep and thought about getting up and exploring the night the way Mudear had done for more than thirty years.

He couldn't say why Mudear was never molested or attacked or disturbed as she gardened at night near the red dirt and asphalt streets of busy East Mulberry and then the narrow roads of the development called Sherwood Forest. It was just hard for him to say why.

Mulberry could be a strange little town like that. A rich old-name white Mulberry man hires two drifters to kill his wife in her bed in her mansion behind high gates with dogs prowling the property, to rip the diamond rings from her bloody fingers, to make it look like a brutal robbery. And an undistinguished black middle-aged woman gardens off the streets of Mulberry alone in the middle of the night unmolested, not even bothered or harassed by idling teenagers that her neighborhood, the development, had plenty of. Spoiled teenagers, teenagers with no thought of a job, teenagers with expensive cars, teenagers who whined for money, big money, to attend a music concert, from what he overheard in the driveways and doorways of his neighbors' homes.

Not like our girls, he thought. Always got a job. Not asking for anything. Doing for themselves.

Mudear would have laughed if she knew that her husband had ever considered her safety. It went against everything that Ernest knew Mudear believed.

"Shit," Mudear used to say. "A man no matter how much he love you will send you out to face the world alone, will sit by and watch your heart break, will let you work yourself into the grave taking care of him and then stand over the open hole and cry and cry and yell, 'Oh, baby, why you have to leave me? Why you have to go before me? Aww, baby, how you 'spect me to live 'out you?'

"Yeah, but yet and still before you cold, he be walking around looking for another fool woman to take care of him while your ass be six feet under.

"A man don't give a damn about you."

Poppa had to laugh at the memory of what he had overheard Mudear tell the girls as she worked their asses to the bone.

He had heard Mudear say so many times if anyone dared to

mention dying, death, or age to her, "Hell, I'm gonna eat the duck that eats the grass off all ya'll's graves."

Well, Esther, he thought again, it didn't work that way, did it?

Then, he felt funny, sneaky for thinking that way about Mudear even though she wasn't still around to give him that look that said, "Negro, have you lost your mind talking to me that way? You got your womens confused.

"You oversporting yourself."

For a while he couldn't remember what he had been thinking or what he was about to do when his dead wife intruded on his thoughts. He had to rub his face with the dry palms of his hands to clear his head. My mind wanders so lately, he thought. Oh, yeah, I was thinking about getting up.

But he realized he had no desire to go walking in the night. That was her thing, he thought.

Poppa picked up the remote control on Mudear's bedside table and fingered it for a while. Mudear had said the remote control was one of the world's best inventions. He clicked on the television at the foot of the bed. It came on one of the home shopping networks. The television was a portable model but a wide-screen one. Mudear couldn't stand the small ones. Said she couldn't make out the screen. She needed glasses but insisted that her eyes were as good as always and better than most because she had night vision. And then, even if she did really need glasses, no optometrist was gonna come out to the house and pay a visit with all his equipment and lenses and frames and stuff in the backseat just for her. Although that's probably what she expected.

She did get one of the girls to get her some of those drugstore reading glasses though. She didn't need 'em for much. 'Cause she wasn't much of a reader. All she ever did was leaf through a magazine or two to look at the pictures or peruse the stack of mail-order catalogs she kept all over the house, next to her bed and her La-Z-Boy and the phones. Mudear loved the pictures, moving or standing still. She called herself a TV baby. Like a baby boomer.

She did love her TV. There were three television sets in the house. All large screens: the twenty-two-inch in the bedroom. The big projection television in the rec room and the thirty-seven-inch Sony in the living room. He had purchased the one in the living room just so he could get to see the baseball games and the boxing matches that he loved. Just watching those young strong bodies at the height of their form punching away at each other and taking it gave him some hope for himself and for all men. Many times he wondered if men, males, "man-kind" as Mudear called all men, were going to survive.

Poppa turned up the sound and watched a few minutes of the woman on the screen selling dollhouses. Even while she was up here in this bed nearly dying, she was busy spending my money, Ernest thought. But I got to admit she didn't waste no money on those little china dogs and doodads that they sold on TV. She went for the good stuff. Equipment and stuff for her garden, light bulbs that were guaranteed to burn for a hundred years, a speed video-tape rewinder.

And then, too, as she would remind him, her girls paid for and sent her just as much stuff as he did. More, really, 'cause they could afford it.

He casually flicked through all the stations, sixty-four of them altogether, including all the movie channels and Playboy. Mudear insisted that she had to have all the stations that the cable com-

pany in Mulberry offered, so she'd know what was going on in the
world. And he had to admit that she did make good use of them.
Mudear was interested in everything that came on TV. She looked
at nature shows, afternoon talk shows, music videos, Sunday morning
discussion panels, feature films, documentaries, the Weather Channel, foreign films, Larry King, game shows, soap operas, cooking
shows, fishing and hunting shows, concerts, CNN, CNBC, and
C-Span. She never bothered with the copies of *TV Guide* that one
of the girls got her a subscription to. She would just turn on the
television and flick through the channels until she found something
that caught her interest. And when her interest waned, she'd just
find another channel.

Cable television, Ernest thought, like catalogs and overnight
delivery service, was just made for Mudear.

CHAPTER 13

I wonder how long it will take before Ernest is laying all the way across that bed. Enjoying the freedom of not having to share it with me. I never could understand why more men aren't found murdered in they beds. I heard on television that most murders are committed in the kitchen. I guess I can understand that, too. I guess I should be mad at the thought of him enjoying my big pretty canopy bed without me in it, but somehow right now I'm not. Actually, now that I'm not there anymore, I'm beginning not to care about that bed. Funny, too, since it used to be so important to me. When I first saw it in that fancy catalog that sold reproductions of antiques, I could just see myself laying up in it, propped up with some big down feather pillows covered with material that matched the dust ruffle and comforter. I never once envisioned that wide old-looking bed with anybody but me in it. Not 'til I walked back in the room right after it was delivered about dawn from my garden and found Ernest laying up there sleeping like he been hoeing rows a' cotton all day instead of just playing out there in the chalk mines.

But that's one thing he refused to do, stop sleeping in my bed. And I sure as hell wasn't about to move from that bed.

Everything about that bed was important to me. The little footstool with the tapestry cover I needed to step up to the height of the big hard mattress. The way the sheets felt, the kinds of patterns in the pillowcases and sheets and spreads, just the right kind of blankets that didn't irritate my sensitive skin, the red plaid and purple plaid flannel sheets that I had to have in wintertime that felt so cozy against my skin that the girls sent me in the big brown UPS truck. God, Ernest was right, that truck was made for me. I loved to see that big brown truck pull up in front of the house.

I spent so much time up in that bed, I guess that's why it was so special to me. Lord, I guess I better start feeling the same way about this satin-lined casket. Although, in my heart of hearts, I can't really believe that this is where I'm gonna really spend eternity. Or else, if it is, then all that "she's gone to a better place" stuff that people love to say when somebody die don't mean shit.

I sure do hope this is not it since I know ain't nobody gonna be coming in here every few days to change the cream-colored satin lining in this box the way one of those girls Betty hired or Ernest did at home.

And seeing how the girls are acting already, I know they ain't gonna be making many pilgrimages back to Mulberry City Cemetery to visit my grave and plant some pretty flowers, maybe some nice big hydrangea bushes around the back of my tombstone to set me off from the other dead folks—I wonder if all them dead folks make the soil acidy or alkaline?—and keep 'em up. They all claim they can't stand cemeteries. They think they so smart talking bad about graveyards like I don't know that they trying to pick at me on the sly just 'cause I sent them those few little times to the graveyard when they was little to get me a few cuttings from those lovely rosebushes growing all over the place.

Best rosebush cuttings you can get . . . from cemeteries. None of these new-time hybrids they try to sell you in mail-order books now that don't hold up to bugs or heat or diseases. But the old-fashioned kind of roses that smell so good, almost like lemons, you want to lick the velvety petals just for the taste.

When I'd see in those magazines with all the lace and flowers and gardening shears on the front that the girls had sent to me every month about putting flower petals in salads and baking 'em in cookies, I'd just smiled. 'Cause I knew just what they were talking about to do that. A garden of flowers is a luscious thing.

It's hard for me to believe that at one time I had stopped getting any enjoyment out of food, all that delicious food I prepared in that dark cramped kitchen in the old house in East Mulberry. Uh, everything started tasting like wet cardboard in my mouth, even my cakes. Wet and papery with a bit of paste thrown in. But I found out afterwards that it wasn't my cooking, it was my life.

At first, when I made up my mind it was gonna be different, I had thought about just walking away. Leaving that house and that kitchen and everything and walking away free and clear of it all. But then, I thought, why should I leave something that was mine? *A nice comfortable house where I had three girls, two of them—and soon all of them—big enough to help with every-thing, the cooking and cleaning and sewing, and a man that I knew inside out who had a steady enough job. And the thought of leav-ing my garden at the old house—I bet I was the only one in Mulberry who had asparagus growing up 'gainst an old fence—made me well up with tears. Leave all that? Just to go off and to tackle the world by myself. Why?*

So, I decided to stay in body. But to leave in spirit and let my spirit free. So that's what I did. And never did regret it, either.

Ernest thought that his messing around with those women downtown at The Place would bother me, hurt me, maybe even make me leave, so he could have the house and his entire paycheck to himself, but I told him right to his face one night when he come in smelling of whiskey and pussy and that cheap-ass Evening in Paris or that Hoyt's cologne that I didn't give a damn what he did as long as I could live my life the way I wanted to and not have to clean up that house or cook dinner myself or stop taking care of my flowers. And I didn't, either.

I tried to tell the girls, tried my best to tell them: a man don't give a damn about you. No matter how much he claim to love you, even the ones who will eat your dirty drawers don't really give a damn about you, not really.

I told 'em straight out. I never did talk down to my girls the way some grown-up folks do with children. I always talked to 'em the way I expected them to be, women. And they understood me, too. Never did come crying to me with some little silly stuff that they knew I didn't have no interest in. I never could stand a whole lot a' childish crying and whining.

"This teacher don't like me, she look at me funny all day."

"So-and-so say she ain't gonna play with me 'cause her mama won't let her."

"I might not have enough credits to graduate."

I tried to show them how freeing it is to discover that and really live your life by that . . . *"That man don't give a damn 'bout me."* . . . To say that and know it ain't got nothing to do with you, that that's just the way a man is. And when it don't hurt no more, then you free.

Once you realize that about the person that you lay your head down next to every night, then you can move on to the other folk in this world who also don't give a shit about you.

Ernest certainly didn't give a damn about me, not even when we first got married and I thought he was really in love with me. I was stupid or innocent enough to think that he just had to care about me, with my little cute self. Keep living, Esther. I feel like a fool just thinking about it now, but I used to write our names over and over on my school pad: Ernest Lovejoy, Mr. and Mrs. Ernest Lovejoy, the Lovejoys, Mrs. Ernest Lovejoy, Ernest and Esther Lovejoy, Mrs. Esther Lovejoy.

It sound so foolish now, but I truly thought that Ernest and me, our getting married was like a wedding of two forces. We would be joining forces, taking the best of both of us, me a city girl and him a country boy, my strong points joined up with his strong points, his best traits and mine. We was gonna take life by storm. I really thought that at one time. That's how I thought it was with my Mudear and father.

And it did hurt for a while when I realized he didn't give no more of a damn about me than the man in the moon. The things he did to me didn't hurt me half as much as realizing that he did 'em 'cause he didn't give a damn.

That's what I was trying to save my girls from. From that time—and it eventually come to all women—when you all deep in what you think is love and you get slapped in the face with a rolled-up copy of the Mulberry Clarion *newspaper or told what you think or what you think you are ain't shit. That you need to wear a bra all the time around the house 'cause your titties funny shaped. Or your rice is always gummy. If you already know that time is coming, then they can't touch you. Then, you ain't even got tears to shed when it happen.*

It was even one of the first things I taught Emily to say when she wasn't no more than a baby, "A man don't give a damn about you." Heh-heh, it sho' was funny hearing that cute little thing saying that. And that time when she went waddling over to her daddy laying in bed and made him lean down and said right in his ear, "Poppa, a man don't give a damn about you." I thought I'd die right then. I laughed so hard behind my hand, I nearly peed in my drawers. I knew that when he came in the house the next day after work smelling like liquor and put all us out to scout around for somewhere to stay for two days that that was what was behind it. But I comforted myself with the look on his face when he heard his own child tell him that a man don't give a damn about you.

CHAPTER 14

Gazing down at the rings the raindrops made on the murky surface of the Ocawatchee River, Emily hummed a few bars of a blues song she liked: "I'd rather drink muddy water. Sleep out in a hollow log."

Mudear had always reminded Emily of an old blues singer, someone like Alberta Hunter: tough, capable, and knowing, with beautiful skin and gold hoops in her ears. Seeing Emily tend her poor bruised teenaged face in the bathroom, Mudear had always told her that she must have gotten her sensitive skin from Poppa's side of the family.

"Even when I first started my period, I never had so much as a pimple," Mudear would say lightly from her seat on the toilet as

poor Emily struggled in the mirror with Noxzema and tubes of
Clearasil to cover and treat her blackheads and zits without crying.
"I think that stuff just make it worse. Make your face look like a
potato grater," Mudear would add as she wiped herself dry and
walked out of the family bathroom without washing her hands.
"That cream is lighter than your skin, daughter, now everybody
can see just how bad your face looks. You look like a dough-face."

Mudear would not have let snatches of blues songs, her favorites, snatch her back from the jaws of death if it was her destiny.
But Emily did. "I'd rather drink muddy water. Sleep out in a
hollow log. Before I let you make a fool out of me."

The irony of the songs always struck some chord in Emily's
life that made her chuckle and eventually head back home.

"Before I let you make a fool out of me." It sounded like
something Mudear would say. "I'd rather drink muddy water. Sleep
out in a hollow log."

"Daughter," Mudear instructed Emily one day after her abor-
tive first marriage when she came upon her middle child sitting
on the staircase in the new house hugging her knees to her breasts,
sobbing over her predicament. "Don't cry over nothing that don't
cry over you." Mudear literally said it in passing as she continued
down the steps to lie on the chaise longue on the porch. At the
time it had just made Emily cry all the more. But a few days later
in school, she saw her seventeen-year-old ex-husband trying to rub
up against a tall light-skinned freshman with a long red ponytail
and realized he wasn't crying over her at all.

Emily had married the first boy who showed any interest in
her. She made no bones about it. As she threw a few things in a
suitcase at the age of fifteen to elope with the boy, she told her
sisters, "I don't know about you, but I'm getting the hell out of
here while the getting is good. I'm bailing out, sisters."

Then, as an afterthought she turned to Betty and Annie Ruth, who was standing watch at the bedroom door for her, and suggested, "Why don't ya'll come with me? You can leave, too."

But Betty didn't think it was such a good idea for Emily to be running off as it was, to say nothing of dragging her and the baby, a very developed twelve-year-old Annie Ruth, off with her and her new husky husband. Emily and the boy (even the bride had trouble now remembering his name) made it across the state line to South Carolina in a raggedy black and white Ford with a broken muffler and to a justice of the peace who didn't care about anything but the requisite twenty-five dollars they had to pay for the license. But when they came back to Mulberry the next day to move in with the boy's mother, Poppa was waiting on the boy's porch to take her home. The affair was cleared up quickly without Emily's prior knowledge or full participation. And the marriage wasn't mentioned except in sly comments from Mudear.

"Daughter, run over to the drugstore and get me a bottle of clear fingernail polish, that is, if you ain't got a fine young man and no immediate plans to run off and get married this afternoon."

Then, it would strike her that what had happened to her was worse than what she and her sisters said they feared and resented the most. She had played her own self for a fool.

How many times had they talked about some other poor stupid girl they knew. "Girl, you know that little knock-kneed, no-talking, tied-tongue boy played her, played her for a fool."

"Oooo," they would all say with a shudder, their eyes shut, their mouths tight and disapproving. To be played for a fool by a boy, a man, none of whom, Mudear had told them, knew shit from Shinola anyway, was the worst.

Mudear had made it so hard for her or any of the girls to love a man. For Emily, love was a serious thing, not something to be made light of or demeaned with casual pointed comments. Visiting Mudear some weekends, Emily would glance out the window at the field of wildflowers in the front and spy a pair of steel-blue dragonflies mating in midflight. It reminded her of her own love life. Of how difficult it was to find love on the wing.

Each time, she had been tempted to share her insight with Mudear—she knew that Mudear would appreciate the sight of the dragonflies, would even take credit for their being in the area because of her garden. But even Emily knew that Mudear didn't give a damn about her love life.

Emily had tried at different times to explain Mudear to her friends, men, and coworkers. At some time or other, all the girls had attempted to put Mudear in a neat, compact enough package to explain her. But Mudear could not be contained in their mere words. Especially since none of the girls felt free to tell the entire truth about Mudear to outsiders. They censored their thoughts any time they spoke to others, weeding out facts and descriptions of their mother and their upbringing in just the way they had learned to excise anything from their childhood chats with Mudear that they thought would bore her.

Even Emily's psychiatrist, a tall thin regal-looking white woman who used a cane and was trying to quit smoking, with whom Emily was unabashedly honest, gave the impression that she was having a hard time understanding Mudear, taking her all in. Emily would try again to explain Mudear.

As little girls, if we were having trouble doing something around the house and going at it the wrong way, Mudear would stroll into the room and say, "You cannot build a chimney from the top. You cannot drive a car from the rear." Or something like that. And I know it sounds crazy, but most times it would really help. She could be wise that way, sometimes. It made it hard sometimes to hate her. I mean, be mad at her, not hate her. I didn't mean that. Didn't mean to say that.

She could be mean, too, so mean she used to scare me just talking.

One day, she said to me out of the clear blue, "Your Poppa, one time when we was real low on money, he was sitting around feeling sorry for himself. So, I suggested that maybe it was time for me to buy me one of those gray and white maid's uniforms and do some day work. Hee-hee."

Somehow, that sounded cruel to me, her saying that to Poppa. I don't know why it sounded that way. But then, Mudear could make just about anything sound cruel.

The idea of anyone in our house cleaning up after white folks was not up for discussion. It was unthinkable. Mudear would say whenever the subject of maids came up:

"Humph, let them wash their own drawers. I wash my own. The world would be a better place if everyone, no matter how rich and no matter how many servants, if everyone had to wash their own drawers."

Religious? Hell, she isn't even superstitious. She doesn't believe in anything. And if she did, she wasn't afraid of anything. Black cats crossing her path, seeing the full moon between the branches of a tree, sweeping trash out the door after dark, nothing. She'd walk under a ladder just as quick as other people would step on a crack. Bad luck? She'd say, "Shit, you make your own luck in this world."

Growing up, I thought Mudear was the most powerful force on the face of the earth.

Mudear would begin any strenuous task, for her that was replanting a bush or fertilizing a patch of garden or taking a long hot bath with big white fragrant moonflowers floating on the water, with the exhortation "Well, Lord," as if she were asking the Lord for strength and guidance in completing this job. And she'd say it so intimately as if she and the Lord were on close, close terms. I told you, Dr. Axelton, Mudear is the most sacrilegious person I know.

She has a habit of quoting spirituals and the Bible and old hymns and such as if she really believed that stuff. Like her favorite one is you'd ask her how she was, you know, in just a conversational way. And she say, real sincerely, "I'm just standing on the battlefield holding hands with the Lord." And she say it with such fervor, such conviction. It would only be us girls who knew her and Poppa I guess who would know what a sacrilegious thing that was to come out of Mudear's mouth.

I guess she'd disagree with us, argue with us really, because at times she saw herself as a very fervent, spiritual person. But actually she's the most carnal person we ever knew. Dr. Axelton, this is a woman who eats collard greens with her fingers. With these four fingers, the thumb and the first three fingers meeting to grasp the shredded leaves of the collards, wet, greasy, ham hocky, juicy the way Betty makes them, and bring them slowly, exquisitely to her mouth. She'd say, " 'Scuse me, I have to eat collards with my hands. This my fork." And she could make it look good, too.

"Standing on the battlefield holding hands with the Lord." What a thing to say and not really believe it. How do I know she didn't believe it? Mudear doesn't feel she h̶ hold hands with anybody for strength or anything else for that matter, that's why.

Besides, she never went to church and she hasn't looked at a Bible since she went to Sunday school. I think she used to go to church a lot when she was a girl. But you can tell by the half-assed mean way she quotes scripture that she wasn't paying any attention.

If she hear me and Annie Ruth and Betty bitching about her 'round the house, she'd call us into where she was laying up in her bed or on her La-Z-Boy and tell us, "Daughters, when your mother and father abandon you, then the Lord will take you up." Then, she'd go back to doing what she had been doing before just like we weren't in the room.

And she certainly doesn't live her life according to any Christian tenets. Nobody would call her religious. Religious, actually, that's funny. Mudear doesn't study any religion except the religion of Mudear. That's what she believes in.

The rest of us? Yeah, we went to church, we girls did. When we were little, Poppa would drive us. We were cute all three of us dressed in matching outfits. Annie Ruth in violet, Betty in blue, and me in pink. Mudear knew about people's colors long before anybody came up with paying however many dollars to some newly divorced, gone-back-to-work suburban matron to "do" your colors. You know that autumn, summer, winter, spring stuff.

Mudear knows a lot. Too much, probably.

But religious? Holding hands with the Lord? Mudear? No, not Mudear. She used to make fun of people who believed. You know, really believed in God and a Supreme Being and a higher purpose other than themselves.

She used to say, "Shit, niggas eat fish off the Bible." Mudear made selfishness into a religion.

After a few weeks of listening to Emily fill her fifty minutes with talk of Mudear, Dr. Axelton had suggested that perhaps the best thing for her was to put some distance between herself and Mudear. She made the suggestion to Emily very gently, gingerly, the way she always talked with her, as if she knew just how fragile Emily was. Besides her sisters, her psychiatrist seemed to be the only person sometimes who realized just how fragile Emily was.

"Sometimes," Dr. Axelton said in her soft flat southern accent, "when we can't change a situation that is painful, a situation that is harming us, then we need to stay away from that situation."

She must have read Emily's feelings through her face because she added, "Yes, Emily, even if the situation you need to stay away from is your own mother."

But Dr. Axelton could tell by her patient's face that Emily was not ready to hear that.

Dr. Axelton was just one in a string of healers Emily had sought out to bring some peace and solace to her life. She went to her in just the way she still consulted a personal psychic routinely and a tarot reader and a telephone psychic periodically for advice, guidance, and support. Her job with the state didn't carry the excitement of television broadcasting like Annie Ruth's or of power and entrepreneurship like Betty's, but the insurance offered government employees made it possible for her to visit a psychiatrist with no set time limit. And after her first visit, she was hooked, looking forward all week to her Monday late-morning appointment. She'd drive out to the perimeter interstate surrounding the city and Dr. Axelton's office seemingly brimming over with talk of Mudear and her own life and her dreams and questions. She could hardly hold herself together until she sat on Dr. Axelton's tweed nubby pile sofa.

She detested the process of sitting at the desk of some young hardly educated white girl in the state government personnel office and discussing her analysis in order to keep her insurance payments coming.

"And so you're telling me that you're compulsive-obsessionate, that's what it says on your doctor's report, and your sessions should be continued?" the chubby woman with splotchy skin would ask Emily in a loud voice after every three-month interval.

Emily wanted to reach across the desk and ball up the report along with the other papers on her desk and jam them all down her fat throat, but she just answered in a voice she hoped was as loud and strong as the interrogator's, "Yes."

The psychic she went to, a caramel-colored fleshy woman who

wore her long thick sandy hair in braids and who lived, conveniently enough, outside of Atlanta on the way to Mulberry, assured her in her very first reading it was predestined that she would have to suffer some indignities before she was recognized for the fully evolved spirit that she was. So, Emily just figured this was part of the plan for her life.

Emily shifted her butt again on the hard ground of the riverbank. She could feel the beginning of a tiny itch between her legs and knew that all the stress and worry of the funeral and life had given her what the girls called "the itch." And the tight jeans she was wearing weren't helping any, either.

She knew that all she had to do was think about the itch to get it. Sort of like herpes, she guessed. But none of her other friends at work or elsewhere ever said that the itch was as suggestive as it seemed with her. She said a silent prayer of thanksgiving to the river god as she imagined her—long-legged and big-butt astride the water—for the sale of Monistat 7 over the counter at the local drugstore and shifted her butt on the shale of the riverbank.

If she were at home in Atlanta, she would go to her own bathroom and fix a refreshing douche to flush herself out with. Mudear had taught her that. Well, she had told her about it. "When I was a young woman and got the itch, I always put a couple tablespoons of baking soda in a douche bag with warm, not hot, warm water, and half a cup of white vinegar. Um, I can still feel those fizzling bubbles just eating up that 'itch.' "

Emily couldn't remember Mudear ever really teaching any of them anything directly. The girls just had to be swift enough to listen to her criticisms and pick up suggestions she dropped in conversation.

The girls rarely told anyone the truth about Mudear. They had discovered early on in grammar school that people judged them by what they thought of Mudear. Besides, it seemed that folks always had trouble understanding how any of the girls could continue to have any type of relationship with a woman like Mudear whom some would have considered such a monster. The very idea that a grown woman would choose to sit down and visit with a woman who for all practical purposes had abandoned her for the better part of her life was incomprehensible to folks who didn't know Mudear.

The girls found it difficult to capture the entirety of Mudear in conversations away from the woman with folks outside the family. Of course, Mudear did some horrible things to them when they were growing up. But it never was personal, the girls firmly believed. Mudear had made it clear over the years that she didn't do anything, not since she had so easily gotten the upper hand with Poppa, *because* of somebody. She was just doing what the hell she wanted to do. If somebody got in the way, well, that was life.

And the girls didn't know how else to put it to strangers, but nobody was really *allowed* to hate Mudear. It wasn't a matter of what she did or did not deserve. Deserving did not enter into it. She lived and played by her own set of rules or lack of them. She made you feel that you couldn't judge her by your piddling standards even if those standards were held by most of the world.

Emily felt she could sum up her and her sisters' relationship to Mudear best by quoting a scene from a movie she had seen on TV about a former Air Force pilot, a survivor of a Vietcong POW camp. He told how his captors used a torture device that tied him up with his hands bound behind him and suspended him from a rope that intensified the excruciating pain in his arms the longer he hung from the ceiling. As he demonstrated a replica of the device he kept in his garage, he was asked how does one survive that kind of daily torture. The former Vietnam POW replied, "You learn to love the rope."

It was how she and the girls felt about Mudear.

Regardless of her abdication of responsibility as mother, Mudear was, as she reminded them from time to time, still their mother. Some respect was due her, Mudear felt, for not throwing herself down a flight of steps when she was pregnant with each one of them.

CHAPTER 15

The automatic timer switch had already turned on the lights throughout Betty's large colonial-style house. The lights timer was as much for Betty's mental health as it was for security. Betty refused to come home to a dark house especially when the days began to get shorter in the late fall and early winter. And tonight with the fine misty rain falling, she was even more grateful for the lights in her empty house.

She dumped her things on a delicate tapestry-covered chair in the hall and picked up her mail stacked next to a bowl of silk orchids on the tall piecrust table beside the front door. Although Emily's townhouse in Atlanta was spartan compared to Betty's elegant home and Annie Ruth's condo was stylishly messy compared to Betty's meticulously neat one, the three did share a few things in common. One was their decorating attitude toward flowers. Any plants or flowers in any of the girls' homes were always fake. None of them would abide a growing plant in their homes. The plants in the front of Betty's house and lining the driveway were taken care of quietly by a lawn care company.

And their hatred of plants was as strong as their love of books. All three women made spaces for their ever-growing collections of books all over their homes. Betty not only had a library with a sliding ladder to get to the top shelves, she had had bookshelves built in just about every sitting room and bedroom in her house. Emily, who still lived in the same pleasantly messy townhouse apartment she had moved into ten years before when her marriage to Ron ended, used every repository imaginable to store her books— wooden bookcases, étagères, filing cabinets, wine crates, utility racks. Her book arrangement formed the only decorating theme in her whole apartment. The rest was just comfortable sofas, chairs, and a bed.

When Annie Ruth had filled up the four beautiful ebony book-cases that a former boyfriend had built for her, she put her books anywhere around the house: in stacks on the floor, in huge Indian baskets she bought on Melrose, propped against walls, on table-tops. In Los Angeles, the fact that she had any books at all in her home was enough to make it a conversation opener at parties. "I know you know this face," hostesses would say introducing her. "Ruth's on TV, but you should see all the *books* she has in her house."

Betty's house, once home to old white southern Mulberry belles having afternoon teas prepared and served by women like Betty who had to wear black and white starched uniforms, had a sweeping staircase like something out of an old MGM movie set. Betty and her decorator had taken down the crystal chandelier that had hung there since the war and filled the top of the two-story foyer with a brightly stained wooden mobile by an artist who had gone to college with Annie Ruth. The artist had driven down from Atlanta personally to hang the piece and attend the reception Betty held for her.

Betty looked around and noted that the house had that special polish to it—the books and shelves in the library dusted, the hardwood floors waxed and buffed, the smell of lemon oil in the air, drapes shaken and pillows plumped—that it wore on the days Mrs. Andrews, the cleaning woman, came.

She made a note on a stack of yellow Post-Its on the table to tell this latest cleaning woman what a good job she was doing and give her a bonus. For a woman as busy as Betty, finding an independent, efficient cleaning woman she could count on was no small accomplishment. She had wasted more than a year going through six other women and one transvestite named Veronica, who was the best of the lot but who had the unsettling habit of disappearing for weeks at a time, looking for a black person who would clean her house as well as she cleaned for some white woman.

As she pictured the cleaning woman going about her work in a slow methodical way, Betty realized with a start that Mrs. Andrews, who wasn't that much younger than Mudear, looked like her, too.

Suddenly weakened by a bout of fatigue, Betty sank into the high-backed chair and let the mail drop in her lap. As a rule, Betty's days started so early and went so long that she was tired off and on all day long and kept getting her second wind over and over to keep going on. She had always kept herself just this busy, not always accomplishing as much as she should because she wasted a great deal of effort on unnecessary chores. Mudear would sit in her La-Z-Boy in the rec room and watch her in the kitchen washing off vegetables for dinner three and four times, reading the same page of a book over and over, and putting the clean clothes in the dryer all at the same time and say, "Ummph, ummph, ummph, look at her in there running around digging kitty holes and cat holes and not realizing all the time that one would do." Then, Mudear would laugh.

Gathering her strength, Betty picked up the mail and glanced through it. The thickest one was her phone bill, which wasn't surprising considering how much she and her sisters were on the phone to each other. She talked to both of them individually at least two times a week and then always held a midweek conference call for them all to get together and share their lives.

She didn't bother to open the gas and electric bills. And she ignored the envelopes with reminders of subscription renewals for herself and Mudear. Some of the junk mail caught her eye, but she was too tired to wade through it. There were two envelopes from American Express: one for her charges and one for Mudear's charges. They were both fat. Mudear hadn't asked for her own card or even who was paying the bill. But Mudear rarely had to ask for anything. That was something else Betty admired about her mother after she changed.

Betty wasn't concerned about the amount on the credit-card bill. She knew it would be what most people considered exorbitant, but money was not a problem for her, had not been for years. Even she was sometimes surprised at how much money she made— without an education—from doing heads.

Even when she was just three or four years out of high school, she was earning enough money at her booth in Delores Beauty Shop, the first shop she worked in, to help Emily out with her extra expenses that her scholarship at Fort Valley State College didn't cover. And by the time Annie Ruth went to Spelman College, Betty was able to pay for all of her expenses even after she went wild her freshman year with all that relative freedom in Atlanta away from Mulberry and Mudear, stopped studying and attending classes regularly, and lost her scholarship. Betty was just twenty-six when Annie Ruth entered her sophomore year, but she had opened her own shop by then and, between her income and Emily's new income with the state, they saw to it that their baby sister had pastel-colored underwear by Vanity Fair, knee-high suede boots, and a bright orange melton jacket for Morehouse College's football games so she didn't look out of place next to the more affluent daughters of doctors and professors and lawyers at the school.

"I know Annie Ruth is as smart as any of those girls at Spelman," Betty would tell Emily as they wrapped up another big dress box of new frocks in brown paper to mail to their sister. "But I want to make sure she look as good as they do."

All her life, Betty had made sure that her sisters—smart girls to begin with—concentrated on their studies even though Mudear warned them that they were "all gonna wind up crossed-eyed from reading so much." It had been Betty who sat proudly in the audience at their graduations wearing a wide-brimmed straw hat so her sisters could spot her representing the Lovejoy family, took snapshots of them getting their diplomas, and took them and their girlfriends out to dinner later to celebrate.

Glancing around her home at the gallery of framed photographs of her family arranged on the entrance table, in the living room on the piano, on the desk in her home office, Betty regretted not sneaking up on Mudear sometime when she wasn't paying attention or was asleep and getting a good snapshot of her. Mudear wouldn't allow pictures of herself to be taken. She said her nose always looked so big in photographs, so, she wouldn't have anybody taking her picture. All Betty had of Mudear was an ancient black-and-white studio shot of Poppa and Mudear right after they were married that Betty had had copied, restored, and touched up by a local photographer.

Mudear hated that picture, too. So, Betty hadn't dared give it to Mr. Parkinson when he asked for a photograph of Mudear. She had had to tell him to print the funeral program without a picture of the deceased on the front.

Mudear never knew that Betty had sneaked the old photograph out of the house for a few days. How could she have known? Betty thought. Mudear never went looking through old letters or pictures or mementoes. She had little interest in the past, and especially a past that had so many painful reminders of how things used to be.

Betty remembered how it was before the change. She was the only one of the girls who truly had memories of their father when he was an entirely different man. Bigger, it seemed, stronger, louder. At one time, she had almost thought that the man who now lived in their house was not the same man she had known before as Poppa.

But that's silly, she had told herself at age eleven as she looked up into the face of the man at the dinner table. But she wasn't sure. All the time that she pretended to listen to the conversation among her mother and sisters about school and plants and local gossip, going back to the stove to get seconds for her family, she examined the man. Starting with his hands and mentally going over his whole body right down to his beat-up old leather slippers. It seemed that not so much about him was changed as much as the things around him. He still placed his chalk-whitened muddy Wolverine work boots at the side of the back door each day, but now they stayed there from evening 'til morning without Mudear snatching them up to clean for the next day. Over time the boots got caked thicker and thicker with white mud until she saw her father take them out in the backyard and hose them down. After that, he rinsed them off himself every night.

In the battle that had been their marriage, Esther had finally won. Not at first, but finally. Betty remembered a time when her mother acquiesced publicly to her father in all matters—money, the children, choices for dinner, or how to line the kitchen trash can in the most efficient way. At that time, it was only in private with her daughters that Esther dared to express her views, how they differed from her husband's and how he was a stupid and underhanded bastard for holding those views and imposing them on her.

Her mother didn't even call this new Poppa "Mr. Bastard" on the phone to her friend Carrie the way she used to. So Betty knew something or someone had changed. Mudear's calling Poppa "Mr. Bastard" had been a game that drew the attention and the life's breath of the entire household. On the phone to Carrie, Mudear would say, "Naw, he ain't here, Mr. Bastard's gone to work," or "Mr. Bastard raised hell 'cause I didn't have his favorite white shirt pressed this morning," or "Here come Mr. Bastard now, I gotta go." Betty couldn't remember her mother calling him anything other than "Mr. Bastard" when he wasn't around until she was eleven years old. The girl would marvel at her mother's ability to use the name selectively. Betty would sit holding her breath sometimes, afraid her mother would slip up and call him that to his face when he threw a clean khaki work shirt, stiff with starch and ironed stiffer, on the floor and said to her, "Wash this shirt again. You call that clean?"

She couldn't even imagine the kind of fight that would ensue in that case. But she never once heard her mother slip up and use the nickname at the wrong time.

Then, when her mother started spending longer and longer periods lounging in bed in her nightclothes, she noticed that Mudear no longer called her father "Mr. Bastard" at any time. At the same time, Betty began to sense a shift in the tension that used to ring the house like the moons of a planet and seemed somehow to keep the family together. Sometimes, she would walk past her parents' room and feel the floor almost tilt with the sudden contradiction her mother would throw out at the man.

"Naw, man, don't fold the paper back that way. That's stupid!"

Betty would grab onto the wall waiting for the explosion of her father's temper to rock the house. But there was no explosion. Instead of feeling relief, the child Betty would feel only confusion and fearful anticipation of the next time it happened. "My God, next time he's gonna kill her." Betty was sure. But it happened again and again and again with no bloody aftermath. Betty finally had to accept that this man who only occasionally railed at his wife out of her earshot and stomped through the narrow halls of their wooden home was truly her father. But he was a changed man.

It all added to Mudear's mystique that she could know just when she could safely change.

It didn't happen as magically as Betty had envisioned it. Esther had waited for this time. From the first year of her marriage, since he made her take a mayonnaise jar along on a car trip for her to pee in so they wouldn't have to stop along the road, her anger at him had been growing, like the tangle of gourd vines that grew from fat black seeds she had dropped in the fertile loamy soil back of her house.

"You just gonna stoop down by the side of the car or go off in the woods like a man to pee?" Ernest had asked her with scorn and amazement as he shoved the large jar in her hands.

By the time their second daughter was born, he was no longer ordering her and her life around with sharp rough words, he was making her do what he wanted with just a gesture. A rude gesture. When he wanted her to do his nails, a ritual she had initiated out of caring and self-preservation because she couldn't bear the thought of him going up in her with those filthy chalk-lined nails, he just glanced at his hands and drummed his nails on the nearest hard surface. She was expected to jump up, go get the manicure kit and her stool, and come do his nails. And she did.

When he wanted more mashed potatoes at the dinner table, he just rapped the empty spot on his plate where the potatoes had been with the tips of the tines of his fork and that was the signal for Mudear to run get the pot of potatoes and replenish his plate. And she did.

Ever since she had discovered that her vision of life with Ernest was sculpted in fool's gold, she felt more and more like a fool for having ever believed in him.

Whenever Poppa drove up in the driveway from work or an errand, one of the girls or Mudear would yell, "Fire in the hole," to warn the household that Poppa was on the premises. The girls didn't know at the time that the yell had been used originally as a warning in dynamite jobs, but when they each discovered its original meaning they had to chuckle.

Betty knew firsthand how her Poppa was, what a hellcat he was, as Mudear had instructed her and as she had seen with her own eyes. She was the only one old enough or cognizant enough to remember the cold nights when Poppa would come home, fight with Mudear, and issue the order, "Get out!" And Mudear would have to pack up the girls and herself and get out in the street and find somewhere to spend the night. Sometimes, it was at her parents' house. Sometimes, at a cousin's who ran a liquor house and had folks coming in all times of the day or night anyway. Then, the next day, Mudear would have to come back to Poppa and apologize for whatever Poppa felt she had done to displease him. Once, she even had to instruct Betty to apologize, too, to get them all back under one roof. "I'm sorry, Poppa," little Betty had said, unsure of what she was sorry for.

The closest Mudear had ever come to defying her husband openly was in the dinner preparation. Each day, she managed to burn the okra for dinner. It was a family joke, if something as pathetic and tenacious and meaningful as a ritualistic burning could be called funny. But without fail, each day Mudear washed off the okra, snipping off the horned end of each tight khaki-green pod, then cut the pods into popcorn-sized pieces. She covered the couple cups of sliced vegetable with cold water, added salt and pepper, and put it on to boil.

Then, she left the kitchen. Betty had watched her so she knew how it went. Mudear would put on the pot over a high flame and go pick up the phone to call her friend Carrie. Or she would take a magazine and go into the bathroom for twenty or so minutes.

Just long enough for the water in the pot to boil into a slimy concoction and long enough again for the slick water to boil out, leaving a sticky residue.

No matter that Betty or one of the other girls would come running to Mudear warning that the okra was about to burn or was already smoking up the kitchen. It still burned. Mudear would always say the same thing, from the phone, from the other side of the bathroom door, from outside in the garden: "Don't ya'll girls dare touch that hot pot. It's already burning. I'll take care of it."

But Mudear never came to see about the pan, Betty noticed, until it was an okra holocaust.

That memory was probably key to Betty's understanding of Mudear and Mudear's stand in the house to never be put in the position of having to "get out!" It probably, now that she thought of it, was the reason she herself had started her own business (Mudear had sanctioned her choice: "Colored women gonna *always* get their hair done") and ran it so smoothly, efficiently, economically. She never as long as she lived and stayed black, as Mudear used to say, wanted to be told to "get out" and have to do it. Any move for her was a wrenching experience. She winced when she drove past someone's possessions sitting on the side of the street and sometimes drove around the block two or three times in hopes of coming on the evicted family to offer help. Even Annie Ruth's profession's peripatetic life-style of big money, quick moves, and whimsical audiences made Betty nervous for her.

Mudear just assumed that none of her girls remembered. But Betty remembered.

While burning the okra, while renaming her husband "Mr. Bastard," while putting aside a few pennies, a nickel, a quarter, Mudear had waited for this time, this contradictory, kiss-my-ass time. She had bided her time and waited.

If she had been a praying woman, she would have prayed for that time to come. But since she wasn't, she had just trusted in the irony of life and waited.

Betty heaved herself up from the fragile chair and began the climb up her curving staircase to get out of her clothes. Although she was exhausted, she had no intention of going to bed before Emily came in.

Looking down at the first floor of her exquisitely decorated home, she wished that Mudear could have at least seen it one time before she died. Betty had used up packs of Polaroid film taking stacks of pictures when she first bought the house and then again at holidays—pictures of the Christmas tree decorated and lit, pictures of the broad front lawn decorated with red, white, and blue bunting and an American flag and a red, black and green National Freedom flag on Independence Day, pictures of the dining room table set for a formal dinner—and given them to Mudear. But after glancing at a couple of photos, Mudear always tossed the stack aside without a comment. Later, Betty would find the photographs on the floor by Mudear's favorite La-Z-Boy chair in the rec room or strewn wet and bent on the screen porch sofa or tangled up in the bedclothes and comforter at the foot of her bed.

She knew better than to press Mudear for a response to the photographs and the accomplishments they chronicled. Her response was always so demoralizing.

No matter what the pictures showed—Betty in her high-school cap and gown, Betty at graduation from cosmetology school, Betty in front of her first beauty shop, Lovejoy's, at its grand opening—Mudear always managed to say just about the same thing. "God, daughter, your butt sho' look big in these pictures."

Even when *Essence* magazine did a short profile of her after she opened her second beauty shop and when *Ebony* made note of the annual hair and beauty show she put on, Betty just left the magazines by Mudear's bed turned to the page with her picture circled. Mudear never did say she read the articles, but she did tell Betty later that she had enjoyed the short story in the issue of *Essence*.

Still, Betty couldn't stop herself from bringing the pictures to Mudear and laying them before her like a burnt offering to Yemaya, the Yoruba goddess of the womb. She told herself that was the least she owed her own mother. Even if her own mother reminded her of Medea.

CHAPTER 16

When Annie Ruth opened the door to the lavender bathroom, so much of Mudear came flooding out that she thought for sure she had opened Pandora's box. And for a moment she stood at the door, her hand over her mouth, and forgot that she had rushed to the bathroom to throw up.

It was as if she were cocooned in a blanket of Mudear. It was as if over the years Mudear had been able to extract the essence, the spirit of herself and sprayed it cunningly placed throughout the house to catch some poor unsuspecting prowler, victim. It was more than the smell of candy cinnamon balls. It was even more than the subtle scent of lavender and rose petals that Mudear used as the basis for the potpourris she created from her herb garden and placed in the bathroom and throughout the house near spots where she lounged. Those smells were smaller, more understated in relationship to this refinement of the essence of the woman. Essence of Mudear. That's how Annie Ruth imagined what was left of her mother. Like a perfume, Essence of Mudear, in a fancy curved crystal bottle. Annie Ruth looked over at the long shallow dressing table with just a comb and brush, a bottle of witch hazel and a bottle of coconut oil, a jar of moisturizer and the small manicure set on it. The feeling of her mother was so strong in the bathroom that Annie Ruth could almost see Mudear floating around the room spraying her Essence of Mudear all over the place.

Like a cat.

The taste of bile coming up in her mouth again sent her racing for the lavender toilet. She knelt at the toilet for what seemed like minutes throwing up watery ginger ale and phlegm. Liquids were all she had been able to keep down for the last two days. But now she assumed she couldn't even drink a glass of ginger ale.

Annie Ruth sat on the side of the tub to steady herself and got a sudden flash of splashing in the bathtub nestled in a ship of safety. Her childhood often came back to her that way, in flashes that she could not immediately connect with an actual remembered event. Then, she remembered when Betty had told her and Emily one night between their beds that all the girls at one time had bathed in the old house's bathtub between Mudear's legs.

"It was a treat for Mudear to lift you into her bathwater after she had finished bathing. She'd say, 'Got some good sudsy water here for somebody who wants to get clean.' And it did feel good settling into her full tub of water with the Ivory soapsuds she had worked up to a lather still floating on the grayish water."

By now Annie Ruth was sure she could clearly recall splashing in the water between her mother's legs. Many of her childhood memories were really born and nurtured in Betty's stories to the girls rather than in actual experience. But Betty told the stories so well that over the years, and especially in their childhood, the stories had usurped even what slim memories they carried of their lives, enriching the reality to the point past true recollection.

Annie Ruth was just as sure she could taste the rolls Betty had told them about:

"Mudear used to make these rolls, not biscuits, but dinner rolls. It seemed that it took days for her to make them. She'd mix up the batter with milk and flour and yeast in little fat envelopes in this big brown bowl with a light blue ring around the top, then she'd cover it up on the stove with a plaid dish towel overnight for it to rise, then the next morning she'd punch it back down with her fists, real hard like a man beating up another man. Then, she'd put it back in the bowl and cover it again with the dish towel and let it rise again.

"It just went on and on. These preparations. Then, when she'd roll out the dough — beautiful white tender-looking dough — she'd take this little juice glass — she only used it for the rolls, never to drink juice out of — and punch out small round pieces about the size of your palm, Em-Em," taking her sister's little hand and holding it up for Annie Ruth to see the size she was talking about. "Sweet small little pieces. And she'd lay 'em on a big ungreased cookie sheet and fold them over one time so they looked like they had little lips. She'd let 'em sit again for a while. Then, just before she put 'em in the hot hot oven, she drizzle melted butter, not margarine, not oleo, but real butter, over each one of them.

"Oh, Em-Em. Oh, Annie Ruth. When those things came out the oven, girl. You never smelled or tasted anything like 'em. They

really were sweet. No, not like sweet rolls and honey buns. It was
like they were naturally sweet. I don't know. Like a cantaloupe is
sweet. Like a warm peach off a tree is sweet. Not with sugar you
put in but sugar that's just there.

"You know how people say something melt in your mouth?

"Yeah, Annie Ruth, like M&M's. Well, these rolls just melt in
your mouth. You didn't even have to chew 'em.

"You put them in your mouth and they just seemed to melt
and just float away to your stomach.

"Yeah, Annie Ruth, like heaven."

Betty told them stories all the time. When Annie Ruth was
eight and Emily eleven, Betty even told them the story of their
impending menstrual periods. She went out and bought a box of
Kotex and a box of Tampax and safe in the family bathroom of
the old house, with Annie Ruth and Emily sitting on the floor
watching, Betty demonstrated how to use both. Then, she gave
her sisters the choice of which one to use when their time came.
"If you use the Tampax, you can still go swimming when you're
on your period," she told her attentive audience. They both nodded, but none of them ever learned how to swim. Mudear would
never allow them to go to the old segregated pool set in the
middle of a red dusty parking lot and after 1964 Mulberry closed
both the black and the white pools rather than integrate them
both. Betty's talk was a mixture of what she had learned from her
own period, from junior-high hygiene class, and from what her
friends at school had told her.

"Having your period is called 'the curse,' 'on the rag,' 'a visit
from your cousin,' or 'having cramps,' " Betty informed them. "In
the books, it says it means you are now a woman, you can have a
baby. They keep telling us at school that it's something you're

supposed to be proud of and happy about. But I don't know any-body who is.

"At school, the women teachers and the gym teacher keep saying over and over how a 'young lady' have to be especially careful to keep herself clean and good smelling when she has her period. And that is the truth. Nothing smell worse than old dried menstrual blood. That's another reason to use the Tampax instead of the Kotex.

"From what the older girls at school say, getting your period also means you're a woman 'cause then you can have sex, you know, Annie Ruth, do nasty. If you do, you called 'fast.' If you don't, you called 'bitch' or 'tease.'

"One girl at school, Velma, say once you start, you can't stop. So, I guess it must feel mighty good."

Annie Ruth couldn't look at a mirrored medicine cabinet with-out seeing herself and her sisters as girls at the family bathroom sink, elbowing each other, jockeying for a place directly under the light to pluck their eyebrows or put on makeup or curl their hair.

Mudear, awakened by their quarreling on school mornings over space at the mirror, would yell down the hall, "Daughters! Pipe down there and take turns. Everybody got to suck at the trough." Of course, it was easy for her to say. She had a bathroom all to herself. Before the house was constructed, she made sure there was going to be a bathroom built off her bedroom in the new house. For someone who claimed to take no interest in the plans for the new house, the girls noted to each other, Mudear had a great deal of input into the house's details. Although Mudear used whatever bathroom was most convenient for her at the time, no one was allowed to use her lavender bathroom, even in an emer-gency. There was another door to Mudear's bathroom off the hall,

but Annie Ruth couldn't recall one time when folks other than
Mudear used it.

She made sure even then, in the early sixties when Poppa had
it built, that everything in the room was lavender, her favorite
and, she said, most flattering color. Then, she sent Betty and the
girls downtown to the local Belk's store to purchase towels, toilet
seat covers, and rugs in shades of rose and pink and lilac and
purple to coordinate.

For years, the girls speculated on what Mudear did in there by
herself for what seemed like hours. They came up with the idea
of bizarre voodoo rituals complete with three little girl dolls that
she tortured with pins and thorns—"She probably stick thorns in
my face just to keep it looking like a potato grater," Emily said
throughout her teenaged years—and fire, suffocating them with
towels and holding their little bodies underwater for long stretches.
But as they got older and after years of fighting for time and space
in the one family bathroom they had to share with Poppa as well
as each other, it finally dawned on them that she was just in there
luxuriating in the privacy, leisure, and convenience of her own
bathroom.

With nothing left in her stomach, Annie Ruth felt better now.
She stood and stared down at the clean smooth surface of the
deep lavender tub. Then, she reached down quickly, so she wouldn't
have time to change her mind, flipped the drain closed, and turned
on the hot water full blast. Remembering, she raced over to her
parents' bedroom door and rapped on it sharply.

"It's just me, Poppa," she said through the door. "Taking a
bath."

Poppa just grunted in acknowledgment, but Annie Ruth knew
the sound coming from Mudear's bathroom must have given him

a start. Hearing his voice on the other side of the door made her think of the times she and her sisters had heard him screaming and cursing them out when they were teenagers. She could just see him emerging from the family bathroom, blood running down the side of his face from a deep nick he took from shaving with his dull razor that one of them had used to shave her legs or under her arms and then replaced in Poppa's "hiding place" over the jamb of the door.

"God, these girls trying to kill me!" he'd yell to the house. "How many times I got to ask you girls to leave my razor alone!"

Then, he'd stomp back into the bathroom dripping rich red blood down the front of his white undershirt. It had reminded Betty of the old Poppa, but it didn't last. He might mutter a bit to himself, but he never really confronted any of them about it.

Annie Ruth took off her underwear and robe and dropped them in a pile on the floor by the door. She took off her earrings, squiggles of gold shaped like two melted question marks, and laid them on the edge of the sink. She lifted the top off a pink china rose—Emily had sent it to Mudear as a birthday gift—on the shelf above the sink and took out two black hair pins. With them, she secured her copperish curls on top of her head. Turning back to the tub, she saw the apothecary jar full of sprigs of lavender sitting on the back of the tub and dropped a few of them into her steamy water. Reaching for a washcloth and big fluffy lilac towel from the rack by the sink, she caught a glimpse of her behind in the full-length mirror on the back of the door.

She turned around and, looking over her shoulder, she stood in the mirror and got a good long look at herself. Umph, she thought, that butt is . . . She had to pause a moment to recall just how old she actually was. That butt is thirty-five years old. She turned to the side and took another look. Not bad, she thought. From the side, she looked down at her stomach.

Looking at her image in the mirror, Annie Ruth tried to imagine her tight, toned, exercised golden-brown body pregnant, really pregnant. Her stomach extended, her hips curved and widened, her breasts full and hanging. It was hard for her to picture. She had never thought of being pregnant. Never been around pregnant women. Now that she thought about it, she may have even avoided her friends and coworkers when they were pregnant, hoping not to be reminded of the teenaged vow she had made with her sisters.

She patted her stomach tenderly and reached over to add cold water to her bath. She had read a story on the air recently about the dangers of hot tubs and saunas to mother and unborn child.

"Don't worry," she said to her stomach. "I'll take care of you." She laughed out loud because it sounded so corny coming from her, but she could feel herself get "full" in the chest like an old woman at a family reunion at the thought of taking care of her child.

She dipped one foot into the water then, eased into the tepid water, and settled in a tub that, as far as she knew, only Mudear's butt had ever touched. She leaned back and tried to imagine how she had felt as a little girl sitting between a young Mudear's short legs, propped up against her stomach, the back of her head nestled between her mother's breasts. Annie Ruth could almost picture it, but she kept losing the picture.

She rested a hand on her warm wet stomach, she was sure she could see a curve to it now, and thought about Emily.

Annie Ruth routinely lost track of chunks of her life, but she knew she would never forget the time she had come from D.C. to Atlanta to accompany Emily to get her abortion. Each moment of the trip seemed etched so deeply in her memory that there seemed no way to carve it out. She had had to fly down because her sister had waited so long to tell her about her plans that she had no time to make the train trip the way she usually traveled. She could tell from Emily's voice on the phone that if she didn't get there and get there fast, there was no telling what Emily would do.

All her years as a television reporter had come back to haunt her with vivid flashbacks of pictures she had seen of pretty young girls and overweight and overworked middle-aged women lying in pools of their own blood with twisted coat hangers still nearby or bottles of household disinfectant drunk at the last minute in desperation. Even she, while still a freshman at Spelman on her scholarship, when her period was late one time, had considered throwing herself down the flight of steps from the top of the third story of the old brick ivy-covered dormitory the way her roommate had and then rolling over three times on the landing to reach the next flight of stairs to tumble down. But instead, she had gone up to the beautiful historic campus chapel before classes and prayed so hard that her period had miraculously started.

Sitting outside the clean antiseptic-smelling clinic waiting for her sister, she had been unable to meet the pleasant businesslike gazes of any of the women working behind the desks. She swore over and over to herself as she took her sister's arm and led her to the waiting taxi and back to her apartment, "I'll never take my birth control lightly, I'll never take my birth control lightly."

Other than her late periods, she had never been pregnant as far as she knew and she had vowed that she never would get that way. Annie Ruth knew, as surely as she knew Emily could not have gone to term with her pregnancy, that she could never go through an abortion. But she felt she had been strong for Emily.

She took her home and warmed up some Campbell's tomato soup with half-and-half and dried basil the way Emily liked it. She held her sister in her arms when she wept and she lied to Emily's husband that she was in town on business when he returned home from the garage. Then, she helped Emily concoct the falling down the outside steps story to tell Ron. She even bandaged up Emily's right ankle to further buttress her fall story.

She didn't let Emily do a thing for the entire weekend that she stayed there with her. She was as strong as she had ever remembered being, but on the train trip back to D.C. she couldn't stop sobbing. She just leaned her head against the cold air-conditioned window of the train and wept all the way up the eastern seaboard.

She and Emily and Betty had all made a vow when Annie Ruth had joined them as women on her periods that they would never get pregnant and have children just to abandon them the way Mudear had done with them.

"Let's just never have any children," Annie Ruth suggested. "Then, we *know* we won't be like Mudear." And it sounded like a good idea to the other two.

"Okay," they agreed, clasping hands and squeezing tight to seal the vow.

"I swear."

"I swear."

"I swear."

Annie Ruth lay back in the tub, closed her eyes, and just inhaled deeply the scent of lavender rising from the water. Mudear would have a fit if she knew I was luxuriating in her personal tub surrounded by her personal herbs, Annie Ruth thought with a satisfied sigh as she sank lower into the water. Through the bedroom door, she could hear Poppa slowly clicking through the channels of Mudear's television. Annie Ruth wondered if Mudear had ever seen her on television. When she had worked in Washington, she had sent a few videotapes home of herself covering big breaking national and international stories. But only because one of the female technicians at the station had gone to the trouble to make copies for her and put them on her desk with mailing cases, labels, and the smiling suggestion, "I know you'll want to send these home to your mama."

The last tape she remembered sending to the Sherwood Forest address had been more than three years before when she interviewed CNN's Bernard Shaw—Mudear's favorite newsman—after his return from the Persian Gulf. Mudear kept one of her televisions tuned to CNN all the time. And so did her daughters.

On her last visit to Mulberry the year before, Annie Ruth had sat stunned as she and her sisters listened to the news conference on CNN at Betty's house. Magic Johnson stood at the microphone as handsome and healthy looking as always and told the world that he had the HIV virus.

Without saying a word, both her sisters swiveled their heads to look her dead in the face. Stating their question was unnecessary.

"No, I never slept with Magic," Annie Ruth said. She wasn't offended. She knew how her sisters worried about her. "Come to think of it, I don't know how we missed each other in L.A. Lord knows I had my share of professional basketball players."

They pondered her observation for a second. Then, all turned back to the wide-screen television set, shaking their heads at Magic's situation.

Even though they didn't discuss it much anymore, the specter of AIDS had a place in all of their minds. They had been or were still screwing around too much not to consider the possibility of contracting the virus. Betty had settled down more or less with Stan even though he hadn't quite stopped dragging the streets for other women. And then there was Cinque.

Emily, usually in and out of quick relationships when she was younger, was not as sexually active as she had been in her twenties, either. Now, she seemed to give off these nervous signals like radio waves to men that told them she would be trouble, she would be complications, she would be complexities, she would be involvement, she would be commitment. She seemed to let men know early on that she was just what they seemed hell-bent on avoiding. And most did. Long ago, Betty and Annie Ruth had given up on introducing her to any men they knew. Those affairs always ended in acrimony and disaster for Emily. And Betty and Annie Ruth usually ended their relationships with the men out of loyalty to their sister.

As she had watched the TV screen with the reporters and lights and questions, pictures of Magic's favorite haunts on Melrose, his Bel Air mansion, his pool, Annie Ruth had been reminded again of how much she hated L.A.——the conspiracy of lies that told the world there was lovely weather there year-round, all that fucking driving on slabs of concrete that even felt more hostile and forbidding than other cities' expressways, the expensive houses jammed onto every inch of the hills surrounding the city, the fact that she had yet to find one good girlfriend, the universal hunger there for fame or for just being noticed, evidence of the damn film industry everywhere you went, shooting films on the street, in restaurants, in shopping malls and stores, in churches. It wasn't just the shallowness, the hunger for fame and stardom that left Annie Ruth so empty in L.A. It was other things——women at parties trying so hard to be noticed that they seemed to arch their backs in pain.

It was the middle-aged black men in silk shirts and their old white women in spandex and silicone, gold jewelry and diamonds. Both·pretending so hard—he that he has a job, she that they are in love. The rows of convertible Jaguars and Mercedeses with their cellular phones parked next to a homeless family's raggedy Ford. The danger from random violence on the street that everyone tried to pretend they didn't understand. Having to go all the way across town to see more than three black people laughing and talking together.

She had had to stop going to parties in the Hollywood Hills because looking down on the smog-choked city below and all the unfortunates who could not afford to breathe unpolluted air made her so melancholy that she would have to find a quiet spot on a deck and weep.

She always hoped to keep all that and the craziness it evoked in her in abeyance during her visits to Mulberry. But she could feel it taking hold of her from three thousand miles away. Just the sight of that "Hollywood" sign on TV up in the hills over the city made her want to spit.

Whenever she complained to her sisters about her new home, they would ask sincerely, "Girl, what you doing out there, then?"

She never could form a concrete sensible answer. Despite her hatred of the place, the people, the "life-style" (she even hated that word), she continued to stay there. Even when news of her on-air nervous breakdown would have made it easier to start anew in another television market, she had taken a couple of days off and returned to her seat between her coanchor and the weatherman as if nothing had happened.

Annie Ruth had forgotten where she was until she shifted in

the tub and splashed water on the floor. The warm bathwater had turned cool while she had traveled back to L.A. and it gave her a chill. She didn't even bother to wash herself. She just flipped the stopper, rose, and stepped out of the tub as she reached for the fluffy lilac towel and began drying herself. She caught sight of her chipped nail polish and made a mental note to redo her nails before she went to bed.

The sensation of lounging in Mudear's tub wasn't nearly as satisfying as she had thought it would be, but she did feel a bit more relaxed and not a bit nauseated anymore.

CHAPTER 17

And Annie Ruth got the nerve to be sitting her butt in my own personal bathtub first chance she got. Other daughters woulda kept their mother's bathroom just the way she left it. Woulda even sort of set it up like a shrine or something. You know. Not let anybody use it and got real mad if someone, a visitor or something who didn't know any better, walked in by mistake and sat on the toilet or washed her hands in the sink. But no. Miss Had a Nervous Breakdown on the Air in Los Angeles and Having a Baby for She Don't Know Who, first chance she gets, goes and stretches her pregnant ass out in my personal bathtub with sprigs of my lavender floating around her.

As a matter of fact, it woulda been nice if one of those girls

had had the presence of mind to bring a few pieces of that lavender down here to Parkinson Funeral Home and spread 'em here
in my casket for me. It would make things so much nicer for me
in all eternity. Of course, the lavender would only keep its scent
for a few years. But at least for that time I could be enjoying the
smell and all.

But then, those girls never did really think about anybody but
themselves.

And they got the nerve to say I'm selfish. People just think
that 'cause I'm short. Even when I was a girl, people just seemed
to get so upset when I spoke up or expressed my feelings on
anything. Said all I thought about was myself and my wants and
opinions. Used to hurt my feelings, too.

But then I realized that most of that was 'cause folks just
didn't want to hear nothing from no colored woman about what
she thought. Not just men, either, just as often it would be one of
my girlfriends or their mothers or a teacher or somebody who
would be criticizing me for having the nerve to express myself.
Humph. "Girl, go somewhere and sit down." That's what they
used to say.

Yeah, I'm supposed to keep every little scrap of junk those
girls send me 'bout their lives—what they did and what they
bought and who they interviewed—but they don't even have the
decency to keep my bathroom as a shrine.

I cannot believe those little women. Bitch, bitch, bitch. "Mudear didn't do this, Mudear didn't do that." At first, I thought it
might have been a reaction to my passing and all. But now, I'm
beginning to think these little witches really believe some of this
stuff. I certainly never taught 'em to whine like that about their
circumstances.

Good God! "Mudear didn't do this. Mudear didn't do that." *Whine, whine, whine.*

Those ungrateful, trifling women! Hell, I coulda just walked out and left them orphan girls. But no, I stayed so they could have the benefits of a mama.

Well, of course, that's not the whole reason I stayed. I'm a person, too, and I had my own needs and likes and dislikes. And anyway I thought, Shoot, I got this house here with my garden growing in back, a man who keep food on the table and usually keep our butts from freezing, three girls — two of them already able to do things around the house. Hell, I had stayed for the hard times, why should I have left just when I saw things getting a little better? Why should I go out in the world and try to make my own way when I didn't have to? But I stayed. Ungrateful hussies!

It's a damn shame you got to die first before you see how your children really feel about you.

God! Those girls got ugly ways about 'em sometimes. It's hard to believe they are my children. They didn't seem to take anything from me . . . but my sense of style. And unfortunately, my bad choice in men. But then, I guess as far as choices go, it don't much matter which one you make in a man. They all alike, none of them worth the hard-on they think they got to offer you.

Now, Ernest is just as good . . . or worthless as the next one, I guess. Sure, he made a passable living . . . except for that one time . . . and we didn't go hungry or anything. But what did he have to offer really? What did he do to make this world a better place than when he entered it? Like the person who invented the remote control. Now, that meant something. Heck, people gonna be smelling and marveling at my flowers growing in the back field long after I'm dead and gone.

Yeah, Ernest did do a few little things like going to get my cow manure from the country and picking up some few little bedding plants and supplies at the garden center. But I got most of my plants and seeds from ads in the Georgia Market Bulletin from people, other gardeners like me in Georgia who would sell and exchange seeds and cuttings and plants. Sure, sometimes he would ride out U.S. 331 or one of them roads in one of his no-account peeing-on-the-floor friends' truck and pick up a stone bench or a trellis or a tree he knew I wanted. But I'm the one who arranged that garden. Told him just where to dig that lily pond. I designed that, too.

I have to give it to him, he could double-dig a garden lot 'bout as good as anybody I ever met. He'd have that soil so loose and friable that I could stick my hands down in it up to my elbows.

Sometimes, I'd have flowers blooming past first and second frost. And that's something. To say nothing of the fact that people in Mulberry gonna probably be talking about me for even longer than they talk about my garden.

And, of course, my girls.

Having them wasn't no big thing. Even a cat can do that. That don't make you a mother, just having them. But I raised my girls. Better than most, in my opinion. They know things . . . about life. I guess now they gonna have to learn something about death.

Yeah, now that old Mudear is dead and gone, they starting to pretend that I wasn't nothing to them. My goodness, people forget so soon.

But I guess I can't complain too much. 'Cause even though I never forgot one single thing that Ernest did to me, I did try to act like I had and that it didn't matter to me one bit. But you know it did. Sometimes anyway.

Well, if those wenches start messing up their lives again, it won't be my fault. I certainly went out of my way to teach 'em a thing or two. I remember when the girls weren't all even teenagers yet, I sat 'em down and told 'em how to make it in this world.

"Now, a man, they like to call theyselves the strongest things in the universe, but let me tell you, listen to me now, if you get a man at the right time. At that point when he all exposed and open and down, that's when you can get him."

"You mean like get him to marry you, Mudear?" one of 'em, I think it was Emily, said. She always was a fool for getting married.

"Good God, daughter, no! Why in the world would you want a man to marry you? I mean get him right where you want him. You know, get the upper hand. Don't be acting like you don't understand just 'cause you a little girl," I told 'em.

I remember Annie Ruth looked kinda confused, she wasn't no more than eight or nine. And Emily, lord help her and look out for fools and babies, always did have that quizzical expression on her face. "But, Mudear," she said. "I want to meet a man and get married." I told her, "Keep living, daughter."

Nobody can't say I didn't do my best to tell 'em how men are. I know it sunk in with the oldest girl who I guess was a teenager then and already starting to attract the boys. Betty ain't never had time for nothing but business. And where she think she get that from?

Didn't do anything for them? What do you call my planting a whole white garden just for them to see at night, I certainly didn't need it. But one of the girls said, "Mudear, can you really see your garden at night? That's hard to believe."

And what did I do? I went right out there and started a garden with nothing but white blossoms and whitish leaves so my family could see the garden at night the way I did. Did I have to do that? Tell me, did I? No.

Didn't do anything for them!

And as if making them the women that they are ain't something.

Yeah, to let them girls tell it now, I didn't do shit to raise 'em, to help 'em out the way a mother should. Yeah, all that time when I kept an eye on 'em when they was at those "vulnerable" stages when I didn't really haf to. You know? Lots of women who turn they households over to another woman, even if it is her eleven-year-old daughter, they don't pay attention to other changes in the household. But I did. Do you think for one minute I wouldn't keep an eye on that man who slept in my bed and make sure he wasn't turning my child into his wife substitute?

Yeah, yeah, I know most folks don't want to think about, let alone talk about, something like a grown man forcing himself on a child and especially when it's her own father. Hey, I may be crazy, but I ain't stupid. If Ernest knew one thing, it was I woulda killed him dead and gladly gone to serve my time in jail for it if he touched one of my girls. 'Sides, the girls wouldn'a let me go to jail.

Oh, yes, I know the kinds of things that go on in this world. I ain't lived "out" much, but I know what I know. It seems I was born knowing some things. I think I tried to pretend I didn't know 'em or forget what I knew I knew. I think I tried to do that for years. But I learned you can't do that and not go crazy.

Heh-heh-heh-heh-heh.

I can't help it, I got to laugh when I think of how I coulda gone on for years and years like I was if it hadn't gotten so cold that winter. And the baby hadn't had whooping cough and Emily had meningitis so bad.

It was almost like it was planned by some holy power or something. What was that show Eartha Kitt was in? Kismet. Yeah, like it was kismet. But then, I always knew I was meant for something big in this life. I really did. Even as a child, I couldn't wait for the next morning to come to see what it would bring. My Mudear told me that when I was just a little thing, no more than five or six, I said to her, "Come on, Mudear, put me to bed early tonight so I can hurry up and wake up and see what's gonna happen tomorrow."

That's the kind of child I was.

rnest tried to stretch out in the bed again and go to sleep, but whenever he closed his eyes he saw Mudear as she had looked the last time, dead in her hospital bed. Her face in deadly repose was as untroubled as it had always been in life. Somehow, he had always thought that Mudear would die screaming and crying, clawing at her sheets and slobbering at the mouth, in pain for all the pain she had caused in her life. But it wasn't like that.

She had been a little weak from the pneumonia infection and a little short of breath, but otherwise she had looked as she usually did: sleeping undisturbed, no lines at the corners of her wide mouth, no slashlike wrinkles under her eyes, her fluffy hair pressed flat and comical by sleep, thick curly black eyelashes like a child's resting on her lids like two sleeping butterflies. He had been there when she breathed her last. She had opened her eyes, looked over at him sitting by the side of her hospital bed, and pointed to the glass of water on the bedside table. Poppa had gotten up, poured a fresh glass of water from the plastic pitcher on the tray, and held the straw to his wife's lips. When he had looked down into her face, their eyes met a moment and she laughed that sardonic Mudear chuckle.

"I always told the girls that you don't never know who's gonna be around to give you that last drink of water," she had said softly. She had chuckled again, then she closed her eyes, breathed heavily, and died.

Poppa knew she was gone because the machine hooked up to her arm stopped beeping and emitted a long flat whine, just like he had seen on hospital TV dramas.

After he had wearily settled up his bill and signed all the papers that the woman at the hospital desk pushed before him, he had walked out the wide visitors' entrance and into the night. Even the hospital clerk, whose job it was to see that bills were taken care of in the midst of grief, was surprised at the amount of insurance the tall thin graying black man seemed to have. He had tried to get in touch with Betty, but no one picked up, and he just left a message on her machine.

Once outside, it took him awhile to find his car. At first, he wandered around the hospital parking lot trying to remember what color his car was. He had to go through all the cars he had ever owned in his life to come to his present one.

Let's see, there was that old raggedy black heap not too long after we got married. Then, we had the tan Chevrolet that we drove to New York in. Esther always did especially hate that car.

Then, the green sedan when I got my first promotion and raise, God, I was proud of that car. Then, the Toyota, first foreign car I ever bought.

When he finally remembered what his current car looked like, he couldn't recall in what lot he had left the brown Ford Tempo. His wandering around the parking lot seemed to do him some good and relieved his pounding head a bit. But he was so weary and sweaty when he finally pinpointed his automobile, he had to lean against the side of the car for a while to catch his breath and get back some strength before going on.

Once he was safely behind the wheel of his car, his first instinct was to head back toward Sherwood Forest and home. But the blood had begun to rush so furiously through the back of his neck and up to the top of his skull when he even thought about walking back into his house now, Mudear's house, seeing her flowers in the ' k, smelling her smell all through the house — cinnamon cand y mixed up with her herbal and flowery potpourris — that he could barely hold his head up.

He started to reach under the driver's seat of the car for the half-pint of Old Forester that he always tried to keep there, but he felt he needed some company as much as he needed a drink. Besides, he could hear his wife's voice saying, when she came upon him on the porch or in the rec room having a little taste, "You know, I heard on TV that it's a sign of an alcoholic to drink alone."

So instead, he pointed the car in the direction of the old downtown district of Mulberry to the corner of Broadway and Cherry. Just driving up toward The Place made him ease up a bit on the grip he had on the steering wheel. He looked over at the car clock and saw that it was only 10:10. He knew that there would have to be some of his friends in there to talk with. But even if there wasn't anyone he knew real well, at least there would be someone there to sit next to and drink a beer or two with. Even if they didn't know they were drinking with him.

The Place was the kind of joint that folks came to when they needed something and couldn't stand to be let down one more time that day. It didn't usually disappoint them. Its real name was the Bluebird Liquor Store, Bar and Grill, but everybody called it The Place. People just felt good in The Place, always had as far as he knew and he had been coming there for twenty or thirty years. More than that, he thought.

The Place must have been standing in the same spot for nearly fifty years, Ernest thought. Thank God that McPherson girl had refused to sell out, to buckle under, and not let them wrecking crews come down through her place the way they did with all the others.

It looked right lonesome to Ernest sitting there in the middle of what had been downtown Mulberry at night surrounded by the flat painted lines and high-intensity lights of a parking lot on one side and the back of a rambling hardware store on the other. At one time, The Place was surrounded by a thriving all-black business district nestled against the general white downtown stores. Three decades earlier on Broadway and Cherry streets, there had been a candy and peanut store, a movie house ("The Burghart Theatre shoulda been put on the National Register, not torn down," Mudear had said, but she hadn't seen the place in nearly thirty years), restaurants, a barbershop, a beauty shop, a grocery store, a fish market, and a record store with a big shiny black forty-five hanging in the window.

He had heard how the town fathers and the developers, who

were one and the same, had tried to wear the original owner's daughter down and bully her and bribe her and scare her into selling and moving out. But that was one black woman who could not be moved.

"It helped to have all that money on her side, too," Ernest said aloud to himself as he turned the corner of Cherry and looked for a parking space close by. He found one right across from The Place and slipped into it with ease. When he opened the dark painted glass door to The Place, he was surprised at the size of the crowd inside the L-shaped juke joint. No matter how few cars there were in the vicinity of The Place, the joint always looked like it was happy hour. Music—old music from four and five decades earlier that the customers still preferred to hip-hop or urban—blared from an old-fashioned jukebox illuminating a dark corner of the bar.

Folks must still come here on the city bus, he thought as he let his eyes adjust to the dark smoky interior. Or else that Mc-Pherson girl must bus in customers just to prove she had been right for not closing up and moving her business out or across town. While still standing at the entrance, he recognized the words of Etta James singing "Roll with Me, Henry."

That song gotta be from the mid-1950s, Ernest thought as he moved along the crowded bar and found an empty stool. The song reminded him so much of how he was in the fifties—so strong, so in charge.

He almost chuckled—that's when he realized he had all but lost his ability to laugh—remembering how after Mudear changed she used to always say real loud, "Ernest just want to get *down town!*"

He would hear her through the heating vents leading to the

bathroom as he waited for one of the girls to bring him the new razor blades he had just purchased on the way home from work. He would hear her say, "Don't go busting your neck to get those razor blades to your father, he just want to get *down town*."

She always said it, *down town,* as if it were some exotic seductress trying to lure her man into its plump soft arms.

It wasn't that she was jealous of his visits to The Place or even that she suspected that he had a woman he met down there, Mudear didn't give a damn about his fidelity or lack of it. She just hated the idea that he had a place where he could be happy for a little while. He knew that.

But, as with everything Mudear did and said, there also seemed to be some other hidden evil message in saying *down – town* the way she did for him to hear. He knew she was also trying to imply that he was a stupid country boy dazzled by the bright lights and sidewalks of a city. *Down town.*

Mudear had been born up north in Harlem Hospital while her family was visiting relatives in New York City. Even though she stayed there in the city all of three days, the first three days of her life, she never let him forget that she was a city-born woman and he an ignorant country boy.

Of course, at first, when he was courting her and she him, you woulda thought that his big country hands and big country feet, his arms used to field work, too muscular for his cheap shirts, were Spanish fly to her. But after the change, she looked on him with actual disdain. He could see her now turning up her nose at him as if she were smelling something, like dog shit stuck to his boots.

Just as he was finishing his first drink, the liquor in the pit of his stomach beginning to warm his cold dead-feeling body, he spied a familiar figure in the corner of the bar over by the jukebox. He almost didn't recognize the woman. She looked so bad in the face. But even after two or three years, there was no mistaking that tight black and white polka-dot dress and the tall dark thin figure inside it. He just wasn't ready for the lined throat and the ashen face he saw above the dress's scooped neckline.

He had just tried to arrange his own face to cover his surprise when she spied Poppa watching her.

"Ernest!" she yelled and put her bottle of beer down on the top of the jukebox and ran over to his stool at the bar. "Ernest, you old devil! I was hoping I'd see you."

She grabbed him and hugged him good and hard. He slipped his arms around her thin waist and hugged her back.

"Man, it's good to see you," she said, standing back and taking him by his broad shoulders to look in his face. He managed a smile when he saw that although she looked like she'd been beaten around the face, puffy and bloated, her jet-black eyes still held the light of joy just as he had remembered.

"Patrice, where you been?" Poppa asked, taking her by the shoulder and leading her back to the bar.

"Oh, I been scouting around different cities. Went down to New Orleans for a while, rode with some folks to Dallas, but I didn't like Texas so I came back east and stayed with some people I knew in St. Louis. But ain't no place like home, and no home like Mulberry, and here I am!"

He went next door to the liquor store and bought a pint of Tanqueray—Patrice liked gin—and came back and ordered a setup of orange juice and ice.

He started to tell Patrice that his wife had just passed. But somehow it didn't seem right. He knew that Patrice would be understanding and comforting. He could just imagine her saying, "Well, if a woman can't have a drink with a man when his wife is just dead, then what kind of friend is she?" Patrice was that kind of woman. But he knew that Mudear would not have wanted him announcing her death to his old girlfriend before he told anybody else. So, he just let her do all the talking about where she had been and what she'd been doing. After the quiet of Mudear's hospital room, Patrice's gay chatter was balm to his soul.

He knew she could see something was upsetting him, but she didn't intrude. She just gave him an extra-hard hug when he said he had to get going and told him, "See me real soon, okay?" and headed back toward the jukebox.

He had felt like a fool then for trying to be loyal to Mudear.

Then again, he thought as he swung his long legs out of the bed, got up, and walked over to the window overlooking the garden in back of his house, Mudear didn't give a damn about him at all one way or the other.

He turned from the window and looked at the wide bed across the room. He could easily imagine Mudear stretched out on her usual side, dressed in a pink or tangerine bed jacket or dressing gown, a pile of magazines strewn next to her on the thick quilted satin comforter, a dripping half-empty carton of Häagen-Dazs chocolate chocolate chip on the tray on the bedside table.

He could hear Annie Ruth in the bathroom next door. Had heard her running water in Mudear's tub, then heard her splashing in the water. He couldn't hardly stand to listen to the bathroom noises. They reminded him of Mudear and the hours she had spent in there entertaining herself.

Even now with her dead, he couldn't give in to hating her completely. It would make it seem as if she had won finally.

He felt that was what she must have wanted all the time, all the time they knew each other. If she got him to really hate her, the way he knew she despised him, then she would have been satisfied. All Mudear wanted was to be in control. Lord knows she controlled her own small insulated world. But that wasn't enough for her, he thought as he turned down the grape-strewn sheets that Annie Ruth had sent as one of her Christmas gifts the year before. Now that the girls had jobs, good jobs, the big brown UPS truck seemed to pull up to their parents' front door every other day.

But then again, Esther had also discovered catalogs as well as the home shopping networks since cable had come to the town of Mulberry. She had said many times how those two conveniences had been tailor-made for a person like her. Like there were other Mudears scattered all over the country, as if she weren't one of a kind.

Then, he shuddered at the idea of more than one Mudear running around the world.

CHAPTER 19

In Mudear's house, there were no doors on the two entranceways to the kitchen. She had had Poppa remove them. She liked to sit in other parts of the house—the dining room or the rec room—and oversee what was going on in there. From her favorite recliner chair in the rec room she had had a clear view of the sink and the kitchen table. From her seat at the head of the dining room table she had been able to see the stove and the sink. She didn't have to say it, but she did: "Ya'll girls can't do nothing without me checking behind you."

The girls would stand at their kitchen stations, Emily at the sink, Betty at the stove, and Annie Ruth at the table, and try their best to ignore Mudear's orders and comments issued from her current throne.

"Betty, don't fry that chicken so fast. It'll be bloody at the bone. And I can smell the grease burning in here.

"Daughter, be sure to run that dishwater good and hot. Don't nobody want to catch all those germs and viruses ya'll pick up out in the street. Let's see some steam coming out of that sink.

"Annie Ruth, if you ain't doing nothing but sitting there reading, you can change the paper in those drawers in there. Don't be so trifling."

Annie Ruth was in high school before she noticed that there were two head chairs pulled up to their dining room table, two chairs with arms. Mudear had insisted on it. "I don't care if you have you a nice comfortable chair or not," she had told Poppa. "But I sure as shooting want one where I can rest my arms during a meal."

Just walking past the table and chairs made Annie Ruth's stomach hurt.

The delicious food that Betty had learned to cook for the family was served with as much criticism as seasoning meat and as much pressure to perform as salt if Mudear decided to sit at the table with the rest of the family for dinner. The girls had learned early that it was always better to get a small plate of food later in the evening when Mudear took her nap before going outside. By then, their stomachs—upset and soured by Mudear's questions and comments, asking about their teachers and friends, about people at the electric company and grocery store just to get enough information to tear them and their lives apart—would have had enough time to settle down.

It was usually at the dinner table that Mudear went after anyone outside who tried to show an active, positive interest in one of the girls. If a teacher ignored her colleagues' warnings to stay away from members of the Lovejoy family, the ones with the crazy mama, and tried to encourage their love for literature or their quickness in debate or their big-legged majorette march, Mudear talked about them so badly, going into their family history and failed romances and business endeavors, that the girls eventually shied away from the teachers just to shield them from Mudear.

At the table, Mudear would say as she heaped piles of mashed potatoes on her plate and sprinkled chopped onions on top, "Miss Matherling so concerned 'bout you, she ought to be more interested in her own family with her no-working husband. Her half-crippled ma out there wasting away in that nursing home. And the brother who has served *hard* time for stealing. I hate a thief. I hear he even stole from her. Miss Schoolteacher."

Mudear left nothing unexplored as she dissected people's lives while she sucked on the marrow of a chicken bone. The girls even realized too late that they had probably provided some of the ammunition for Mudear's attacks. Then, they had felt stupid and on edge as if they had pointed out the best place to chop off their own legs.

As Annie Ruth came slowly through the dining room, she didn't see anyone in the kitchen but noticed that the overhead light was still burning in there.

Well, she thought, I know that cats can't turn on lights. And she walked bravely into the bright yellow room and she saw her father sitting at the kitchen table dressed in his pajamas, faded washed-out striped pajamas that she had sent him for one of his birthdays years before, with a cup of coffee in front of him. Now, Poppa know he got better-looking pajamas than those old things, she thought.

"Couldn't sleep, Poppa?" she asked as she stood in the doorway. She didn't wait for him to answer. She really didn't expect him to. She just came over and pulled out a chair to join him at the tiny round kitchen table.

"No, I guess not," he said.

They sat in silence for a while.

Then, Poppa asked, "You want some coffee?"

"I'll never get to sleep if I drink coffee now, Poppa," Annie Ruth said.

"It's decaffeinated."

"Alright. I'll have a cup with you."

He got up and turned on the flame under the kettle.

Annie Ruth turned up her nose slightly when she saw her father take the orange jar of instant coffee from the cabinet. She hated the watery taste of Sanka, but she didn't stop him. At least while he made the coffee, it filled the room with noise and movement, and she didn't have to try to think of anything to say to her father.

But watching him, she asked herself with something akin to shock, "Who is this old man shuffling around the kitchen?" She wanted to say, "Pick up your feet! Pick up your feet!" But she could just hear Mudear's exasperated voice saying the same thing and she censured herself for the thought.

"Annie Ruth?" he said as he put the steaming coffee in front of her and took his seat next to her.

"Yeah, Poppa," she answered.

"Do you know what I do at my job?"

"Of course, Poppa," she said, puzzled that he would ask that. "You work at the kaolin mines, the chalk mines. If you haven't taken a new job." She smiled at him because Poppa had worked at the same place all her life. She reached for the can of Pet evaporated milk and poured a splash into the cup—the tall thin gray china mug she always used—of coffee. Um, my cup, Annie Ruth thought as she stirred in the cream. She wondered if Poppa knew it was her cup or if it was just by accident that he picked it.

"Yeah, but do you know what I *do?*" He was going on about his job.

"Sure, you're the foreman of the grading division there."

He looked at his little redheaded daughter and gave a wistful smile. He could see some of Mudear in all the girls. And just then she looked like his wife when she felt she was being patient with her stupid husband.

"And what that mean?"

"It means . . . it means you head up that division at the mine. You're the supervisor of that section." Annie Ruth wondered where this conversation was coming from and where it was going. The only thing that stood out in her mind about her father and his job was the ruckus Mudear had put up when she found out Poppa was bringing home chunks of kaolin for the girls because they liked the taste of it. Annie Ruth had only been about eight when she heard Mudear telling Poppa what an ignorant country Negro he was for passing those stupid country dirt-eating customs along to his children.

"Actually bringing that filthy white dirt home from your job for your own daughters to eat! Damn, a man ain't got no sense!"

Talking with her father this way about his job felt as if they were both negotiating strange and dangerous new territory without a map, feeling their way along without knowing where any of the pitfalls were, the quicksand traps, the slippery spots, the unmarked caverns. She couldn't remember a conversation with him that was not about money or business that had gone on this long.

Discussing his work at the chalk mines reminded Annie Ruth of her flight earlier that evening into Mulberry. Right outside of town, while she was trying to keep her mind off of the cat she had seen on the first leg of the trip, she had looked out the window and noticed for the first time, she thought, the very plant where her father worked.

Against the gray overcast day, the mining site with its plumes of ghostly chalky smoke spewing from a number of stacks and vast white pits chiseled in the earth surrounded by huge pools of aqua water shaped like triangles, squares, and diamonds rimmed in the powdery white clay looked like a movie set. White dust covered the cars in the parking lot, the company's sign, the buildings' roofs, everything.

"You know, at the mines I got one of the best records for showing up for work. The least absenteeism, they call it. I get a award every year for that, not missing any days."

"Really?"

"Annie Ruth, I worked like a dog out there."

She was taken aback by his bluntness. "I can imagine it was hard work, Poppa."

"Naw, girl, I'm not just talking about how hard the labor was, I'm talking about how hard *I* worked."

"I'm sorry. I don't think I'm following you." Annie Ruth was beginning to feel as if she were back at work conducting an interview, a difficult one.

"I didn't let one weekday pass 'out my being at that place punching that time clock and hauling and cutting and grading that limestone," he said after a while.

"That's how you got such a good record." Annie Ruth could hear herself talking to him like he was an idiot, but she couldn't do any better. This conversing with her father was so new and strange to her that she didn't know what to say.

Mudear had had the knack for being able to talk with Poppa where he didn't have to make much of a contribution. Annie Ruth could see Mudear now sitting in her favorite recliner or stretched out on the big chair and ottoman on the porch talking a mile a minute about something she had seen on television about the legal system or something she had discovered on her own about horti-culture in the experimental garden along the eastern side of the house. Poppa wouldn't even have to say a polite "Ummm" any-more. Over the years, he had learned how to pace his silences just so that his *not* saying anything in a certain way, certain nuanced silences, adequately held up his side of the conversation.

"Shoot, Annie Ruth, the record itself didn't mean nothing to me. That's not why I worked like a dog out there at those white people's mines. I worked like that not just to keep a roof over ya'll's head but to give you girls and your mother a little better. To put you and Emily through college so you wouldn't have to work like I did, work like a dog, to make a daily living. That's why I didn't never show up at ya'll's graduation exercises. I was working some overtime. Woulda sent Betty to college, too, but when I tried to talk to Mudear about it, she said Betty didn't have no interest in higher learning. And by then, she had already started making a few dollars doing hair."

Poppa kept looking down at his fingernails and then back at Annie Ruth as if to see if she was listening. Annie Ruth had an interested look on her face because she was. But she was having a hard time not looking confused, too.

"I know both ya'll got scholarship, I was proud of that, told the mens down at work 'bout it, but it was still so expensive. Your mother didn't seem to realize how expensive it all was. But then, you know how Mudear was."

He just sort of let that hang in the air. And Annie Ruth just murmured, "Ummm," and took a sip of her tepid coffee.

"Not that I'm trying to throw up to you what I did for ya'll. Not at all. I was just doing what a man s'posed to do for his family, a real man. And God knows you girls have been more generous than any children I know with your mother and me. Shoot, you all spoiled Mudear rotten. I guess we all did.

"Your mother knew it, too. Whenever I'd say anything about how good you girls were or try to brag on you, she'd shut me up. Say, 'Don't be telling me about my girls. Shoot, they the hand I fan with.' That's what she say, 'They the hand I fan with.' "

There was another pause, so Annie Ruth said, "Well, Poppa . . ."

"She didn't know the price of nothing, whether it was the cost of a college education or the price of a bottle of shampoo. It's sort of funny 'bout that. 'Cause she always played me so cheap. Always played me so cheap. Everything I did or bought or earned, she played so cheap.

"You girls, too, played me cheap. I guess she taught you that."

Annie Ruth was close to shocked. Not only had she rarely heard her father talk so much to anyone, especially his family. But she had never heard him utter a word against Mudear.

He was almost as surprised as Annie Ruth at his candor. But his talking about Mudear seemed to embolden him. He continued to speak as if he were throwing himself into an ice-cold pond.

"Do you remember when you were about five or so and you got real sick? Sick with the whooping cough?" he asked.

Annie Ruth shook her head. "No, Poppa. I didn't even know I ever had whooping cough."

"Well, you did," Poppa said, seeming to brace his spine against the straight back of the chair. "And your sister was sick, too. Emily had meningitis real bad. For a while, we didn't know if she was gonna make it or not."

"Now that you mention it, Poppa, I do remember Betty talking about us being real sick once."

"Well, you were. The doctor kept coming and there was so much medicine to get. And the doctor had to keep coming to see 'bout ya'll. I never been so crazy in all my life. I remember I felt like any minute I might lose my mind."

" 'Cause we were so sick, Poppa?" Annie Ruth was truly touched by her father's show of concern. She and her sisters had figured that Mudear was right all the times she had told them that Poppa didn't give any more of a damn about them than a stranger in the street would, like any man would.

"Well, yeah, because ya'll were sick. You girls and Mudear was just about all the family I really ever had to call my own, my very own. And the thought of losing any of you . . . losing any of you . . . especially to lose ya'll because of my stupidness and pride."

He hung his head in shame over his coffee cup.

As soon as Poppa had mentioned the memory of that cold winter day without heat or lights to Annie Ruth, he had regretted it. How can I ever get this child to understand something that I'm still trying thirty-some-odd years later to figure out myself? he thought.

He had run the events leading up to that cold day over and over in his mind like a reel of tape perpetually set on PLAY.

It was in the Lovejoys' twelfth year of marriage that he had gotten his first promotion, something that didn't happen very often to a colored man at the chalk mines. That spring, he was so full of himself, he didn't think his feet stank. He finally felt that the folks who thought he was just a plodder had been taught an exquisite lesson. Word gets around, so Poppa wasn't a bit surprised to get a late-night telephone call from Mudear's people who lived in New York City. Poppa extravagantly, grandly, foolishly sent the money—$250—to Mudear's aunt's husband in the North for jail bail. Even Mudear gently tried to tell him her people up north couldn't be trusted. But he felt duty bound to show all those Negroes up "nawt" that a colored man in the South could take care of himself, his family, and even his people who were stupid enough to migrate north just when things were starting to get better down in Georgia.

It was a mistake that he could never forgive himself for.

The summer of that year passed without concern for the repayment of the $250. Poppa was having too good a time reminding Mudear where her family, most of whom had moved north unlike his stupid country people, had to come when they needed something. As the fall came, however, money was not quite so free for him and he began to wonder aloud when those trifling northern Negroes were gonna pay what they owed. By the time it started dropping down near freezing at night, Poppa was near panic. For the first time in his married life, he had overextended himself. One night, he had even set up the regulars at the bar at The Place. Now, he *needed* his money.

But he couldn't get anybody to even take his calls up north. "He ain't here" was all he got. And he needed his money. He had been able to keep up the mortgage payments on his little two-bedroom house in East Mulberry. There were groceries in the house and the water was still on. But by the time the white man with the hard hat and tool belt came to turn off the gas and electric, Poppa had no money, expected none for another month, and had nowhere else to get any.

That's when Annie Ruth, the baby, started making that crouping sound at night.

"Look like we just 'bout gon' lose your father," Poppa heard Mudear inform the girls one day after they had all recovered and the lights and gas had been back on awhile.

Ernest did feel as if he wanted to die. He could hardly make himself eat every day and he had dropped so much weight from his already slender frame that even his buddies down at The Place noticed it. But something in his face kept all of them from saying anything. They sensed this was not something open to casual questions or comments. As if someone had pulled down his pants in public, and he looked small and withered.

He kept going to work every day because besides still being the breadwinner, the man of the house, he told himself, work was the only place he could go just then that did not remind him of his stupid, prideful mistake. He could go every day to the kaolin mines and dig and haul in the dry white powdery pits until he was so tired he didn't have the strength to think during the day.

Lord, where would we be now if I had had enough sense to tell them folks we ain't got it to spare or even if I had sent half of what I sent. Hell, if I'd sent a tenth of what I sent, it would 'a been more than they had. And I wouldn't of been left hanging, strapped the way I was.

He couldn't get it out of his mind. Again and again, he remembered getting the money from the bank, counting it over and over just to give himself the satisfaction of ownership, going to the Western Union office on Poplar Street. Waiting in line, waiting his turn in line. The way the white man's tissue-thin hair stood up on the crown of his head. The feel of the orange pencil in his hand as he signed the receipt for the money he sent up north.

Forever afterward, he hated all things northern.

"Don't let your pride get your ass in trouble. I knew better than to send those low-down, worthless northern Negroes my money. But I couldn't help it. I wanted to show them all. They always treated me like . . ."

"Treated you like what, Poppa?" Annie Ruth asked. She was beginning to get interested. The conversation with her father was almost like the ones she and her sisters had shared with Mudear when they were growing up and the woman felt like having them around.

Mudear would urgently call one of the girls to her side. Then, when she arrived to see what emergency Mudear had run into, she would be greeted with the question, "Daughter, tell me now, what does this woman on TV look like?"

It was not a casual question. It was test material. The Lovejoy girl would look at the screen, screw up her face squinting one eye, and appraise the target and say, "She looks like a blond Nancy Wilson."

Mudear would give her delicious rich laugh and clap her hands at her daughter's insight and perception and say, "Girl, you know you can call it!" And with that bit of praise, mother and daughter would return to their routines.

When Poppa realized that he was sitting at his kitchen table talking to Annie Ruth in the middle of the night, he had no idea what he had just thought and what he had actually said. Annie Ruth leaned forward the way he had seen her do when she was interviewing someone on television. Annie Ruth could always make it seem that for that moment you were the most important person in the world.

"What happened, Poppa, with the gas and electric?" Annie Ruth wanted to know. "What happened? How did you pay the bill, Poppa?"

When he didn't answer, she continued, "With Emily and me sick, I guess you had to do something mighty quick to get it turned back on, huh, Poppa?"

Two or three times in as many seconds, it seemed that Poppa was about to open his mouth and answer his youngest daughter, but just looking at her reminded him of Mudear. He couldn't chance seeing Annie Ruth look at him with wicked disdain the way Mudear did.

Annie Ruth thought he was going to cry.

Instead, he dropped his hands to his lap, leaned forward from the waist, and brought his head down so hard on the table he rattled their cups of Sanka and cream. Then, he slowly brought his head up again and upset the cup and saucer before him. The cup and saucer flipped over against his chest and fell down into his lap, leaving the front of his pajama top and bottom soaking wet and stained. But he didn't seem to notice. Poppa just kept banging his head on the tabletop and moaning a bit.

Annie Ruth was past shock at her usually quiet, even-tempered father and his show of grief. She wondered what he was drinking in that cup. He looked and sounded like legions of mourners at wailing walls, at funeral pyres, at mass graves. She tried to stop him from dropping his forehead so heavily on the table, but all she really accomplished was to sort of pat her father's head as he brought it up from the tabletop. After a few seconds, he stopped on his own and sat stiff and sad with tears in his eyes.

She felt so sorry for him. "Come on, Poppa, it's time to go to bed."

Annie Ruth leaned over to help him up from his chair. She fully expected to smell liquor on his breath. How else could she explain his talkativeness, his rambling, his strange extravagant behavior except to assume that he was drunk? But, other than the spilled coffee, she didn't smell anything but the fading scent of Old Spice. She was surprised the combination didn't make her sick.

Slipping her arm under his arm and around his back, she tried to lift him from his chair, but he seemed to be dead weight, much heavier than she had imagined, and when she remembered that she was pregnant, she let go of him so suddenly that he made a plopping sound as he fell back down, nearly missing the seat of the kitchen chair. Well, I can't leave him just sitting down here crying by himself, she thought.

"You gonna have to give me some help, Poppa," she said, steeling herself again to help him to his feet.

The sound of her voice seemed to bring him back to himself and he mumbled, "Yeah, yeah, right, I gotta help my children. Right. I can stand up." And he rubbed his hand over his face a couple of times as if to clear his head.

He stood up shakily without any support from Annie Ruth. But he reached for her broad shoulders as he began to wobble. Seeing her father so unsteady, Annie Ruth could hear her mother's voice instructing the girls, "Your father's just an old fool. Don't pay him no mind."

As they headed for the steps, Annie Ruth asked him, "You want to just stretch out on the sofa tonight, Poppa?"

But he was adamant and said in a strong voice, "No! I want to sleep in my own bed. In your mother's and my bed."

"Okay," Annie Ruth said, but she thought, suit yourself and choose your poison.

She thought they would not be able to navigate the short flight of stairs to the second floor. But Poppa walked up the steps almost unaided. Then, he nearly collapsed onto Annie Ruth. She leaned him against the wall and then sort of scooted him through the first door on the right, to his and Mudear's room.

Finally, laying him in bed, she started to take off his wet pajama top and bottom soaked with Sanka and canned Pet milk, but she remembered the look of shame in the eyes of old men she had seen when she was an investigative reporter covering mistreatment of the elderly in nursing homes. As strange women in white uniforms roughly took off the old men's shirts and stripped them naked of their soiled and streaked pants as if they were store dummies, Annie Ruth would watch from her spot in a corner masquerading as a nurse's aide hired through a temporary service. Torn between averting her eyes and watching closely so she could make notes for her news report later on, she noticed that the old men in the bed would always manage to catch her eye with a look that begged that she not look any longer, that she not witness this indignity that they could no longer control.

But she watched.

As a new shift of nurses and assistants and attendants came in to hold their old dicks so they could pee, stooping beside patched-up wheelchairs as the men tried to help by tapping the side of their penises against the curved lip of the elongated plastic slop jars. In trying to coax urine from the eye of the lifeless piece of meat, sometimes an impatient attendant would turn to the low sink by the bathroom door and turn on the faucet of cold water in hopes of encouraging the old men's flow.

Eventually, all three of us Lovejoy women gonna probably have to take our turns undressing Poppa, washing his wrinkled old genitals, and wiping the spittle from his cheeks. It'll come soon enough. Let him keep some of his dignity now, she thought, and just pulled Mudear's pretty wine-colored comforter up over her father's sleeping figure before heading back to her room.

At the door, she turned and said, "Good night, Poppa," even though she felt he wasn't awake to hear her.

"Annie Ruth?" he said just as she was about to close the door to the bedroom.

She turned and came back to the bed.

"Yes, Poppa?" she asked leaning over him.

"Your mother."

"Yes, Poppa."

He started to reach out for his daughter's arm, but he stopped himself and put his hand back under the cover. "Your mother, no matter what she was when she died, no matter how she ended up. She was a sweet girl when we met."

All Annie Ruth could bring herself to say was "Ummm." Then, when he closed his eyes again, she patted his shoulder and repeated, "Night, Poppa." And left the room.

CHAPTER 20

He's damn right I was sweet when we first met. I couldn't help but be sweet. I didn't know no better. I was like my Mudear had been her whole life. She was a woman who always had a smile on her face. She loved her family and her life and it just seemed to love her back. We didn't hardly have nothing. Daddy seemed to work hard, but I think we rented our house all the time I can remember. But it didn't stop Mudear from seeming to love life. She was the kind of woman who hummed while she did her housework. She actually hummed a happy kinda tune while she went about her day.

I just assumed I had inherited that knack from her naturally. You know, like mother, like daughter. But that was before I came out from under that roof and found out how the world really was. Before I married Ernest.

CHAPTER 21

Betty had meant to just go upstairs, change her clothes, and go back down to the kitchen to make a cup of tea and wait for Emily to come in. But after taking off her clothes and putting on some sweats, she didn't head back downstairs. Instead, she found herself drawn to her office desk across and down the hall from her bedroom even though she dreaded facing the piles of correspondence, accountant ledgers, and magazines there. Even with her home computer tied up to the ones at the shops, she seemed to have more and more paper flooding her office. But Betty was the kind of person who liked to put her hands on her work. That's why she loved the feel of books in her hand.

The room had almost as many shelves covering the walls as

the library downstairs did. They were all crammed with books. In the library the books were shelved in order by subject matter or alphabetically by author. The majority of the library book collection had come with the house. The family of the original owner had amassed an excellent collection of American and European classics as well as an extensive collection of old reference books and atlases. And Betty had added her own extensive collection of hardback books to the library. She had taken such pleasure in removing the old musty-smelling books from one section of shelves and replacing them with first-edition copies of fiction and poetry by black women writers. Betty even had a thin steel ladder that slid along the bookcases of one wall to enable her to reach the volumes on the top shelves.

But in her office the books were put in haphazardly, casually, paperbacks next to leather-bound reference books. A biography of Madame C. J. Walker next to a grocery-store-purchased romance novel. Books on business management next to *Blacks in the Military*.

Sitting in the cool leather of the large desk chair made Betty pull her sweat suit tighter against her body. She got up and went to the thermostat on the opposite wall of her office. She turned up the heating dial and smiled as she felt the rush of warm air blow through the heating vents on the floor beneath her.

When she sat back in the wine-colored leather chair, she almost instinctively opened the drawer where she kept her personal family album. She smiled as she always did when she opened to the first photograph on the first page of the thin laminated book. It was a picture of the three Lovejoy sisters when they were girls dressed up for church. Standing by the passenger door of the family black car, shining in the bright sun of a long-ago late summer day in Mulberry. The three of them dressed in identical dresses in different colors. They all had printed skirts in muted colors with white short-sleeved tops and matching vests. The entire color picture had faded to an overall mellow yellow like a stain, but Betty could remember every detail about the dresses, the day, their lives.

She had been thirteen, Emily was nearly ten, and Annie Ruth was six. And Betty remembered that they were talking about Mudear like a dog among themselves just before their father snapped the picture. Later, they had examined the photograph for hours in search of telltale signs that they had just committed the unspeakable . . . they had spoken.

The girls had not started out feeling so free to talk about Mudear the way they did now. Until Betty became a teenager, they were all afraid that anything they said about their mother would be magically telegraphed back to her and leave them open to some ghastly punishment. Anytime one of them began complaining about Mudear and how her ways infringed on everybody else in the household, the other two would shut her up.

"Don't be talking like that about Mudear," they would say in urgent tones. "Good God, she may hear."

They didn't trust themselves to talk about her in the house, out in the yard, at school, on the bus downtown to pay the bills or buy new shoes. Nowhere, they felt, was safe enough to be out of ear range or spirit range of Mudear.

But one summer day just weeks before Poppa had snapped the Sunday morning photograph, they made a discovery.

All three of them had been invited to a wiener roast in the backyard of one of Betty's schoolmates. And Mudear had agreed. The girls were so excited about going that they had done all their housework and their homework on Friday evening and early Saturday morning. Then, at the last minute, while Betty was ironing crisp cotton shorts for all of them to wear, Mudear decided she needed Betty to wash, straighten, curl, and style her hair for her. And that would take half the day. It shouldn't have taken half the day, but Mudear was so particular about her "personal appearance." She wore her hair then the same way she wore it when she died nearly thirty years later. She had Betty keep her coarse thick hair bobbed just at her earlobe. Betty curled it all over with small hot curlers and brushed it back from her face into a light froth of shiny black curls.

Mudear called it classic.

With Betty doing Mudear's hair, the two younger girls couldn't go across town on the bus without their big sister, so their plans for the wiener roast were off.

The girls were stunned with disappointment. But they knew better than to even raise the question of the wiener roast with Mudear. They never cried and pleaded for anything to Mudear. They had discovered early in life that those ploys, sincere or feigned, were useless with her after the change. She would tell them straight out, "Don't be coming bothering me with that little petty stuff. Fix it, forget it, figure it out, or get over it yourself." Even when a sudden thunderstorm came up and awakened the girls in the middle of the night, they knew better than to go crying to Mudear. She always slept right through the worst storms, with lightning and thunder cracking around the house, and could not stand to be disturbed. She had told them that sleeping through a storm was some of the best sleep you could get. The girls would just have to close their eyes, put their pillows over their heads, hug themselves in their little beds, and try to go back to sleep.

But they had wanted to go to the wiener roast so badly. The party giver had told Betty at recess that week that they planned to roast hot dogs on straightened-out coat hangers that each guest made and held herself over the open fire. She had told Betty that her father had already dug a big hole in the backyard and filled it with oak wood for the fire and that her mother was going to make chili to go over the hot dogs. Then, for dessert each guest was going to use her coat hanger to roast marshmallows.

All week, the girls had hardly been able to contain themselves. They planned the route they would take to get to the party in Pleasant Hill. They discussed what they would wear and how many hot dogs they would eat. They made Betty ask if they should bring their own coat hangers.

And to have their raised little spirits, their high little hopes, dashed so quickly, so casually was bitter enough to make them retch. They all felt that they were as powerless as insects.

It was so unfair. The girls really rarely asked to go anywhere. They had a lot to do in the house usually on weekends when the two younger girls helped Betty with the major cleaning, shopping, and cooking projects. There was little time left over for outings. Once in a while on Saturdays, Poppa would drop them off at the Burghart Theatre to see a matinee while he did some household shopping or drank a couple of beers at The Place. But that was a rare treat.

And they seldom had company at their house. Anyone visiting the girls would have to stay outside in the yard to play because no other little girls were allowed to come into the house and disturb Mudear. The sisters had gotten used to these rules fairly easily, but not their friends. Their little schoolmates thought the rules were strange and insulting—having to run home to the bathroom or for a drink of soda—and rarely came back. But the Lovejoy girls rarely felt deprived because they had found each other to be the best possible company.

So regular visits weren't even considered. But this one time they had really wanted to go.

Of course, Mudear hadn't cared about that. She didn't even seem to notice that they wanted to go to the wiener roast so badly.

With all their work and Mudear's hair done, they had spent the late Saturday afternoon just roaming around their own back-yard, being careful to avoid stepping on Mudear's plants.

In their boredom and anger, their talking about Mudear seemed as natural as listlessly drawing circles in the dirt with a stick.

"She so mean and low-down," Emily said first.

"Yeah," Betty agreed. "She don't care nothing 'bout nothing but her own self. Now, she upstairs in that house just looking at herself in the mirror with nice clean hair."

"She think she so cute," Annie Ruth offered and was gratified that her little input was greeted with amens from her older sisters. It emboldened her.

"Wearing those old funny-looking flowered pastel robes all the time," she added.

"Yeah, like she sick all the time," Emily said. "She make *me* sick."

And they all giggled at Emily's little joke.

They were just getting revved up. There in Mudear's garden, next to the marigolds and tomato plants, they talked about her lovelessness, her heartlessness, her lack of motherliness.

"Yeah," Emily said. "She's the reason we don't get invited anywhere hardly as it is. They think we as funny acting as she is. And nobody want to come visit us if they can't even go to the bathroom."

All of a sudden they knew something was amiss. It seemed that the very breeze had suddenly stopped blowing in the yard.

They all looked up to the house's back porch at the same instant and saw her standing at the screen door dressed in a fresh flowered pastel housecoat, listening.

They nearly fell to their knees right on the spot, waiting for the bolt of lightning called up by their mother to strike them all dead. Emily even brought her hands together in a plaintive gesture of supplication. And Annie Ruth started whimpering in fear.

But Mudear just looked out at the girls and her garden around them and went on back in the house. Neither Betty nor Emily could remember vividly the last time Mudear had switched their legs with a stripped branch of a forsythia bush from outside. And Annie Ruth had never been stung with the switch. But they began to prepare themselves for the beating of their lives.

"Oh, God," Betty whispered. "She going to get a strap!"

She wished with all her heart that she had not encouraged her sisters to do so much reading. Now, all the scenes of punishment they had ever read or heard about came back to them in vivid Technicolor pictures.

And all three of them did actually fall to their knees together and start praying. They just knew that anyone as powerful as Mudear, a woman able to re-create herself overnight, able to change the patterns of her household without a fight, able to boss their big strong father around without even lifting her voice, would mete out the kind of punishment they only had read about in the Bible at Sunday school. So, they prayed to God, the towering white-bearded God they had seen in pictures, to help them, to protect them, to save them from their mother.

They must have stayed that way, with their knees to the ground, their hands clasped, their eyes closed in prayer, for some time.

When they next heard Mudear's voice, they opened their eyes to find that the sun was setting and a summer dusk had fallen on the backyard of their house.

"It's nearly dark out there, daughters," Mudear yelled from the window over the kitchen sink. "Don't be stepping on none of my plants in the dark."

It was all she said. Then, she dropped the pink and white checkered curtains back over the window.

When the girls tried to get to their feet, they found they could barely stand, their knees were dirty and achy, their legs wobbly and cramped, their nerves raw and frayed. They held onto each other as they made their unsteady way to the house. Bolstered by prayer and the support of each other, they were ready to meet their fate. But Mudear didn't say a word to them about their overheard conversation discussing her.

"Ya'll didn't notice any worms on my collard greens, did you?" Mudear asked from her tall wooden stool by the sink as Betty automatically started taking out pots from the refrigerator and began warming up food for their dinner.

Emily stopped taking the plates down from the cabinet and looked to Betty. Annie Ruth, brushing crumbs from the checkered kitchen tablecloth, looking to Betty, too. All three were sure Mudear must be hearing their hearts pounding.

"I—I didn't see any, Mudear," was all Betty could manage to sputter as she put on water to boil to make a fresh pitcher of iced tea for dinner.

The girls felt as if they were merely going through the motions. But they accomplished a table set for dinner as well as eating the prepared meal. After dinner, Poppa went upstairs and lay across the bed with his clothes on. Mudear tied up her fresh hairdo with a flowered chiffon scarf and stretched out on the sofa to look at television.

The girls washed up the dishes in silence. But they hurried through the chore. They couldn't wait to get up to their room to talk. But when they finally closed the door to their bedroom, no one wanted to say it first. They sat on their beds facing each other.

Finally, Betty spoke. "I don't think Mudear care whether we talk about her or not."

They sat there awhile, sly smiles on their faces, considering the possibility of their luck. Looking at the windup clock on their chest of drawers, Betty said, "Time to get ready for bed." Then, Betty got up and started running water for their baths. The other girls laid out their underwear and socks for Sunday school the next morning and got in the tub. While Emily and Annie Ruth bathed, Betty ironed their new matching dresses she had bought at Davison's downtown.

But when they got into their beds, they didn't sleep. The girls stayed up all night talking about Mudear.

CHAPTER 22

Betty was still sitting up watching CNN on the small red portable television in the kitchen and sipping hot tea in her thick cotton sweat suit and slippers when Emily finally let herself in the back door with the key from under the heavy straw doormat.

"Mulberry must be the only place left on the face of the earth where people still feel they can leave their own house key under the doormat," Emily muttered to herself as she walked into the kitchen and threw her wet suede coat across a chair. "You got three hundred thousand dollars' worth of stuff in here and you still leave your back door unlocked for all practical purposes. Humph, and Mudear say I'm supposed to be the crazy one."

Betty pretended not to notice drops of muddy water dripping

off the sleeve of the coat onto the heavy oak antique table she used in the kitchen. She knew Emily hated for any of her sisters to imply that they disapproved of something she had done.

She must be hanging out down by the riverbed again, Betty thought, and said a silent prayer that they would never find her dismembered, decomposed body rotting down there. She may still leave her own house key under the doormat, but she knew that a woman alone wasn't safe walking down by the river after dark.

"Want some tea, Em-Em?"

"Betty, you know as well as I do what a disaster it would be if Annie Ruth actually had a child to raise!" Emily didn't even bother to sit down. "You saw what kind of shape she was in when she got off that plane. That's a mother?"

Betty thought that they would at least have a decent period of chitchat first, but Emily wanted to get right to it.

Emily never did know how to make small talk, Betty thought as Emily plunged into all the reasons Annie Ruth shouldn't even think about having the child she was pregnant with. Emily's inability to chitchat when she had something burning on her mind made people uncomfortable, always had, but then, Betty thought, most of what Emily did made people uncomfortable. She gets that from Mudear.

"Now, Betty, you know as well as I do that Annie Ruth don't have no business with a baby." Emily was saying over and over as she began to take off her wet boots.

"You remember how she used to just throw her old dolls away when she got bored with them," she continued. "Hell, that's how she treats people sometimes. Look at all the men—good men, men other women would have died for—she's just had and thrown away. Good God, Betty, Annie Ruth use men like she uses new improved maxi pads. She even rates 'em like that. Are they comfortable? Are they dependable? Are they easily disposed of? When you're with one, can your mind be free to think of other things? What are they worth?

"Just what do you think she's gonna do with a child, an infant completely dependent on her? Just throw it away when she's tired of it? A child ain't a maxi pad."

Betty started to respond, but she didn't feel like this conversation now. She knew she was tired and the hour was late because she could feel giddiness sneaking up on her. Everything Emily was saying was starting to make her giggle.

"Remember that real nice guy named Tommy, the editor at the newspaper in Washington we met when we visited Annie Ruth that weekend? You notice how he disappeared all of a sudden?"

"Oh, yeah, Tommy, he was nice. I forgot about him," Betty said, remembering the husky young country man who had moved to the big-city newspaper from a small North Carolina town. "What did happen to him?"

"Annie Ruth told me it was over giving head," Emily said with a didn't-I-tell-you smirk. "Annie Ruth told me he was sort of fumbling and hesitant about it. So, she asked him if he had ever done this before and he said, noooo, but he'd *try* to see what he could do.

"Then, Annie Ruth told him, 'Well, don't be coming up in through here if *try* is the best you can do.' "

"And that's why he disappeared so suddenly?" Betty asked, laughing. She laughed so hard she got choked on her tea and had to bring her feet off the table and sit up. "She actually told him, 'Don't be coming up in through here'?"

"And you think this is funny, Betty?" Emily was indignant and hurt. "I was just telling you that to show how she is."

Betty couldn't catch her breath from laughing to reply. She

just held up one hand and rested her face in the other. When she was able to speak, she asked, "And that was the end of his cute husky country ass?"

This time Emily had to laugh, too. "You know it," she said and chuckled with Betty over their baby sister. "Sister girl made him get up, put on his clothes, and get his no-pussy-eating self out of her apartment immediately."

The sisters laughed together so comfortably it sounded as if they were singing in harmony. They all three had felt at one time or another that the sound of them laughing together was their only line to sanity and safety. When all three of them laughed, in a department store or restaurant, the entire room turned to look for the source of the melodic merriment.

Betty decided to take advantage of the lull in the afterglow of their laughter.

"Oh, I didn't even check my answering machine," she said, pretending to remember with a glance over at the flashing red light. She got up, turned her back to Emily, who continued to take off her wet clothes, and pressed the blinking button. Even though she knew it was inevitable that Emily would return to Annie Ruth's situation, she thought she could at least postpone it for a while.

"Hey, baby," the first message went. "It's me, Stan. I heard about your mama. I shore am sorry. Am I gonna see you tonight? Call me at school. Bye."

"Betty, it's Helen. I need your okay on the latest changes for the show. And I need to know the new regulation heights for hair styles. Please call me when you get a chance. Bye."

"Miss Lovejoy, you told me to call and remind you that to-morrow is the day the health inspectors come to the shops."

"Hey, baby, it's me again. You want me to pick up some fish for you to fry tonight?"

Betty hit the stop button with her fist and turned back to Emily.

"Good God," she said, shaking her head. "Mudear laying up there on a cooling board in Parkinson Funeral Home and this man expected me to fry fish for him. Mudear was right, a man don't give a damn about you."

"Hello, Miss Love—I mean Betty. It's Cinque. I went by the shop to fix the light in the reception area and they told me about your mother. I'm sorry. . . . I'm sorry I missed you, too." There was a long pause, then, "If you feel like it, give me a call."

Emily looked up at Betty smiling down at the tape machine. "If you feel like what?" Emily asked her sister and laughed, too.

Betty hit the stop button again.

"Em-Em, I know I don't have any business with this child. But, God, he's so gorgeous—how come boys we went to school with didn't know nothing 'bout lifting weights?—lord knows he's at his sexual peak and since I tied him to my bed like Annie Ruth said—he nearly tore my brass bed down, too—he thinks I hung the moon."

"Don't sound bad to me," Emily said, not even trying to hide her envy.

"Hell, it's better than that. He told me the other day I was the smartest woman he ever met. Then, he thought awhile and said, 'No, you the smartest person I ever met.' This boy even think the few little gray pubic hairs I'm starting to get are cute and sexy. He calls my pussy 'slamming'!"

Emily chuckled. "I guess the irony was lost on him?"

"Irony!" Betty hooted. "Shoot, nineteen-year-old boys don't

know nothing about no irony. And his music does give me a headache."

"But he has other attributes, huh?" Emily said.

"You got that right. But really I guess I know this is just a passing thing. I'm trying to help the boy get into some kind of school somewhere."

"Uh-huh," Emily said with the emphasis on the second syllable heavy with sarcasm, like a character in a television sitcom.

"No, really I am, and once that's done, I know that'll be it."

"Why you say that?"

"Oh, Emily, he's a sweet kid and fun, too, but I know he ain't nothing but a baby. Sometimes when I see him slumped down in a chair, his leg flung over the chair's arm, I want to reprimand him, 'Sit up, baby, sit up straight, you gonna ruin your back.' I have to stop myself from sounding like his mother.

"I guess I'll probably end up with Stan or somebody like him. He's more my speed, I guess, my age and everything. You know. . . ."

She hit the message button again.

"Hey, baby, it's me again. Never mind about the fish, I'm going to a game in Atlanta tonight. Talk to you tomorrow. Bye."

Emily didn't even have to say anything. The look she gave Betty said, "Keep living, daughter."

Shoot, this ain't no better than trying to cool Emily down about Annie Ruth and her baby, Betty thought as she hit the button to save the rest of the messages and turned back to face her sister. She was missing that evening glass of wine more and more.

Emily was almost half undressed now. She stood in the middle of Betty's kitchen and continued to take off her wet clothes and drop them on the floor. She finally stood in the kitchen dressed in just tight red cotton bikini panties and a lacy pink plunging underwire bra. Betty smiled at her sister's voluptuous figure and her skimpy underwear.

"You gonna need a knitting needle to take those panties off," Betty said with a chuckle and went over to the big restaurant-sized gas stove to put the teakettle on the burner.

Emily looked down at her body as if in surprise to see it and, reaching a finger inside the rubber leg band of her panties, snapped the bikinis into a more comfortable position. Then, she just giggled and shrugged her shoulder as she left the kitchen in search of something to cover up with.

Betty watched her bounce out of the room, her butt, breasts, and hair jiggling in rhythm with her pace, and thought, even with her extra weight, Em-Em is still as cute as she can be. Despite all the expense, effort, and time the three women all spent on their looks, their clothes, their hair, their makeup, their bodies, their skin, it still caught Betty by surprise sometimes to realize how attractive they all were. That was Mudear's doing, Betty thought as she turned back to the stove and cut the fire up under the kettle.

Mudear had drummed it into their heads before any of them had gotten out of that ugly awkward preteen stage of life not to count on their looks in this world.

"Pretty women, daughters, are a dime a dozen," she informed them over and over again. "My Mudear used to tell me, 'Pretty is as pretty does. Beauty is a gift from God.' But gift or no, pretty ain't gonna get you where smarts will."

Mudear amended the truism for any locale and occasion. If one of the girls came in on a Sunday and told her that someone at church had commented on how cute all three of them looked in their outfits, Mudear would say, "Pretty girls in a southern country church are a dime a dozen, daughter."

If she picked up the phone to listen in on a conversation and heard a boy sweet-talking Betty about her looks, she'd say right into the phone, "Pretty women in a southern country town are a dime a dozen, daughter."

Even after Emily's skin had cleared up so nicely at Fort Valley State, Mudear was quick to tell her, "Pretty women are a dime a dozen at a little country college, daughter." She repeated the warning to Annie Ruth when she wanted to run for Morehouse's homecoming queen, Miss Maroon and White. "Daughter, pretty women are a dime a dozen on Spelman College campus."

Annie Ruth had told Betty and Emily that Mudear had even pulled the old saw out when she moved to L.A. "Pretty women sho' 'nough a dime a dozen out in Los Angeles, California, daughter," she had warned Annie Ruth over the phone when she called to give her and Poppa her new address and phone number.

Betty poured hot water over the little straw holder of chamomile tea in Emily's favorite cup and tried to ignore the pile of wet clothes in the middle of the floor. She couldn't do it. She hated mess and disarray.

Emily came back in the kitchen wrapping a cover, Betty's dark-blue velvet dressing gown, loosely around her.

"You keep it so hot in this house that I don't really need to wear *any* clothes," Emily said as she headed for the refrigerator and searched through the contents until she found some antipasto, vegetable pasta salad, and one walnut brownie with fudge frosting that she brought back to the heavy oak table. She put her booty on the table beside her steaming cup of tea and plopped down on the smooth seat of a high-back oak chair.

"Don't people bring food and stuff by the house anymore when folks die?" Emily asked.

"Oh, somebody from the shop left a case of Cokes on the back porch. And some of my older customers came by first thing this morning and gave me little pieces of change. Five dollars, ten dollars. You know. But which one of Mudear's friends you think gon' come by with cakes and pies?"

Emily just bit her lip and nodded her understanding.

"Whew," she said, "it really is hot in here."

"You know me, I will *never* sit up in a dark house and I will *never* sit up in a cold house," Betty said as she spread Emily's clothes out on the table in the laundry room to dry. I sure hope that suede jacket has been weatherproofed, she thought and returned to the kitchen. "Mulberry Gas and Electric will never turn off my services."

"Mudear would tell you, 'Keep living, daughter,' " Emily said as she opened the container of pasta salad and took a bite of the brownie.

Emily felt the same way Mudear did about never knowing what's going to happen in your life or what you'll do in any situation. Emily had come close many times to having her heat and electricity cut off and her telephone service was a month-to-month arrangement. She made so many calls to Southern Bell customer service to get an extension on paying her bill that she had formed a chatting relationship with the supervisor she usually talked with. If it had been a male supervisor, she would have dated him by now. After sixteen years with the state government, she wasn't doing any worse than most working people. She just couldn't seem to hold on to any cash. She looked to Betty every few months to bail her out of penury. And Betty always came through cheerfully. She couldn't stand to see her sisters do without.

My money's just running away from me, Emily would think as she pored over her confusing bank statements.

Betty shivered and pulled her feet wrapped in knitted slippers up under her. "God, your mentioning Mudear gave me the all-overs just now. Like she touched me on the shoulder," she said.

"Knowing Mudear, with Annie Ruth's mess and everything, where else would she be?" Emily asked. "She was never around unless you *didn't* want her to be."

"I hope you didn't think any of this was gonna go smoothly," Betty said. "Mudear would probably feel she'd have to sit up in that white oak casket just to get things going if she thought for one minute that things were going to go smoothly."

"Betty, going smoothly is one thing. But a true disaster is another. I know I can't tell Annie Ruth nothing, never could. But she'll listen to you."

"Emily, you know as well as I do that Annie Ruth doesn't hardly listen to anybody when she's decided something. And I know it's hard for you to accept, but I think Annie Ruth's decided to keep this baby."

Emily dropped her fork back into her salad. "Why do you say that? Did she tell you that? Did she?"

Betty reached over and patted her sister's arm. "No, Em-Em, she didn't say a word to me. But that's the feeling I get."

"And that's okay with you?" Emily was incredulous.

"Emily, if that's what Annie Ruth decides, then it's going to have to be okay with me. It's going to have to be okay with all of us. Right?"

Emily was quiet for a while playing with her brownie.

"It's just that, Betty, I'm so afraid for Annie Ruth. Pregnant!

"Either way she go, I'm afraid for her. I know you don't think so, but I know what she's facing and I know how she feels."

Betty didn't know that much about Emily's experience of her abortion. Emily just couldn't bring herself to talk to Betty about it at the time and the more time passed the easier it was to just let it rest. Annie Ruth had told Betty about it, but Emily had never said a word.

"Ron must have some mighty strong sperm," Annie Ruth had said to Betty. " 'Cause Lovejoy women take their birth control very seriously."

It was strange the things Emily could share with Betty and the experiences she was too ashamed of even to talk about. But it had been Betty who Emily had called when a man she dated had started an argument in a restaurant, grabbed up her bag and pushed her out the door, and then slapped her a few times in the car outside.

She had finally managed to get back to her apartment with a cut lip and the beginnings of a blue line along her cheekbone. She put some ice on her face and tracked Betty down on the phone in Mulberry and sobbed out what had happened.

"He just slapped me around a couple of times," she tried to say after calming down.

"Anytime a man hit you, Emily, and he bigger or stronger or anything that makes it so you can't protect yourself, then, he kicked your ass," Betty insisted, trying hard to control the anger she felt at Emily for being in this situation and the anger she felt at herself for judging her sister. "We just got to find a way to make sure you safe from that happening again."

Emily finished off the brownie and continued:

"When I got pregnant before Ron and I broke up and Annie Ruth came down, came down on the plane, from Washington, to be with me here for it and afterwards. Lord, Betty, I thought I was gonna have to be there for her myself. She nearly passed out at the clinic waiting for me. Then, when she brought me back home to the apartment, she became so unglued, dropping dishes and walking around in front of Ron in her underwear, that I told her I was better than I was and she could go back to D.C."

"Well," Betty said, "maybe that just goes to show you that Annie Ruth shouldn't consider doing what you did. That for her having her baby is the right thing."

"How can you say that *any* of us having children could be the right thing? Good God, Betty, she could turn out to be like Mudear!"

It was a sobering thought that left them both sitting silent sipping their tea.

"You know, I drove past our old house in East Mulberry tonight before I came here," Emily said after a while. "I go by there every now and then just to see what it look like."

"Em-Em, what in the world you want to do that for?"

"Oh, you know, I just like to see things," she said. "You don't ever drive by there when you go to the shop?"

"Naw," Betty said, getting up to pour herself more hot water. "Never."

"Well, you ought to sometimes. Mudear's old garden is all grown up and the house is empty right now. But there are still flowers peeking through the weeds in back."

Betty got up and rinsed both their cups out at the sink. She didn't respond.

"You know, Betty, that yard was where we swore to each other that we would never have any children."

"I know," Betty said wearily, her back still to Emily.

"And I stuck by my promise," Emily said in a strong voice.

Betty stood at the sink looking out on the wet shiny leaves of a magnolia in the backyard and combed the hair down on the back of her neck with her fingers. "I know," she said. "But we burying Mudear in two days. Maybe it's time we turn that promise a-loose."

CHAPTER 23

When Betty awoke the next morning and realized she not only had to take Annie Ruth and Emily to the funeral home to view Mudear's body, she also had to be at the old shop sometime before noon to oversee the plans for the annual hair show that her businesses were cosponsoring and get back to the funeral home to do Mudear's hair and makeup now that Poppa was moving up the funeral, she wanted to turn over and sleep forever. She felt like the elderly woman she had seen sitting in the foyer of the mortuary the night Mudear died toying with her checkbook and pen.

"Lord have mercy," the older woman had said to Betty as she raced through the door frantically looking for one of the Parkinsons. Betty had just come home from Stan's house around mid-night when she had checked her answering machine and heard Poppa's message of Mudear's death. "Why don't folks ever die when it's convenient?"

She knew just what the harried mourner had meant. This was such a bad time for Mudear to die. Like Mudear ever gave a damn about whether her actions were convenient or not to anyone else, Betty thought as she kicked off the covers and stretched out as far as she could in her big brass antique four-poster bed. She was glad to see that the sun was streaming through the pale shirred drapes at the window. The dramatic aspects of tromping around Mulberry preparing for her mother's funeral in the rain were a bit more than she thought even she could handle.

Okay, she thought, trying to organize her day. But all in the world she wanted to do was pull the covers back up over her head and let somebody else take care of it, take care of it all.

But she immediately heard Mudear's admonition each time she tried to cut a corner, do for herself instead of her family. "Well, daughter," Mudear would say, "if your conscience doesn't con-demn you, why should I?" Mudear had said it when Betty was about to open her second shop and finally got up the nerve to tell Mudear that in the future she was going to have to pay someone to come by their house a few days a week to clean and make sure she and Poppa had meals prepared instead of doing it herself every day.

"Well, daughter, if your conscience doesn't condemn you, why should I?" Mudear had said, then she hung up the phone in Betty's face. Betty, standing with the dead phone in her hand, could just imagine Mudear turning back to the wide-screen television and with the remote control turning the sound back up, ending the audience. It was one of the two ways she had dealt with her children for at least the last thirty years: either she drifted off to her own thoughts while they talked or she cut them off dead.

It was one of the reasons that Annie Ruth said she called Mudear so seldom. Annie Ruth said it infuriated her to have Mudear just hang up in her face whenever she was tired of talking. "It just makes me want to go through the phone and rip her throat out," she would hiss into the phone to one of her sisters. She always had to call one of them after talking with Mudear just to calm herself down. "First, you got to hope that Poppa's there to answer the phone, 'cause you know *she* won't. Then, you got to practically beg Poppa to beg Mudear to even come to the damn phone so you can hear to see if she still alive. Then, right in the middle of a sentence, if she sees a pretty bird in the yard or if something interesting flits across the TV screen, she just hangs up right in your face."

While I'm thinking about it, I better put a pair of hot curlers and some makeup that'll suit Mudear's complexion in my bag, Betty thought as she jumped up and went to her dressing table. The table looked like a cosmetics counter in Bloomingdale's. She picked out some foundation a shade or two lighter than her own skin and some pale cheek color and lipstick.

Mudear never did use much makeup. As far back as Betty could remember, she couldn't recall Mudear in anything more than a brush of rouge from a flat round fifty-cent-piece-sized compact and red lipstick. But this was back in the days when Mudear came out the house from time to time like other mothers. Then, after the change, she didn't bother to put anything on her face. When Poppa had ruled, Betty had heard the arguments that he and Mudear had over any ornamentation Mudear tried to add to herself.

Once, she had heard Mudear try to laugh off her husband's protestations that she looked like a whore going out the house with her two daughters downtown with makeup on. His own mother never wore it, he had shouted at Mudear as she stood at the mirror in the tiny bathroom of their old house and rubbed the red stains from her cheeks and lips.

As she put the electric hot curlers in her work bag, Betty thought about all the times she had done Mudear's hair in her life, standing on a little stool at the kitchen stove to reach Mudear's head in the old house, at the kitchen table, in her bedroom, in her La-Z-Boy in the rec room, wherever it was convenient for Mudear with enough light for Betty to see to do a good job.

Mudear insisted on a certain standard of service. She told her daughters as she ordered them around, "When I was cleaning a house, I always kept a beautiful comfortably clean well-run house. Betty she remember that. And I knew how important it is. That's why you girls so well trained."

So, she didn't accept anything, whether it was a cold glass of water or a plump Christmas goose, that was not top drawer. The girl knew there were standards to be met. And met they were.

Betty knew it was time to get up and get started, but her warm rumpled bed with the electric blanket turned to five was too inviting and she dove back under the covers headfirst when she finished packing her makeup bag.

God, what is Annie Ruth thinking of considering keeping and raising this baby? Betty thought. She can't even deal with Mudear being the way she has been practically all her life preferring the sight of a painted bunting to her own daughter's voice let alone a child who's going to turn out God knows how.

"Well, we'll jump off that bridge when we get to it," Betty

said aloud and forced herself to leap out of bed as if she had the energy to do it. Since she was eleven, she had somehow found the energy to do whatever it was she felt she had to do.

Betty couldn't stop thinking something that her mother used to say all the time whenever anyone the family knew died. "When you dead, you done. So, let the good times roll."

Mudear's the only person I know who you can't say that about. "When you dead, you done."

It had never crossed Betty's mind to do anything other than take care of her family. From the time she made baloney-and-graham-cracker sandwiches for herself and her sisters when she was eleven. From the time she figured out how to use the old rusty washing machine and ruined a few loads of clothes before she taught herself about separating the colors from the whites. From the time she collected all the girls' report cards and made sure they were signed by one of their parents and returned to school and wrote all the notes giving permission for field trips.

She had felt it was her duty.

She could never forget what she had heard through the faded pink flowered wallpaper of her bedroom wall the night she first had to feed her sisters.

Betty remembered it clearly as the exact time that she knew that she was alone in this world, really alone, an orphan without a mother. Her stomach was beginning to cramp up on her and make funny noises.

Betty had just turned eleven at the time, and though she shot up in her early teens, she was not tall enough yet to reach the loaf of Colonial bread someone had thrown all the way to the back on top of the refrigerator behind the tin bread box. Even when she pulled a kitchen chair up to the refrigerator and stood on it, she couldn't reach the bread at the back. The baby, Annie Ruth, had started a low irritating whine for food. And the box of crackers had been left open on the counter. So, she took what she could reach and made baloney-and-graham-cracker sandwiches for her sisters and herself.

I hope our dinner don't make us sick, she thought as she looked over her sisters asleep in their beds next to her. The three cotlike beds were lined up like little soldiers in the small room the three of them shared. There was just room between each of them for three little girls to hunker down tight together and weather a storm. This was in the old house over in East Mulberry where there were only two bedrooms and of course her father had insisted on the bigger room, " 'cause I'm a big man," he had said. There was no further discussion of room assignments.

When she heard her father's sharp voice in her parents' bedroom next door, she sat straight up in bed.

"You been laying around in bed all *day?*" Her father's voice, even through the bedroom wall, was strong, unbelieving, and angry. "Did you get up at all today?"

All she could hear of her mother's voice was a sleepy muffled sound.

"What about the girls?" He was almost sputtering with rage. "You been looking after them? Good God, the baby just got over being sick. Did you even fix them someum to eat?"

Another muffled sound and a long stretch—Mudear—in reply.

"Woman, don't you hear me talking to you? Your family's hongry!" Poppa shouted.

There was a slight pause and then Mudear said, "I done et, and when I done et, my whole family done et."

Poppa seemed as stunned by the statement at Betty was. The little girl could hear her father take two steps toward the bed in his heavy chalk-covered work boots. But Mudear's voice stopped the advance.

"And cut up that heat on your way out," she said. Then, Betty heard the rustle of sheets and quilts as Mudear settled back to sleep.

Everything was silent for a while. Betty held her breath waiting for her father to explode on the other side of the wall. But even after what seemed like minutes, there was still no sound from her parents' room. Then, she heard the slow slow clump, clump, clump of her father's footfalls as he left the room and softly closed the door.

She didn't know why she did it, but when Poppa opened the door to their room to look in on them, she pretended to be asleep. What she really wanted to do was ask, "Did you *hear* what she said? Does that mean what it sounded like? From now on Mudear's only family is *Mudear?* What's gonna happen to *us?*" But instead she lay there as still as death. She knew that in their house no one was ever allowed to question Poppa. And after a second or two, he pulled the door to and walked slowly into the bathroom. Then, all was silent.

Although she closed her eyes tight and covered her ears, she couldn't drown out in her head what she had heard Mudear say.

"I done et, and when I done et, my whole family done et."

If I don't feed us, the child thought, we could all just waste away and die. But she thought it more with wonder than with anger and resentment.

Early on, Betty didn't even blame Mudear for abandoning all of them in favor of her own wishes. She hated going downtown on the bus to pay the bills and deal with white folks in the stores by herself after she turned about twelve or thirteen. But she really didn't mind the responsibility. Actually, most of her new duties she shared with her sisters, which lightened the load. And besides, at first Mudear hadn't dumped *everything* in the house on her girls. She just, bit by bit, let go of what she didn't feel like doing. And the girls picked it up.

Sometimes, for Mudear, doing just what she felt like doing meant cooking a good hot dinner every day for a week for her family. Some days, she even had it waiting for Poppa and the girls when they came home from school and work. But that was more cruel than not cooking at all because each time Mudear did something in the house like the old days, before the change, it got the girls' hopes up, made them believe in their mother, just to have their hopes dashed in the next day or so when they came home from school and found Mudear still lying in bed in her gown eating two bananas and reading a picture magazine.

But most days, it meant fixing something scrumptious for herself while the girls and Poppa were away at school and work, then sleeping through dinnertime, leaving her family to fend for itself. Sometimes, she'd clean up the bathroom a bit. Nothing big, just wipe out the sink of globs of dried green toothpaste or rinse out the tub after she finished. But never anything as strenuous and distasteful as scrubbing around the inside of the toilet or mopping the floor.

But over the months after Mudear's change, these simple duties she chose to perform became less and less frequent with all the girls taking up the slack Mudear left. Until the time when everybody in the household seemed to look up and discover that Mudear didn't do a damn thing in the house. And since the house and garden were the only places Mudear ventured, that cut out just about all her nonpleasant chores.

There was no real discussion of what had happened and what that now meant. Other than the girls' and Poppa's muttering under their breath as they tried and failed, tried and failed at some task that Mudear had done seemingly effortlessly.

At first, Betty was just barely able to keep herself and the girls relatively clean and fed because they had a washer and dryer and Poppa gave her enough money when he took her to the grocery store to keep the refrigerator full of food. Then, after a while, Betty discovered that she was actually good at keeping house.

Betty, in fact, was relieved when Mudear finally stopped doing everything in the house. The uncertainty was beginning to make her an eleven-year-old nervous wreck. She'd sit in school trying to anticipate the situation at home, deciding what she would cook if Mudear hadn't prepared anything, if she and her sisters had clean clothes for the rest of the week, if she had remembered to remind Poppa of all the bills that needed paying that month.

Betty was just grateful that the baby was long out of diapers and almost ready for kindergarten by the time Mudear changed.

Of course, Betty's studies suffered along with her psyche. She loved reading and studying, but now she knew she had other things to learn. And she never did seem to catch up with her own class in school. But she took pride in her sisters' good grades and made sure they did their homework every night. That's when she finally learned her own lessons—four and seven years late as she went over her sisters' homework. "Oh," she would say with a real sense of revelation as she praised one of Annie Ruth's own hand-drawn maps. "*That's* where Madagascar is!"

The only thing Mudear insisted on doing herself was washing

her own panties each night. She told the girls to do the same. She said, "Everybody in the world ought to wash out they own drawers. This world would be a better place to live if everybody had to wash out his own drawers."

So, a pair of Mudear's sparkling white cotton briefs, purchased by Betty from Woolworth's downtown in packages of three, hanging over a towel rack in the bathroom or on a big lavender bush outside was what greeted Ernest and the girls each morning when they arose.

For years, Annie Ruth and Emily, even in their thirties, had to fight the impulse to throw their panties in the bathroom sink each night after they took them off. Annie Ruth had broken herself of the panty-washing habit when she found herself crawling around on the floor of her bedroom in an ocean-front villa on a Caribbean island in the dark trying not to wake her current lover while she searched in the jumble of their discarded clothes for her black flowered silk bikini panties.

Emily still struggled with the quotidian ritual. Some nights, she could go to bed and go to sleep when she hadn't washed out her panties. Other nights, she lay awake fighting the urge to jump up and at least rinse her drawers out in clear water. Sometimes, she triumphed, and sometimes, Mudear's indoctrination won out.

Betty didn't even try to fight the years of teaching. She, like Mudear, washed her panties out each night before retiring.

Mudear's natural bossiness had been a plus, too. Since Mudear seemed to love controlling things, she did enjoy overseeing the duties, the responsibilities, the running of the household, even if she had no intention of actually participating in the work.

And at first, it actually helped the girls get organized to have Mudear shouting orders at them from her resting place. They all had done little chores around the house before the change like making their beds or emptying the trash or helping to wash the dishes, but taking care of an entire household was a different matter. And the girls found that a "Did you put the clothes in the dryer?" or "What ya'll gon' take to school tomorrow to eat?" yelled from Mudear's bed kept the pace of the housekeeping moving along.

The only thing Betty truly hated handling was the telephone calls and visits—curious, hurt, confused, frantic, insistent, indignant—from Mudear's former friends inquiring about her sudden disappearance. "Mudear say she fine, better than fine. She just don't feel like coming out or talking," Betty told the women over and over. The only calls Mudear took sometimes were from her childhood friend Carrie.

But the uncertainty in the aftermath of Mudear's change had its effect on all the girls. Emily, especially, was unhinged by the sudden unexplained shift.

Betty did her best to help her sister. At night, the three of them would sit on the floor between their beds the way they had before the change when their father fought. They would huddle there on the floor like survivors of a village raid who suddenly found they had to deal with a new unknown leader. Knowing in their little stomachs that things were different, strange, altered, never ever to return to their original state. Like raid survivors surveying the burning rubble that was once their homes, their meeting places, their gardens, and knowing that, even rebuilt, they would not ever be the same. Not familiar, not safe, not comfortable, not ever again.

Sitting there, Betty would try to answer Emily's questions: "Who do we ask for permission now?" "Who's going to take us downtown for new shoes?" "Can we go downtown now whenever we want to?" "Who do we believe?" "Who has the final word now?" "Who cooks now?" "Who will tell us things about life?" "Who is who now?" "Will we change like Mudear sometime when we get bigger?"

The girls had to shift the focus, the line in which they were growing, when Mudear changed, became as she called it "a woman in her own shoes." They did not know at first if they liked it better this way or the other way, when their father was in total charge. They just knew that this change left things so different, so strange that it was frightening.

Betty stood under the steady spray of the shower for longer than she had allotted for herself because she had discovered that with the six shower heads aimed directly at her body, surrounding her, it was the only time her mind wasn't spinning with plans and memories. She was always grateful after a shower that she had had the money to install the specially designed fixtures in her modern bathroom shower stall. She also had a Jacuzzi in her tub and a hot tub on the balcony off her bedroom, but she never seemed to have time to lounge in either one of them. Sometimes, after working out, Cinque took her up on her offer and came by to soak in the hot tub, leaving his scent throughout the house.

When Betty came downstairs, she found Emily still in the X-large T-shirt she slept in but already up and sitting in the big glass atrium drinking a cup of steaming black coffee.

"Morning, sugar, how you feeling?" Betty asked as she came in with her own cup of coffee in the bone china she had bought for herself when she opened her second shop.

Emily just lifted one hand and sighed in reply. "Just standing on the battlefield . . . ," she said softly.

Betty felt sorry for Emily. Betty herself had only gotten a couple of hours of sleep, restless tossing sleep but at least she had dozed off a bit. Poor Emily probably didn't close her eyes all night, Betty thought as she passed by her sister and patted her on the shoulder. Emily was a terrible insomniac, unable to fall asleep each night until nearly dawn.

"You better think about getting dressed," Betty said. "I'm going to go by the shop for a second, then go to Sherwood Forest and pick up Annie Ruth, then swing back by here and pick you up for the funeral home. In about an hour and a half? Okay?"

She put down her coffee cup and headed for the kitchen. At the door she turned to Emily and said, "Em-Em, go easy on Annie Ruth today, okay? We got enough to handle with Mudear."

Emily didn't reply. She just sat there biting her bottom lip.

CHAPTER 24

When Betty pulled into the driveway at Sherwood Forest, she saw Annie Ruth sitting out on one of the beautifully weathered wooden swings in Mudear's back garden with a big mug in her hand. She sat watching flocks of birds—fiery cardinals, tiny blackpoll warblers, goldfinches, cantankerous bluebirds, brown thrashers, and mourning doves—swoop and eat around the dozen or more bird feeders placed around the yard. Dressed all in black with a flash of red and yellow at her throat and wrists, Annie Ruth looked like a bird herself, a red-winged blackbird perched on the edge of the swing.

The feeders—some built and painted like little woodland cottages, others made of clay or stone or glass or copper and terracotta shaped like domes or half a clamshell—gave added variety and personality to the thick lush garden that already carried Mudear's stamp on every square foot of dirt. The whole garden was homey and inviting, like the hard yellowish gourds Mudear had hung from wires for martins to make their nests in.

"How's it going, girl?" Betty asked as she came up one of the cypress-chip paths Mudear had had Poppa lay throughout her garden. Brushing a huge leggy bush with small violet flowers, she brought the smell of rosemary with her.

Annie Ruth reached up for Betty's hand and pulled her down next to her on the swing.

"Just standing on the battlefield," she said with a smile. "Poppa still sleep. I didn't bother him."

"Poor thing," Betty said and shook her head.

"Yeah, but this is a man who slept next to Mudear for the last forty-some year. Hell, the least he deserve is to sleep late."

They both laughed, but then Annie Ruth turned serious and added, "Um, he had a kind of a rough night."

"I don't doubt it," Betty said looking up at the split-level house that Poppa kept up so nicely. "I'm surprised Mudear let me get any sleep at all last night."

"She was probably too busy out here in her garden last night to bother us," Annie Ruth said, rocking the swing softly.

"It's funny you should say that," Betty said. "I was just thinking last night that this would be where Mudear would show up if she were to come back."

Annie Ruth looked around. "It is quite a place. I was noticing really how truly beautiful and well laid out this garden is. Mudear's garden is just so beautifully groomed and taken care of. I mean this woman only did work in this garden during the nighttime and there's no sign of a weed, no stinging nettle, no dollar weeds, no tufts of nut grass sticking up like unrelenting hairs out of an old man's ears. Nothing unwanted anywhere."

"Mudear had Poppa put down so much mulch and compost on this soil over the years that weeds didn't have much of a chance to appear let alone take hold," Betty explained.

"It's not that I'm surprised that it's so well taken care of," Annie Ruth said. "Mudear took better care of this garden than she ever took of us. But I really don't think I ever really appreciated how beautiful it is."

"How could you?" Betty asked as she picked an angel-wing jasmine bloom from the vine crawling up the trellis over the bench and examined its long fragrant petals before throwing it over her shoulder into a tangle of sweet william and scented geraniums.

"But, Betty, it's so green. I don't think I ever remember it being so green back here."

"That's 'cause it rained last night," Betty said matter-of-factly. "But this is how it usually looks 'cause Poppa put in an automatic watering system a few years ago."

Annie Ruth still just shook her head in awe at the show of garden glory. At her feet were tiny alyssum blooms and English thyme used as a ground cover that exuded the sweet smell of a kitchen when she walked over it. Behind her, a line of loblolly trees set in huge tubs guarded her back with their fragrant Cherokee-roselike flowers peeking out at the tips. Behind the loblollies, a cluster of tall magnolias with their thick shiny leaves blocked out all the other ranch-style houses on the next street. Mounds of hydrangea—Mudear had adjusted the pH of the soil with extra lime to make the blossoms white—ringed a section of the garden that made a private space filled with roses and a small maze of tea olive hedges. Lamb's ear sat like plump rabbits ready to munch on the exotic red and green and purple lettuces nearby that Annie Ruth had sent the seeds for from a California nursery.

Betty looked around the yard dispassionately. "You know what I noticed after I moved out of this house? Mudear grew a buffer around this house. The plants and the trees and flowers set us off from this whole neighborhood. Even when she let us visit around here or go to a basement party, we were still set off. As soon as a boy walked you back home, they could see from our house, we were strange and different."

The plants and trees continued on through another lot and up to the next street of the development because Poppa had bought the lot behind them when Mudear had looked at the plans for the house and announced, "You expect me to garden on that little piece of land back there?"

Betty had told the girls how proud Poppa was to have been able to secure another loan for the land behind their new house. She had heard him on the phone talking about it. But all the girls had heard Mudear tell Poppa any number of times, "I certainly hope you don't think I give a damn about this little piece a' house out here on Pork n' Bean Row. It don't mean shit to me and my girls. I could make it anywhere with or without a house."

And the girls had believed her.

"All kinds of flowers, tropical flowers, grow in southern California," Annie Ruth said as she surveyed Mudear's garden. "Birds of paradise next to people's driveways, exotic palms in front of run-down apartment buildings. But even with that mild climate and all that water they pump out of neighboring states and use to water that dry desert land in L.A., you never see anything as naturally beautiful as this." Annie Ruth got up and walked to the side of the house to look at the last of the wildflowers growing in place of a lawn in front. Mudear hadn't even bothered to let the contractor lay sod. One night after the Lovejoy family moved into the new house, Mudear went out and strewed local and regional wildflower seed she had been collecting and exchanging with Georgia gardeners through the mail.

"God, I miss the South." Annie Ruth rubbed her hand over the velvety moss growing on the outside of a huge strawberry pot and smelled her palm. She sounded as if she might cry as she touched the tongue of a stone frog set among a bed of frilly ferns with the toe of her boot and came back to the swing and sat down.

Betty didn't even bother to ask anymore why, feeling the way she did about Los Angeles and the South, why Annie Ruth was there instead of here. She and Emily had been trying to get her back home for years. But Betty knew what it was like to try to put some space between herself and Mudear. She reached for Annie Ruth's cup, but her sister pulled it away.

"You don't want this," she said fingering the rim of the mug. "It's Poppa's Sanka."

Betty just chuckled.

Annie Ruth smiled, too.

"You don't know everything, Ms. Betty Jean Lovejoy. It's not because of the baby. It just seems that my bouts with PMS have been getting out of control lately. I read caffeine makes it worse."

"Oh, so now we've moved on to calling it 'the baby'?" Betty asked.

Annie Ruth just looked at her sister.

Betty kept talking. "Well, you won't have to worry with PMS, then. They say it gets worse as you get older, but better after you have a baby."

Annie Ruth sat tearing the ivory petals off a tiny iceberg rose-bud.

"Don't say anything to Emily about it yet, okay?" Annie Ruth's voice sounded pleading. "About me planning to really keep this baby."

"I don't have to, sugar. She's already on the scent. We all know each other too well to try to keep secrets."

mily was waiting outside when Betty and Annie Ruth pulled up in the winding gravel driveway to get her. Emily, dressed in a bright red long-sleeved knit dress cinched at the waist with a wide black and red leather belt, climbed into the backseat, leaned forward, and kissed Annie Ruth on the cheek, leaving a slash of red lipstick there.

"Emily, you *know* you in that dress. And you look pretty in red," Betty said to her sister as she reached over and pulled out a tissue form the car's console and handed it to her. "But you got a booger in your nose."

Emily took the tissue and they all chuckled. " 'Lovejoy women *keep* dirty noses,' " she recited, laughing again. "And as Mudear say, 'Just when you dressed up and think you looking cute, too.' "

Emily leaned forward again and checked her nose in the rear-view mirror. She noticed Betty running her fingers through her hair. Whenever Betty was trying to figure something out, she ran her hand through her cropped, permed hair, really just over the top of it. It was hardly long enough to get her fingers through.

Betty's hair was barely longer than a boy's with practically nothing in the back, but she kept it straightened to within an inch of its life because she liked to have it grow down the back of her neck without forming nappy little balls of hair at the nape; Mudear called them "pepper pods." When the girls were teenagers and straightened and permed each other's hair in the kitchen and family bathroom, Mudear would look up at their French twists and upswept hairdos and point to a brush—not hers because she didn't like anybody using her personal things—and say, "Daughter, take that brush and crack them pepper pods in the back of your head." Mudear made it sound as if the girls had cooties or lice. She couldn't stand "pepper pods."

One time when Betty was a teenager, she got Emily to get Poppa's razor from where he "hid" it up over the bathroom door-jamb so the girls wouldn't use it to shave their legs and up under their arms and give her a "tape"—shaving the hair from the nape or "kitchen" of her neck. The idea was to give a smooth, clean edge to her hairdo. But Mudear protested.

Lovejoy women don't get no tapes, Mudear told her daughters, it makes you look common and hard, like wearing an anklet. Only whores and sluts got tapes and wore anklets, according to Mudear. But then, Mudear had a long litany of things Lovejoy women did and did not do.

- Lovejoy women *love* pretty clothes.
- Lovejoy women are *strong as mules.*

- But Lovejoy women go to *nothing* when they get a cold.
- Lovejoy women can cook.
- Lovejoy women *keep* dirty noses.
- Lovejoy women can arrange *weeds*.
- Lovejoy women don't get no tapes.
- Lovejoy women don't wear no anklets.
- Lovejoy women don't take no tea for the fever. (She had to explain that one. "It means you don't take no shit. You so bad you won't even take a soothing tea to break your fever.")
- Lovejoy women have shoulders like men.
- Lovejoy women are terrible liars.
- Lovejoy women don't wear no cheap clothes.
- Lovejoy women don't wear no Hoyt's cologne.
- Lovejoy women don't wear no costume jewelry.

Over the years, the list had grown into a type of mythology: "The Lovejoy Women." Mudear would start and the girls would join in as if they were reciting a mantra.

Whenever Mudear caught the girls making light of "what Lovejoy women do and don't do," looking at each other out of the corners of their eyes when they didn't think Mudear was watching, she'd smirk and say, "Well, there must be something to it. 'Cause married or not, I notice all ya'll still go by 'Lovejoy.' "

As usual, the girls couldn't say anything, couldn't dispute her. It was true. After both of Emily's marriages and even while Betty had been married briefly, they still kept their maiden names. Even Betty's shops, Mudear would point out, were named Lovejoy's 1 and Lovejoy's 2.

But Mudear did that regularly with her girls, said something so true, so insightful that it would fairly take their breath away in its indisputability. Even when it cut to the quick.

Where Betty's hair was thick and coarse, Annie Ruth's was

just the opposite. Mudear called it "little t'in t'in hair," then she laughed. It was baby fine and thin. Annie Ruth had done just about everything imaginable to her hair to thicken it up: henna rinses, falls, conditioners that claimed to leave a coating on each strand of hair, teasing, setting it with beer, body-building haircuts. Betty, who always loved to play in folks' hair even as a child and did all the Lovejoy women's hair from the time she was ten or so, started experimenting with her baby sister's hair when they were girls and she had never stopped. Lately, she and Annie Ruth had settled on a fluffy brown mass of short curls—some hers, some fake—that framed her face and complemented its oval shape. With her hair styled in curls, she looked younger than her already fake age, like a moppet. But in her harried condition before her plane trip back to Mulberry, Annie Ruth had forgotten her small hairpiece and had to make do with just her own thin hair. She knew that Betty could have picked up a hairpiece for her from one of her shops, but Annie Ruth felt Betty had enough to do without worrying about her hair.

Emily's hair style changed nearly every week. She had what Mudear called fast-growing hair. "Like dead folks," she said. Emily's hair and fingernails did seem to grow overnight. The manicurist at Lovejoy's 1 told her, "Miss Lady, I've seen lots of hands in my time, but I ain't never seen nails grow as fast as yours."

Every Saturday morning when she drove the two hours down to Mulberry for her standing eight-fifteen hair and nail appointment, she had no idea what she was going to look like when she drove back by noon. She liked that. It made her feel like the mutant she was. She changed to accommodate the men she dated, to appease her coworkers, to fit into her family.

Even more than her sisters, Emily was the family chameleon, changing with what was expected of her. She tried so hard to be whatever was asked of her that she routinely lost track of what she felt was the real Emily. Betty felt this was why her sister acted so crazy sometimes, it was what people expected of her. And her older sister had to routinely tell her, "Okay, Em-Em, come on now, come on back now."

But Emily had no intention of "coming back." She liked it out there on the edge of the ravine, the chasm between sanity and insanity. Even as she signed the checks for her regular appointments with her psychiatrist, she knew that she would allow herself to be helped to normalcy only so much. She felt at home down by the river at night smoking a joint and thinking about life and Mudear and how she was going to get this man, whoever he happened to be at the time, to marry her.

What I got to "come on back" to reality for? she'd ask herself. Even the edge of insanity felt safe to her compared to the chaos and loneliness she saw in her own life. Her reality was a steady government job, a garden apartment, a hair and manicure appointment every Saturday morning, and twenty extra pounds on her ass that she had to get rid of.

Actually, what she was seeking was a little peace, a little connection, and even though everything in her life—her upbringing, her family experiences, her own marriages, her sisters' lives, her mother—told her that in the arms of a man was the last place she would find it, she couldn't stop searching. Even her sisters said that Emily was looking for a man harder than anyone they knew.

"Girl, Emily looking for a man with a flashlight," Annie Ruth would say, even in front of Emily, with a sad chuckle.

Emily didn't take any chances. She never put a hat on her bed because she knew that meant a man would never sleep there. On New Year's Day, she made sure that the first person to walk in the house was a man for good luck. She always threw kisses at every red bird she saw so she would be assured of seeing her lover that day.

During the Gulf War she had even sent dozens of letters with her picture inside addressed to "An Officer and a Gentleman" to the front hoping to find a man in what she herself called a weakened state of war. She packed up care boxes with sunglasses, Girl Scout cookies, disposable razors, soap, suede work gloves, writing paper, and extra stamps and sent them off to Saudi Arabia with her hopes packed up in there, too. Her sisters were surprised when she got back a number of responses from the front. Most with photographs of healthy-looking young soldiers, black and white, so happy to have someone back home care about them as they faced death on the sandy battlefield. But after the conflict died down and the "boys" returned home, she never heard from any of them again.

Of the three girls, Emily was the most scarred by her quest to find happiness with a man. But she also had insight about relationships that seemed to evade her sisters.

The year before at Thanksgiving when all three of them had been together in Mulberry the last time, Emily had seemed especially down.

"Em-Em, what's the matter?" Betty asked as she pulled the giblets from the twenty-pound turkey and turned off the water that was running over the thirty pounds of chitterlings in the sink.

Emily shared her news.

"James Patrick got a man? James Patrick got a *man?*" Betty was dumbfounded.

"Not only does he have a man . . . he married him."

"James Patrick got *married?*" Betty couldn't believe it.

"Not only did he get married. But the man left his wife to marry James."

"Left his *wife?*"

"Left his wife of thirteen years to marry James Patrick."

"Left his wife of *thirteen years?*"

"Left his wife to marry James in a church ceremony."

"Shit, did he wear white?"

Emily just silently handed over the Polaroid.

"Damn," Annie Ruth said. "He look good, too."

"You know," Emily said finally, taking the photograph back and dropping it in her purse, "maybe we can learn something from gay men."

"Like . . . ?" Betty wanted to know.

"Well, I haven't completely figured that out yet, but knowing James has made me see it's more than one man just wanting another man. You know, I've been working with James for five or six years and I've been watching him."

"Hell, that shows what a sad state black women have come to in this world that now we got to watch gay men to get pointers in getting men," Betty said shaking her head.

"Well, like Mudear say, 'Keep living, daughter,' " Annie Ruth reminded her.

"Anyway, I would see him at work every day and he would have *men* coming 'round all the time to see him and ask after him."

"That just goes to show you how few straight men there are out there for us to have," Betty said.

"Yeah, that, too. But it's something else."

"Like what?" they both wanted to know.

"Well, I think it's the way he lives his life that attracts men rather than how he has sex. I mean if it all had to do with how good you are at sucking dick, then none of us would have any problem. James Patrick has a real joy in his life, in the way he lives it, in knowing who he is and what he is and not just accepting it. But reveling in it. I mean, how many women do you know who live their lives like that?

"God, James Patrick can make his lunch break into an event, an intriguing interlude. He'll run to the bank at lunchtime and come back smiling. And I'll say, 'James, what you smiling about?' And he'll say, 'Oh, I just met this guy.' And I'll say, 'In the last fifteen *minutes?*' And he'll lay the whole thing out for me.

" 'Well, I was in a real hurry, you know, 'cause I only had a few minutes, so I cut through the MARTA train station at the corner to save time and I passed this guy in this real nice-looking suit, and after I passed him, I turned around to look at him and he was turned around looking at me and I said, "Don't I know you?" and he said, "Don't I know *you?*" So, he walked to the bank with me and we had a nice conversation.'

"Then, James Patrick just looked at me and smiled. Annie Ruth, Betty, he was just glowing!"

"Oh, Emily, you talking crazy. You know as well as I do that in this world we live in it's close to suicide to just strike up a conversation with some strange man on the street. In the first place, most of them don't want a pleasant exchange, they just want to say something mean and degrading to a black woman. And second, you don't know what kind of psycho you might pick up, to say nothing of what else you might pick up in the process. Hell, that's what got James Patrick and his friends dying all over the place now," Betty said.

"Well, Betty, you know gay men ain't the only ones dying from AIDS, we black women right behind 'em. But you are right about the ugliness that black men always greet black women with," Annie Ruth said.

"Now, I don't know who James fucking, other than his 'husband' now, but that's not what I'm talking about. I'm just talking about a pleasant unplanned encounter in the middle of the day. Seeing a good-looking good-smelling man and smiling at him and having him smile at you . . ."

"Come on back, Em-Em," Betty said chuckling. "Now, you know as well as I do that that ain't even the way black men and women deal with each other. I mean when's the last time you had one of those spontaneous sweet meetings in the street?"

"I know, that's just what I mean. When did we let it get that way between us, when did we let it get that way? That we so angry and hateful with each other that we can't even speak on the street anymore? What made us let it get that way between black men and women? Isn't that something we ought to be thinking about?"

"What makes you think *we* let it get that way, that our generation let it come to that? My God, look at Poppa and Mudear. We didn't invent this internecine bloodletting," Annie Ruth said.

"Yeah," Emily admitted. "But we sure as hell seem to have perfected it."

"Oh, what you complaining 'bout, Annie Ruth, you always got a bunch of men," Betty had said. "Right now, there's Delbert, the record executive, Edwin, the college professor, Rick, the technician from the TV station, Hank, the musician, Steve, the bum-slash-screenwriter . . ."

"Yeah, but you know I think most of the men I see want me 'cause they know everybody sees me on TV. I can just imagine most of them sitting in front of the television at ten telling their buddies, 'Had her.' Maybe I'm being unfair, but ain't none of them nothing I want. Don't none of them really please me. You know what I mean?"

"Yeah, I do. I been seeing Stan off and on for more than ten years. And I guess we get along okay. We used to each other. That's the best I can say. And that ain't saying nothing. But you know there ain't much to pick from here in Mulberry . . . or anywhere for that matter."

"At least, ya'll got somebody to complain about," Emily said sadly.

"I don't know," Betty said. "At the Christmas party last year, Stan was there laughing and talking and being charming, and two women behind me said, 'Look at him,' meaning Stan. 'He done had every woman in this room.' Then, the other woman said, 'Present company included?' And they both just left the room laughing.

"And it's the truth. I know that. Later on that night, I walked into the back room. Stan was on the phone. Before he saw me standing there, I heard him saying, 'Merry Christmas, baby.'

"And he even got the nerve not to go in for an AIDS test. The biggest fight we ever had was about him using a condom. Says he knows how to take care of himself, he been out there too long to make the wrong decision about a woman. Like he can look at somebody and tell if they HIV positive."

"But Betty, you and Emily know as well as I do that we all just playing a slowed-down game of Russian roulette with our bodies," Annie Ruth said. She had a resigned sound to her voice. "I mean what does safe sex mean to people who have been fucking just who they want for the last fifteen or twenty years? What's a condom gonna do for the past?"

"Maybe it's like Mudear says," offered Emily, who had carried condoms in her purse since high school. " 'When you dead you done, so let the good times roll.' "

CHAPTER 26

When the car fell silent, Betty looked in the rearview mirror at Emily.

"Emily," Betty said suddenly, noticing her sister in the backseat rhythmically bouncing her left breast in her right hand. "Do you realize you always clutch your titty when you're thinking or worried? Do you do that out in public, too?"

Emily stopped rocking and looked down at her breast in her hand. She looked up and smiled sheepishly at her sisters.

"Yeah, I guess I do. I catch myself doing it at the most embarrassing places. Standing in line at the post office, waiting for the Xerox machine to warm up . . ."

"I bet the guys in your office love to see you think!"

Emily bit her lip and shrugged. Then, she glanced down at her breasts again.

"I was talking once to some women at work," Emily said. "One of them, Regina, you remember her, came to work looking like she hadn't gotten a wink of sleep. when I asked her what was wrong, she said, 'Girl, I was up all night talking to my mama. I don't know what I'm gonna do.'

"So naturally, I said, 'I know how mamas can be. What she bothering you about?'

"Regina said, surprised like, '*Mama's* not bothering me about anything. That's why I called *her* to try to help me out of this mess.'

"I guess I looked funny at her because she said, 'Emily, you know my mother makes me as crazy as everybody's mother does. But you know how it is when you need a little comfort, who else can you turn to but your mama. You know.'

"I still didn't have anything to say to that.

"So she said, 'Come on, Emily, who do *you* go to when you need a little tit? When you need to suck on a tit for a while, when you need to cry in somebody's arms?'

" 'I called my sisters,' I told her.

"By this time, the other women standing around were looking at me funny, too.

" 'You mean, when you really need that mother comfort, that tit, you call your sisters over your mother?' one of the other women in the office said, shocked like.

"So, I told them, 'Well, I sure as hell wouldn't call Mudear, especially if I was in a weakened or stressed-out condition.' "

"You said that to those strangers?" Betty asked, surprised.

"Yeah, I wished I hadn't. Knew I shouldn't have as soon as it was out my mouth. I could just see these women just pull away, you know, just distance themselves from me after that."

"Oh, yeah, like all of them had Mother Teresa, no, Mother Hale with the little AIDS babies, for mamas. I hate that." Annie Ruth turned in her seat with her nose wrinkled in distaste, making the light sprinkling of dark freckles that all the girls had inherited from Mudear when they reached their thirties dance on her face.

"Naw, Annie Ruth, I don't think it's that," Emily said. "I don't think it's that they don't know what I was talking about. It was more like they rather not think about it because then they have to think about their own lives and mothers and even what kind of mothers they are or will be, know what I mean?

"It's like as long as we all keep talking and thinking like every black mother in the world is this great wonderful self-sacrificing matriarch . . ."

"Right, not counting the women who have children on welfare or who are drug addicts or who are children still themselves," Betty said.

"You know as well as I do that those women aren't considered 'real black mothers.' They just lazy black 'hos," Annie Ruth said. "That is, 'til they are of a certain age and become grandmothers themselves, taking in their babies' babies."

"Yeah, then they real mothers," Betty offered.

"Well," Emily said, continuing her thought, "it's like as long as we don't think about our mothers as anything but these huge black breasts oozing chocolate milk on demand, we keep all our demons in check."

"But now, you know, Mudear always bragged on the fact that she breast-fed all her children," Betty said with a sly smile. It was a fact that Mudear had tossed at them when she sensed any inchoate rebellion growing among her ranks.

"Yeah, she breast-fed us alright, but she didn't never give us no tit," Annie Ruth said.

Then, the whole car fell silent again.

"But you know there is something about what Mudear gave," Emily said softly. "You remember that time I was ready to quit my job because that cracker son-of-a-bitch supervisor was making my life miserable because I wouldn't screw him, said he was the only one in the office I wouldn't screw. He was about right, too.

"But you all know how I feel about that. As far as I'm concerned, white men have gotten all the black pussy they gon' ever get in this country.

"Well, one night I couldn't sleep I was so stressed out and was driving around town like I do and ended up on I-85 coming down here to Mulberry. It was about three or four in the morning when I pulled into the driveway. Right away, I saw Mudear doing her gardening in one of those flowered voile dresses she liked to wear as some kind of joke. I wanted to run right over to her and bury my face in the front of that voile dress and cry 'til I had no more tears to shed. But you know how Mudear hated that, for us to come crying to her. So, I just rolled up the windows and sat in the car with my head on the steering wheel and sobbed.

"When I looked up. Mudear was standing in front of the car, standing right in the beam of my headlights like some kind of ghost. Nearly scared me to death. She was looking at me like I was one of her flowers that wasn't doing too well and she was wondering whether she should cut back on water, fertilize me, or snip my head off.

"When I rolled the window down, she stepped out of the beam of my lights and walked up to the driver's side of the car and waited for me to say something.

"I told her, 'I can't go back to that office.'

"She reached out to me and for a minute, just a minute, I thought she was actually gonna wipe my tears away. But she didn't. She reached up in my hair and picked something out, a leaf or a string or something that was stuck there. She took this little piece of something out of my hair and examined it in the light from the car. Then, she threw it down on the ground and wiped her hand on the skirt of her dress.

"Then she asked me, 'Emily, you like that little piece of job you go to?'

"I didn't even have to think before I said, 'Yeah.'

"Then she said, 'You like putting on your pretty clothes every day and your makeup and perfume and going downtown and sitting behind that desk?'

"I said, 'Yeah.'

" 'You like that little work you do, shuffling those papers or whatever it is you do?'

"Again, I said, 'Yeah.'

" 'Then, daughter,' she said, 'don't you let nobody steal your joy.'

"She sucked her teeth lightly the way she do. Then, she turned and walked back into the dark of her garden.

"I only sat there for a minute more, then I put the car in reverse, backed on out the driveway, and drove on back to Atlanta. 'Don't let nobody steal your joy.' Umph, umph, umph.

"I went into work the next day and told him if he ever said shit to me again, I was filing a sexual harassment suit. And that was that. Mudear saved my life that night. I wonder if she knew that?"

"Humph, I wonder if she cared," Annie Ruth said.

"Mudear could do that sometimes," Betty said from the front

seat. "You know, give you just what you needed with all the other stuff cut away."

"What do you mean, 'the other stuff cut away'?" Emily asked.

"You know, just the basic, the real deal, the bottom line without the hand-holding, without the sympathy, without the 'umph, umph, umph' that we go to each other for. You know, without the tit. Like a piece of chicken without all the fat and skin and bone and gristle and the crust . . ."

"And the seasoning!" Annie Ruth cut in.

"Yeah, and the seasoning cut away. She just give you what you needed, you know, that little piece of wisdom without any of the flavoring to make it taste better.

"I guess that's what we all wanted so bad," Betty said. "We wanted that seasoning from Mudear."

"Maybe, she didn't have it to give to us," Emily suggested timidly.

"Stop it, Emily," Annie Ruth said. "You know as well as I do that Mudear had everything she ever wanted or needed. She just didn't want to give it up."

"I don't know, Annie Ruth, maybe that piece of chicken was it," Betty said. "Maybe that was all she had to give. It was all Em-Em needed that night, wasn't it?"

"Oh, the both of you getting too soft. So, now we gonna start remembering Mudear as this sweet saintly little woman just 'cause— 'God rest the dead'—she *dead?*"

"I didn't say nothing 'bout Mudear being no saint," Emily countered. "But when she'd talk sometimes, even when we were kids, I'd feel, I don't know."

Emily seemed as if she were groping for something.

"It was like she was giving up some message from some higher power, like she was channeling the message that helped us," she said finally.

"Okay, Em-Em, I'm 'bout with Annie Ruth on this if you start that New Age bullshit. Next thing you know you gonna be calling up your psychic adviser and saying we ought to have a seance and call up Mudear's spirit."

"And you don't think we can call up Mudear's spirit talking about her like this?" Emily asked. "She probably somewhere now trying to get Saint Peter or whoever to let her come back one time just to get our little asses straight."

"Look, if we coulda called up her spirit or anything having to do with her, don't you think we would have done that long ago as much as we talk about her whenever we get together?" Annie Ruth asked.

"Yeah, but she was in control then, now I don't think she is," Betty said.

"Really?" Emily asked sincerely. "I can't imagine any situation, even death, when Mudear ain't in charge. It's just her nature, to be in charge."

CHAPTER 27

L ord, these girls still talking 'bout what they think
they didn't get, from the tit on up.

Such complainers!

That's why they keep those ugly looks on their
faces all the time. Because they have such bad attitudes. Those
girls can't seem to see the lighter side of things.

You would think we didn't never have no good times together
in that house, and the old one, too, to let them girls tell it. Hell,
if it wasn't for me, they wouldn't 'a had nothing in neither one of
those houses. Their father sho' wasn't about to make things nice
for 'em.

And what about all those good meals I made sure they cooked?
Sitting around the table eating, that was fun.

And we laughed and talked a lot.

"Tell me something, daughters," I'd ask them after I'd call them up to my room. "Now, this here woman on television is letting this man with a microphone and camera crew interview her with those pink rollers in her hair. Now, she's out at the shopping center. So she had to get in her car and come out in public like that knowing people were going to see her. She didn't even have the decency to put on one of those thin chiffony scarfs. Now she's gonna let this man take her picture and put it on television for all the world to see."

"Um-huh," the girls would say.

"Now, tell me. I have one question. Where is this woman going tonight that is so important that she has to keep her hair up in curlers, not just in the mall, but on television?"

Then, we'd try to figure out where this woman was going tonight.

Annie Ruth, the baby, was real good at it.

Those are some of the times I felt closest to my girls. Us all sitting around talking 'bout people.

Guess they don't remember none of that.

God, those girls got ugly ways!

CHAPTER 28

When they arrived at Parkinson Funeral Home at the corner of Poplar and Pringle and caught a first glimpse of the row of big shiny ebony hearses with faded maroon satin curtains at the side and back windows, all conversation ceased in the car. Emily wanted to shout from the backseat, "I don't want to see my mother riding in one of those dead wagons!" But she kept her counsel and closed her eyes a moment to collect herself.

She had a distinct but distant memory of Mudear sitting on a small round stool at the side of Poppa's chair in the old house in East Mulberry. Mudear had seemed to Emily, who was small herself, so tiny and defenseless sitting there with her knees nearly up to her breasts. Her father sat in his overstuffed chair with his slim dark hand resting indolently in a soup bowl of soapy water on a tin tray perched on Mudear's knees. Next to the bowl of water was a small travel manicure set.

On Mudear's face, a look that appeared to Emily to smell like burning brimstone, sulfur, the odor she associated for life with burning, white-hot hatred.

That face, Emily thought, lies lifeless inside that building. Lord, Lord, Lord.

Betty, who had been there the day before and had already seen Mudear's body, knew what to expect. But seeing the funeral home with her sisters, sensing their reactions to the accoutrements of death made her feel a bit woozy, too. She didn't realize it, but her body went kind of limp behind the steering wheel and she let her foot rise from the accelerator. The car coasted to a stop a few feet away from the funeral home door.

Betty put the car in park automatically and put the hand brake on without thinking. As they sat in silence in Betty's big steel and black Town Car, a side door to the mortuary flew open and two men in black suits and ties and plain white shirts rushed out, propping the door open and signaling in the direction of the line of parked hearses. One of the hearses started up and pulled up to the mortuary door as if by magic. Just as the funeral car pulled up to the door, the two men standing there whipped inside and returned immediately wheeling out an ornate black casket on a collapsible gurney. Then, the rear door of the hearse seemed to suddenly pop open.

The three Lovejoy women, still sitting in Betty's car, had all jumped when the hearse door swung open. It was the first time since they had rolled to a stop that Betty was able to pull her gaze away from the mortuary and get herself a smoke. She rolled down

her window and reached in the purse next to her for her cigarettes. As Betty lit up, Emily cleared her throat and rolled down
her window, too.

Then, they went back to staring at the black hearse pulled up
to the side of the building with its rear door swung wide open
ready for that final trip as if they expected something to come
flying out.

"I never once thought that we would all be here doing this
for Mudear," Emily said from the backseat. "Not once."

" 'Keep living, daughter,' " Betty said, because nobody else would
say it. But after she did, Emily intoned, "Humph, humph, humph."

Annie Ruth hadn't said anything. Her sisters hadn't noticed,
but ever since they pulled up, Annie Ruth had been edging back
into her seat, seemingly trying to wedge herself into the crack
between the door and the seat.

Annie Ruth wanted to tell her sisters that she was frightened
of the gang of cats that she saw hanging around the door and the
wide brick gate with the initials P. F. H. etched on the front of
the portal. She just couldn't get out of the car and make the few
paces up the front stoop and into the cool quiet airless room
where Mudear lay. Not through that barrage of cats.

But the cats weren't the entire problem. Even if she had not
seen them prowling around the entrance to the building, Annie
Ruth couldn't face Mudear. She couldn't do it. Annie Ruth knew
she couldn't go inside and see the woman that she feared and
hated and admired and cursed, the one who had brought her into
the world, the one who didn't throw herself down a flight of steps
early in her pregnancy, the one who had given her life, lifeless.

She could not imagine how Betty was going to be able to bear
to stand there and do Mudear's hair and makeup. Everybody knew

that Betty was the strongest one in the family, but this, Annie Ruth felt, was asking too much. It would have been for her. But then, neither Annie Ruth nor Emily could have stood to remain in Mulberry all these years in such close proximity and heavy service to Mudear. But it was never even discussed that Betty would leave Mulberry to live somewhere else.

When Betty finally glanced over at Annie Ruth, she looked as if she had seen a ghost. And at the sight of her sister's face, Betty nearly paled, too.

"Good God, Annie Ruth, what's wrong?"

But Annie Ruth couldn't find her voice. It seemed frozen in her throat. So, she just kept shaking her head.

Emily jumped out of the backseat and ran to Betty's side. "What in the world is the matter?"

"I think this is too much for her, Emily. She's not up to seeing Mudear now."

At first, Betty suggested that she and Emily go in to see to Mudear quickly while leaving Annie Ruth in the car. But then, they both looked down at Annie Ruth in the car and they hadn't the heart to leave their wild-eyed sister out there alone.

Betty stood at the side of her car for a while with her hand still on the door handle. She was so torn.

She could just picture Mudear inside the mortuary, lying there with no color in her face and her hair standing up all over her head from sweating in the hospital. She knew she could do something for her, make her look like her own self with some makeup and the hot curlers. It was her duty.

But she kept glancing down at Annie Ruth in the car, curled up on the seat with her face buried in the upholstery as if she were afraid to look out the window at her sisters.

"Y'all hold on a minute," Betty said and dashed into the building and was thankful to see one of the Parkinsons who worked with the bodies standing at the desk. Even though he didn't usually work with live customers, he came toward Betty with a solicitous mortician's face and his arms extended. Before Betty could lock her elbow with her arm stretched out in front of her to block the man's assault, he was on her, softly feeling her up through her flowing silky dress and murmuring cooing mournful sounds in her ear. Betty just sighed, counted slowly to three, giving the mortician time enough to caress her shoulder and back, then she broke his embrace and cut in on his running line.

"Hi, Billy, thank you so much, I do, my whole family really appreciates your condolences and your assistance. Oh, they're fine, they're fine. You'll see them later on. Yeah, pretty as ever. You know, Billy, there is something you can do for me. My father wants to move the service up a couple of days. To tomorrow. Anytime. Thank you. Now, one more thing and I'll be out your way. Oh, what a sweet thing to say. Well, I have to go run a quick errand and I wanted to come back by here in a half an hour or so and do Mudear's hair and makeup. Yes, I know it's a closed casket service, but I still want to do this. Could you have her ready? Thank you, Billy. I knew you'd understand. You always were my favorite Parkinson. What? Oh, if you could have her in her casket so I can see how her hair is gonna look against the satin and everything, that would be wonderful. Uh-huh. The light oak. Yes, it is a beautiful thing. Very simple. Yes, just like my Mudear, beautiful and simple."

When Betty ran out of the building to her car, Emily was already behind the wheel with the motor running. Betty jumped in back and Emily pulled off without saying a word.

Betty felt she just knew what was going to happen on the ride home. Emily ought to have enough sense to see that Annie Ruth is in bad shape, Betty thought as Emily easily negotiated the late-morning traffic. But sure as she's born, no sooner will we turn the corner before Emily lights into her with some more of that talk about the baby.

But Betty was wrong. Emily didn't say a word to Annie Ruth all the way back to Betty's house. As she drove, Emily kept her eye on Annie Ruth and two or three times reached over to pat her arm, but she didn't say a thing about a baby or anything else.

Betty looked over the seat a few times to see how Annie Ruth was breathing, but she kept quiet, too. Once, Emily had to pull over to the curb to let Annie Ruth lean out her open door and retch into the sewers of Mulberry before driving off again.

As they pulled into the long gravel driveway of Betty's house, Emily thought the car felt like it belonged in a funeral procession.

CHAPTER 29

It felt funny to Poppa to be off from work more than two days in a row. So, he rose at 6:00 A.M. as always and went down the hall quietly to the family bathroom to shower and shave as he did every weekday for work.

Moving quickly around the family bathroom, he cleaned up after himself and left. He wanted to be finished and back in his room by the time Annie Ruth awoke. Poppa couldn't bear the thought of facing his youngest daughter after he had allowed himself to weaken and even cry in front of his child. A bit of the night before was still fuzzy in his mind as if he had been drinking. But he remembered enough to know he was ashamed and ought to be.

Losing control of himself, knocking over his coffee cup, having to be put to bed. It woulda been better if I'da just told her the truth, he thought.

Back in his room, dressed and ready for the day, he sat on the side of his bed. He didn't think about making the bed. Mudear liked her bed rumpled and loose so she could get back into it during the day if she liked. In a while, he heard Annie Ruth get up and start moving around the house, first in the bathroom then up and down the hall. She stopped at his door on her way toward the stairs and stood there listening awhile. Poppa didn't move a muscle. She knocked softly on the door. Poppa didn't respond. And after a while she went on downstairs.

Down there, he could hear her moving around in the kitchen and rec room. When he heard the kitchen door close, he got up and went to the back window and watched Annie Ruth walk out to Mudear's garden. She gonna ruin those high-heeled boots, Poppa thought. He watched her stroll up and down the paths of cedar chips edged in white gravel looking over the garden and stopping every now and then to stoop and examine some plant or pot more closely.

When she got to one of the garden's freestanding cedar swings, she sat down in her tight black outfit and high-heeled boots and began swinging with her cup of coffee in her hand.

After a while, he heard Betty's car pull up in the driveway. He could tell it was Betty just by the sound of her car. How many times a week does she come out here to see 'bout us? he wondered.

He stepped back from the window when he saw the girls look up to the house and point at his room. After a while, he heard them come in the house for Annie Ruth's things and then leave together.

When he heard them pull off, he went downstairs. There was a yellow Post-It on the hall mirror from Betty: "We've gone to Parkinson's. Get something to eat."

He didn't want anything to eat, but he made himself put one of the carrot raisin muffins Betty had left in the bread keeper for him into the microwave oven. He ate it slowly with a cup of Sanka as he stood at the back window overlooking Mudear's garden in back.

He saw a number of things he knew Mudear would probably want him to do. The new camellia bushes she had ordered had arrived a few days before and he needed to dig some holes and get them planted. Mudear had told him where she planned to put them. It was time to do some pruning. It was a job Mudear enjoyed, but she had almost let it get away from her so late in the season.

He looked at the big steel structure in the middle of the garden covered with vines and flowers and remembered the struggle it had been to get it moved and positioned just right. How his muscles had ached in his back and his legs.

He hoped if he worked hard enough for a few hours now, he could tire himself out enough to be able to go downtown to the funeral home and face Mudear with her daughters. He wondered if Annie Ruth had already told the others about the spectacle he had put on the night before. He rinsed his empty coffee cup out and put it in the sink and headed outside to get the pruning shears.

CHAPTER 30

Even after Betty and Emily had brought Annie Ruth in the house, helped her to lie down in the living room on a comfortable overstuffed sofa, and fixed her a cup of herbal tea, she and Emily were still gravely concerned about their baby sister. For about an hour she had been deathly silent. Not even responding to her sisters' questions and suggestions. She lay tight and stiff on the sofa under a soft wool blanket Emily had spread over her with her clothes and boots still on. Emily took off her own shoes and settled into a chair across from the sofa to watch her.

She still didn't respond to Emily, but Emily noticed after a while that she seemed to relax a bit and breathe evenly. Betty came in a few times from the library where she was trying to conduct some business over the phone—moving appointments around, conferring with her managers, canceling a trip to Aruba she had planned to take Cinque on after Thanksgiving, trying to reach Poppa—to check on Annie Ruth. But Emily, who sat reading a magazine and playing with her hair, would just look up, biting her bottom lip, and shake her head slowly.

Annie Ruth lay quietly for about an hour more. Then, she started muttering a bit to herself. As Emily caught snatches of words and phrases, "There he is . . ." "It's a big one . . ." "No, a baby . . ." "Don't let 'em get me . . ." "Kill that cat . . ." she realized Annie Ruth was talking in her sleep.

Finally, Emily walked over and gently shook her shoulder. "Annie Ruth? Annie Ruth?"

Annie Ruth opened her eyes, then sat up laughing. Emily was relieved to see it.

"What you dreaming about that's so funny?" Emily asked.

"Annie Ruth. Betty. Emily," she said and started laughing again.

This time, Annie Ruth's laughter did not make her feel better, it made her uncomfortable. It was as if she, Emily, were the butt of the joke.

"What you laughing at, Annie Ruth?" she persisted, but she was uneasy.

"Hell, do you know anybody else our age with names like Betty Jean and Emily Mae and, the best one of all, *Annie Ruth?*"

Emily didn't know what Annie Ruth was talking about. She thought she might still be half asleep.

"No, I'll answer that for you, no, you don't," Annie Ruth continued. "You know why? 'Cause other mothers put some time and thought and energy and, yes, let's say it, love into the naming of their children."

Betty, hearing Annie Ruth's voice, came hurriedly into the living room smoking and smiling expectantly when she saw Annie Ruth sitting up. But as soon as she got in the room and saw her face and Emily's, she knew the situation hadn't gotten any better. Annie Ruth just kept on talking.

"Hell, I would have preferred to be named Laquita or Chine-akqua or Shaquithra or Urethra or any of those names that people make fun of teenaged mothers for laying on their children. At least those mothers . . . I can hear some of those young girls now talking about their babies and what they plan to name 'em. Maybe it's the name of their favorite actress on the soap operas or it's a name they made up and had to spell the best way they could. Or something they read somewhere. We did a story once at my TV station in Washington on names and a woman named her baby Female and pronounced it *Fe-maul-i*. She did. But she was so proud telling me how she saw it on a document and it reminded her right away of the kind of name she wished she had. And she just knew then that that was the kind of name she wanted to give to her little girl."

Betty came all the way in the room and leaned against the arm of the sofa Annie Ruth was sitting on. She could hear the pitch in her sister's voice going higher and higher. And she was getting more and more worried. She felt she should stay close by.

"I asked Mudear one time why she named me Annie Ruth. She thought awhile and you know what she said? She said, 'I can't recall right now, daughter.' Good God, Betty, Emily, she didn't even remember why she named us what she did. And I finally figured out that the only reason she called us 'daughter' so much is that half the time she couldn't even remember what our real names were."

Emily was picking up Annie Ruth's teacup full of cold sweet tea from the dear little side table near the sofa, but she put it down and looked crestfallen at Annie Ruth's last remarks.

"I always kinda liked it when she called me 'daughter,' " Emily said.

Annie Ruth just shook her head at her sister. "Did you now, Emily?"

Betty looked over at Annie Ruth in surprise at the depth of her sarcasm toward Emily. Annie Ruth continued looking at Emily.

"Oh, you saw it as an endearment, huh, Emily?" Annie Ruth asked.

Emily just shrugged.

"Tell me, Em-Em, how many times did Mudear tell you she loved you?" Annie Ruth asked.

Emily chuckled nervously and walked over to the wide mantel over the huge stone fireplace on the north wall of the room.

"Yeah, I know," Annie Ruth said as she struggled to unwrap herself from the soft blanket Emily had placed over her. "If she ever said it to you at all, she probably said, 'I love you, daughter, but I hate your ways. You got ugly ways sometimes.'

"Am I right? That's what she said. That was her expression of motherly love. I love you, but I hate the way you are," Annie Ruth said.

"Annie Ruth, you know that was how she was." Emily was examining the crystal figures and onyx stones on the mantelpiece.

"Well, I never believed her. Even when I was a little girl, I didn't believe her, I didn't believe she loved us. I think she really hated us."

Emily spun around at the fireplace. "Speak for yourself! Maybe she hated you. But she didn't hate me!"

"Oh, grow the fuck up, Emily," Annie Ruth shouted. "If she hated me, she hated you. She hated you, she hated me, she hated Betty, she hated Poppa, she hated the house she lived in, she hated Mulberry. She hated all of us. Don't you really know that? God, I am so sick of you playing that innocent shit. You've played it to death and I'm sick of it."

Betty stood up. She had decided it was time to break this up. Even though they were all safely inside her big warm well-lit house sitting on beautiful old well-made furniture, sipping tea from bone china cups, Betty could feel the whole scene with all the Lovejoy women inside whirling out of control. But Annie Ruth brushed past her and rushed on.

"Sister girls, I don't know about you, but I am sick and tired of a lot of stuff. I'm so tired of trying to pretend that she was something she wasn't. I'm so sick of coming home for holidays and sitting around the dinner table like nothing's wrong. And sending gifts home to Mudear like she was the mother goddess Giya as offerings. Like   got something to make up for. Then, sneaking around like sc ,ed children talking 'bout her in hushed tones, running our phone bills up going over and over something she did. And then, trying to pretend this is all perfectly normal."

"Annie Ruth." Betty tried to interrupt. But her sister just turned on her with her eyes blazing.

"Betty, you know you just as tired of this crazy shit as I am!" she shouted.

Betty took a last draw on her cigarette and stubbed it out in a pretty flowered ashtray.

"I was just gonna remind you, Annie Ruth, that Mudear is dead. And all that is behind us."

"*Behind* us? Surely, you don't think this all just ends because

Mudear's dead, do you? Hell, I got up last night to throw up and I smelled her, *felt* her in the bathroom. Shit, I feel her hanging around me all the time all the way out in that godforsaken L.A.

"I'm so sick of pretending that we had something we didn't that I could just about die myself. But that's just the thing now, 'cause I'm gonna be a mama now and I want to turn loose some of this crazy shit. *She's behind us now?* God, girl, ya'll expect me to go out and have an abortion, get rid of my child because of the kind of mother we had. Does that sound like all this, all of Mudear's shit, is *behind us?* No! I don't want to *not* be a mother because I'm afraid Mudear's gonna jump out of me and ruin my child like she ruined us. I'm tired of her ruining my life. I won't have it anymore. And I won't have her ruining it from the grave."

"See, Betty, I told you!" Emily stormed toward her big sister. "Annie Ruth wants to have this baby, wants to have Mudear's grandchild. I can only *imagine* how screwed up that poor child will be. Look at us!

"Betty, say something! Say you agree with me. Say you haven't lost your mind or forgotten how it is to be Mudear's child or how it feel to be the crazy woman's child. Say something that make some sense. If *you* don't make sense, then what we gon' do?"

Betty just took Emily's arm and sat her down in the nearest chair.

Annie Ruth continued as if no one else had said anything.

"I could think about Mudear sometimes and just think I want to die. I don't want to die anymore and finally, I don't think I am gonna die now. But Lord knows I do want a change.

"Not by delving into it and discussing it and reliving it and being rehurt by it, but forgiving it and turning it loose and moving the hell on with it."

Now, Annie Ruth was pacing back and forth over a deep rich maroon-design rug worn soft and thin with footsteps, dragging the baby-blue blanket behind her.

"It's not like you and me and Emily don't know all the shit that's fucking up our lives. Sure, we know. Good God, Emily, how many thousands of dollars have you spent with your Dr. Axelton to find that out? I certainly know that none of us knows how to appreciate anything, knows how to find or even see joy in life 'cause we didn't never see that when we were growing up.

" 'I don't take a vanilla wafer for granted.' That's what she used to say. But it was a lie. She took everything for granted. And didn't give nothing in return. All in the name of her freedom.

"We were never taught to appreciate anything, whether it was a roasted marshmallow on a stick or a ten-course meal. Shit, I've been sunning myself on the deck of a chartered sailboat in the Caribbean with folks running back and forth trying to please me. And in the middle of it I see my reflection in the brass work and my face is all screwed up and you'd think I was out in the hot sun digging ditches or down at the paper plant working like a man. And I have to remind myself, 'Enjoy this, Annie Ruth, enjoy this, girl, this is nice. Take that ugly look off your face. This is great.' But no, I'm sitting there chewing on some evil shit Mudear did to me or to you or to Emily back when, or something she said the last time I called. I'm sick of it."

Annie Ruth kept talking and pacing in her high-heeled black boots. As she did, she also kept getting the blue blanket she trailed behind her caught between her legs and tripping over it. She jerked it free from her legs and threw one corner over her shoulder like a toga.

"Look at you, Betty. You took care of us, all of us, all your life. You didn't get to go to college like Emily and me even though you were probably the smartest one of us. You stayed around here doing right by Poppa and Mudear. Doing better than right by them. And look what you accomplished in the process. You got two thriving beauty shops, everybody knows they the best, classiest places in Mulberry. You even been quoted in *Essence* magazine on hair care.

"Do you ever sit back and appreciate what you've done? Sit back and be proud of yourself, and rightfully so? No!

"And I won't even go into Mudear and Poppa," Annie Ruth said, recalling her nighttime kitchen chat with her father. "Mudear got that old man out at the house in Sherwood Forest weeping into his coffee and banging his head on the kitchen table, for God's sake. How the hell were we ever supposed to see how love worked, men and women are supposed to act and love and get along? We sure as hell didn't get any instruction about a loving relationship other than 'A man don't give a damn about you.' We taught our own selves about loving each other 'cause that's all we had.

"Hell, I used to read books just to find out how normal people, families live. That's why Mudear hated to see us reading."

Betty and Emily exchanged glances.

"Oh, no, Miss Things, you're not gonna do that, try to shame me into not saying what we all know is true. You both can give each other all the knowing looks you want. It doesn't change the truth of what I'm saying and you know it.

"Sure, we know all about Mudear, we know all about ourselves, but when we gon' start making a change? Seeing some joy, having some appreciation?

"I'm sick of being a product of Mudear, sick of it.

" 'Don't let nobody steal your joy,' indeed! What you think *her* purpose in life was?

"You know what, I want to get big as a house and have this

baby and love her and sit and rock her and brag on her and bore people to death talking about her and making them look at pictures. Before she's even born, I want to think about her and worry about her and name her, name her Betty Jean or Emily or even Esther, no, not Esther. But name her something that has some meaning for me and will for her. So when I look into her face I think of something I love, when I call her name I remember tenderness. I don't care if I call her 'Turnip Green,' at least when I say it, I'll remember how good and sweet turnips are when Betty cooks 'em down with a little fatback and a long red hot pepper."

Annie Ruth was out of breath and leaning against the wide doorjamb leading to the hall for support, but she wasn't finished.

"It's the truth. I hear myself thinking while I'm talking sometimes, and I realize I'm still editing myself according to what I think Mudear might think. Sometimes, I don't edit, I translate. And when I open my mouth, Mudear's voice comes out. And I have to cover real quick for something real mean and evil I said. Are we supposed to keep on tiptoeing around Mudear and her mess and the trail of pain she's left everywhere she's been even after she's *dead*? I don't believe so because then that means we ain't never gon' be free of her. And I can't live like that, I refuse to live like that. I put three thousand miles between her and me, went to live in that godforsaken Los Angeles and I still drag her around like a dead stanking corpse tied to my leg, like some cat rubbing up against my leg.

"I'm turning her a-loose. And I'm telling her so. As a matter of fact, I'm going right back down there now and tell that bitch so right to her face."

"Annie Ruth!" Betty jumped up from the sofa, shocked.

"Don't 'Annie Ruth' me. I know I'm the one who had the

nervous breakdown, I'm the one who went out. I'm the one who can't make a cross-country flight without seeing cats on the plane— Shit!"

"You seeing cats, Annie Ruth?" Emily asked, more interested than shocked.

"Maybe so," Annie Ruth shot back. "But that don't change nothing. I don't know about you two, but I know I got to tell Mudear this stuff. All the things we've always been too afraid to say to her face. Like Mudear some kind of powerful goddess who can strike us mute or dead for some minor transgression.

"Well, she's not. She's just a woman with no heart and no feeling who cared more about herself, her creature comforts, sleeping late, gardening at night, than she did her own children, her own family.

"But I'm wasting my breath telling you all this. You know it. I'm going down to Parkinson Funeral Home and tell it to the person who should be hearing it. I'm gonna do what *she* always told us to do to men to put them in their place. I'm gonna pull the sheets off that woman." Annie Ruth headed for the back door.

"For God's sake, Annie Ruth, don't be going out of this house shaming us in the street," Betty said, catching her sister by the arm in the kitchen and pulling her back into the hall.

Annie Ruth snatched her arm away.

"Betty, you the smartest one of us. Don't you get it? We ain't never done nothing to shame us in this town. Hell, we ought to be proud we still alive and just *slightly* crazy.

"And this town ain't done a thing to us. It couldn't touch us. Don't you know who made us feel shamed?"

The question, asked right out, stopped her sisters where they stood, about to pounce on her as if they wore white jackets and had a straitjacket ready to take her to the crazy house in Milledge-ville. Their pause gave Annie Ruth enough time to snatch up Emily's car keys slung over her purse in the hall, dash through the kitchen, and bolt out the door to her sister's red Datsun in the driveway. She jumped in, locked the car door, and screeched out into the street before her sisters were down the steps. Bumping a yellow light at the corner, she raced through the intersection, shifting the gears like a race-car driver, speeding toward the funeral home.

Even though she didn't see them in her rearview mirror, Annie Ruth knew her sisters would be following close behind.

CHAPTER 31

Would you look at that child driving like a bat out of hell.

Surely, she don't plan to actually come down here and get in my dead face with all that crazy talk about wanting to let me go.

I wonder if they been smoking that marijuana again.

CHAPTER 32

When Annie Ruth burst into the wide carved wooden front door of Parkinson Funeral Home, she looked like a well-dressed wild woman. On the crazy drive over, she had let her window down to yell at some woman to get herself and her three kids in a minivan out of her way, she was coming through. Now, her thin windblown red curls stood up all over her head. But her close-fitting cat suit, more snug than usual, still looked stunning on her and the African beaded jewelry she wore with it stood up to her drama. One of the funeral director's assistants, a sturdy round-shaped young man with a bounce to his step and a large white apron on, watched her with admiration from a small window in the back of the establishment. The drive from Betty's house and her fury had given new, unexpected color to her face. The man thought she looked like an avenging angel would look if angels were to wear skintight black jumpsuits.

And that's how she felt, like an avenging angel striding through the halls of the funeral home in her high-heeled black boots looking for the deceased.

She hadn't even noticed if the gang of cats that had been hanging around the entrance to the funeral home earlier was still there when she entered. She couldn't even tell anybody where she had parked Emily's car or if she had turned the engine off.

And she didn't even think about trying to find one of the Parkinson family to direct her to Mudear's body. She just went tearing from memorial room to memorial room of the elegant old building, her heels clicking on the parquet floor. Yanking open single and double doors, Annie Ruth went in search of Mudear. In the first two chapels, she came upon funeral services in progress. People were crying and moaning. And to both crowded rooms, Annie Ruth said the same thing. "Mudear? Mudear? Excuse me, I'm looking for my mother."

Then, she backed out of the rooms and slammed the doors shut, leaving two sets of mourners puzzled and irritated by the disruption. Annie Ruth moved across the hall to the next door. The room was empty.

By the time she reached the fourth door, she was nearly running, muttering, "I'm looking for Mudear." She pulled the door open and ran straight into the chest of a man coming out of the last chapel. The chest of his dark suit smelled deeply of carnations.

"Why, Annie Ruth!" Billy Parkinson took her into his arms so adeptly that she was enveloped in his flowery embrace before she realized it. "I wasn't expecting to see you this afternoon. But you know it's always a pleasure. Except under these circumstances." He still had not let her go.

She was having trouble breathing and she could tell she was on the verge of an anxiety attack. All the time Billy talked, Annie Ruth squirmed and struggled to free herself from his grasp. But he just pulled her closer to him.

"I saw your pretty sister Betty this morning, and she told me what she needed, so your mother is all set up in the Light and Shadow Memorial Chapel right here. I thought this might be a little more comfortable for you girls than being in the back with all the . . . ah, others."

Annie Ruth still struggled like a kitten in a wet croaker sack to get away from the mortician, but he seemed to anticipate her moves and outmaneuver her.

"I have your mother in her casket and this room isn't scheduled to be used for a few hours, until eight tonight. So, you and your sisters— By the way, where is that fine Emily? Will she be here today? She's put on a few pounds lately, huh? but she *still* look good. —you and your sisters can take care of your mother undisturbed. Okay?"

Annie Ruth was about ready to scream. Instead, she just reached up with the one hand she was able to wiggle free and clawed at the man holding her in his clutches. Three of her bright crimson fingernails caught him at his throat and drew blood.

He let out a little yelp of surprise and let go of Annie Ruth to clasp his hand to his throat.

Annie Ruth stepped back and leaned against the door to get her breath. She looked up at the mortician who was standing there touching his throat and examining his hand. Three red lines appeared on Billy's pale neck and at the end of one of them a drop of blood began making its way down to his stiff white shirt collar.

"Whew, you clipped me there. Don't worry, don't worry. It's okay. A death in the family is a very stressful time. Don't upset yourself." Billy tried to sound like his usual confident self, but the whole time he talked he continued backing off from Annie Ruth, putting as much distance between them as quickly and politely as he could.

"When your pretty sisters show up, I'll tell them where you are," he added as he started toward her for a last squeeze. Then, he thought better of it, turned, and quickly headed toward the back of the building.

Annie Ruth made sure he disappeared down the hall and then slipped inside the room and closed the door quickly behind her. She was still having trouble catching her breath and her heart was vibrating in her chest. She could almost hear it in the silence of the room. This place must be soundproofed, she thought. She couldn't even hear the organ music or the wailing from the two services in progress across the hall.

She closed her eyes a few moments as she leaned against the door. When she opened them, her gaze went directly to the front of the chapel and she let out a long, deep breath.

Under a single soft light shining from the ceiling, Mudear lay on champagne-colored satin in her white oak casket, illuminated like a Madonna. A tall candleholder stood at each end of the coffin with a fake lit candle atop.

It had been a few months since Annie Ruth had seen her mother, but seeing her in a coffin, still, motionless, but not asleep, made her feel five years old again.

Annie Ruth slowly walked to the front of the chapel. Heavy velvet maroon drapes with silk tassels sewn along the top border were hung across the front wall of the room. There was a low platform stretching in front of the drapes and a narrow lectern off to the side with a purple nondenominational streamer draped over the front.

Mudear's white oak casket rested on a collapsible gurney on the low platform. The gurney was like the one they had seen outside at the side of the mortuary. Billy had adjusted the legs of the wheeled stand so Mudear's body came up nearly to Annie Ruth's breasts. Annie Ruth moved in closer.

Mudear's beautiful brown skin looked tight and hard as if it were frozen and glazed with ice. And when Annie Ruth tentatively touched her shoulder through her navy blue dress, she wished she hadn't. It, too, felt hard and unhuman. Mudear's hair did need some hot curls put in it, but brushed back from her face the way she wore it, it looked natural and right. Billy must have put a pillow or block behind her head for Betty to do her hair because the crown of her head was tipped forward a bit with her chin on her chest. The small gold hoops in her ears seemed to hang back against the pillow.

The simple string of pearls Betty had put around her neck still seemed to glow next to Mudear's dead ashen skin.

As Annie Ruth looked down at her dead mother, she realized that she was still furious. Annie Ruth thought that the rage would have drained from her the moment she saw Mudear's body. But it hadn't. She was about to lean down closer to Mudear's face and speak vile mean words when she heard the doors to the chapel crash open. She turned to see her sisters come in.

Betty and Emily burst in the chapel door like henchmen. But they stopped to turn and close the door behind them so no one could see and hear what was going on.

"Still sneaking around closing doors and making excuses, trying to protect her from this town, huh, sister girlfriends?" Annie Ruth asked as she leaned back on the edge of the coffin with her elbows. The whole thing wobbled a bit.

"Annie Ruth! I can't believe you," Betty said in a harsh whisper from the door. "Even if you are pregnant and upset. This is too disrespectful even for you. Too disrespectful of Mudear, disrespectful of the dead." She came racing up to the front of the chapel.

"*Disrespectful?* Oh, I'm supposed to be showing some *respect?* Did you hear that, Mudear?" she said, turning around to face the woman in the coffin. "Betty here thinks I should be more respectful. Well, this is as respectful as it gets.

"I told you both I was coming down here to tell this woman how I feel and that's what I'm gonna do."

Betty grabbed Annie Ruth's arm and motioned for Emily to take the other one. Emily hurried down the maroon runner of the middle aisle with her purse flying behind her. "This is too much, Annie Ruth. You've gone too far. We're not gonna allow you to go on with this. Tomorrow, you'll regret it. Come on, we're taking you home!"

"I'm not going anywhere 'til I've done what I came to do," Annie Ruth said and tried to snatch her arm away, but she accidentally hit Betty in the jaw with the back of her hand. Seeing her sister wince, Annie Ruth stopped and reached out to comfort her. When she did, Emily saw her chance and grabbed Annie Ruth around the waist. Emily tried to grunt quietly. Annie Ruth, feeling tricked, spun around on her high heels and, peeling Emily's arm away from her waist, she pushed her away, causing her to bump into Mudear's casket. The coffin rocked a bit on the gurney with its accordionlike legs, then steadied itself. The movement made Mudear's head seem to shake "no" two or three times.

Emily found her footing, too, and, straightening her red knit dress and throwing her purse over her shoulder, she came at Annie Ruth again. Betty was still rubbing her face, but she had recovered from the blow enough to act. She grabbed one of Annie Ruth's elbows while Emily clasped the other in both her hands.

"Annie Ruth, settle down!" Betty hissed at her sister as they turned her away from the coffin and in the direction of the door.

"I will not be told to go somewhere and sit down," Annie Ruth said in a loud voice. "That's all we've ever been told in one way or another. And I won't be dictated to like that, shuffled aside, brushed aside like so much garbage." And grateful for developed biceps, she yanked her arms away from her sisters. Then, she spun around to face Mudear again.

"I've had a lifetime of that from you, Mudear," she began to shout in her mother's face.

But in spinning around, she somehow lifted one leg and got the sharp heel of her boot tangled up with the long gold and black leather strap of the purse Emily had hanging from her arm and began to fall. Reaching out to break her fall, Annie Ruth let out a little cry and grasped for Betty's broad shoulders beside her. But she caught Betty off guard and brought her sister crashing down to the parquet floor with her. Emily, still hanging on to her purse, lost her balance, too, and was pulled down with her sisters, her hair swinging around her.

They fell near the first row of chairs in the Light and Shadow Memorial Chapel right in front of Mudear's casket, holding on to each other and letting out little cries of surprise and pain as they hit the floor and each other. The soft folds of Betty's royal blue skirt ballooned gracefully up around her chest. As Betty and Emily tried to disengage and right themselves, Annie Ruth just tried to escape. She inched along the wooden floor, dragging her sisters with her because they refused to turn her loose.

As they struggled on the floor in a tangle of high-heeled shoes and purses and silk skirts and lacy garter belts and arms and legs, Betty and Emily attempted to keep their voices down so no one else in the funeral home would hear them. But Annie Ruth was screaming at the top of her lungs and kicking her feet back and forth on the shiny floor. "Let go of me! Let me up," she yelled at her sisters. "I haven't finished telling this woman what I came down here to say."

As she flailed around, trying to elude the grasp of her sisters who still held on to her, she rolled closer and closer to the foot of the gurney that held her mother's coffin aloft. But just as she was finally making some progress, struggling to rise to her knees, her high heel got caught in the accordion spokes of the gurney and, twisting in the space, caused one end of the table slowly to collapse.

The girls all heard the small creaking noise, even above Annie Ruth's shouting, and all three of them turned and sat back on the floor to watch as the gurney collapsed. The end of the oak wood coffin holding Mudear's head tilted toward the floor, then slowly slid off the surface of the gurney. The shiny wooden box gained some momentum when it fell farther off the low platform and sailed across the waxed surface of the floor, coming to an abrupt stop at the edge of the maroon floor runner and tipping over.

Emily let out a small cry as Mudear's body popped out of the satin-lined casket onto the floor like an ice cube out of a frosty tray and came to rest right at the girls' laps.

They all sat or lay on the mortuary floor in silence. The girls were stunned. They sat quietly together on the funeral parlor floor as they had when they were girls and huddled close between their beads and talked. Only this time, Mudear was with them.

They looked down at their mother, stiff and straight as a little Popsicle. They didn't know what to do. They were afraid to move or cry out for fear of upsetting the delicate balance of the situation. But their dead mother was practically lying in their laps.

Finally, in the soft light of the Light and Shadow Memorial Chapel, Emily reached out and touched Mudear's hand stretched out grotesquely as if pointing to the enormous rip in Emily's new red stockings. She reached out and pulled down Mudear's dress hiked up to her thighs and began to weep softly.

For the first time in their lives since the change, they all looked Mudear directly in the face, and because she didn't insult them or shoo them off, they talked to her. They all spoke from the hurt in their hearts.

"Mudear," Emily began, "you shouldn't have told your own daughter that her face looked like a potato grater. That was wrong. Look, my face cleared up years ago. My skin's as pretty as yours, Mudear."

Annie Ruth, in the middle, sat up on her knees and spoke next.

"Was being free, like you always said, Mudear, was that the most important thing? Being free. Shit, what did that mean? Did it mean you were free to hurt us, your own children, to abandon us? To cut yourself off from the world and put the burden of your survival and ours, too, on us? If it hadn't been for us bringing you the world, you would'na had a life! And you didn't even appreciate it. Even though you were there, you might as well have thrown us away like so much trash. Even women who leave their babies in trash cans must think about them once in a while.

"Did you? Did you ever think of us?"

"No, I can answer that," Betty cut in, automatically backing up her sister. She sat right at Mudear's face. Annie Ruth looked at her in surprise. Annie Ruth felt seeing Mudear dead and stiff on the floor had changed Betty as it had touched her. "*No.* 'Cause, Mudear, the only person you ever thought of was yourself, the only person. And Mudear, that was wrong. God, that was so wrong. 'Cause you can't live in this world like that. Not and not crush everything you breathe on and touch and claim to love or give birth to.

"I remember how it was for you before, but did you have to go and be like *him?*"

Annie Ruth spoke again.

"Mudear, I don't give a fuck about your freedom. And I know that that don't matter to you 'cause we don't matter to you. But look at you now, Mudear, you dead and gone and free, I guess. But look at what you left us all here with. You left us here with all your garbage to tote around."

"Don't you have anything to say, Em-Em?" Betty reached across Annie Ruth and asked. Emily hadn't stopped weeping since she touched Mudear's stiff hand.

"I just always wanted a mama," Emily said softly and broke into sobs again.

Annie Ruth reached beside her and took both her sisters' clasped hands.

"I know you wish you could just reach up out of death and slap our faces, Mudear," Annie Ruth said. "Slap 'em the way you slapped Betty when she told you about Emily running off to get married. I can feel you wanting to slap me. To tell the truth, I wish you would, wish you could. 'Cause, God, Mudear, I don't want this to be the end. Can't it be better than this? I think it can."

At the memory of Mudear's hot handprint on her face, tears began to well up in Betty's eyes, too. When she had walked into the chapel and seen Annie Ruth leaning on Mudear's casket, she had thought it was the most sacrilegious thing she had ever seen. But now, with Mudear stretched out in front of them like one of those hard plastic life-sized colored dolls they sold when she was a girl, just a corpse like every other human that had to face death, the idea of Mudear didn't seem so sacred to Betty anymore. She picked up where her sisters had left off.

"It was Annie Ruth's idea, Mudear. But we all came down here to tell you we gonna *make* it better than this. Starting right now, we came down here to tell you that we know we crazy, like all of Mulberry think the Lovejoys are. But now we gonna work on happy and peaceful and appreciative and joyful." Betty looked at Annie Ruth and smiled a bit. "After being with you for forty years, we got being a 'ranting, raving maniac' down pat. Now, we want to move on."

Annie Ruth smiled back and continued. "So, we gonna put you in the ground tomorrow, Mudear. And we're gonna try and bury a lot of pain and hurt and being mad with you.

"We probably won't be able to do it all at one time. We can't stop being the way we are overnight. But we gonna work on it. I'm gonna work real hard the next eight or so months 'cause, Mudear, I'm pregnant. I may not know who the father is, I may have to wait until it come out to see who it favors, and I may not even tell Delbert or any of them they could be the father. But I tell you one thing, Mudear. I sure as hell am gonna be a mother."

Then, at the thought of motherhood and the idea that her

body was going to be swelling soon like Mudear's did with her three pregnancies, Annie Ruth began to cry, too.

"That's about all what we had to say, Mudear," Betty concluded, with tears rolling off her face. "We gonna put you in the ground tomorrow. I'm sorry for you that you won't have some good old friend stand and raise a prayer for you or one to raise a hymn for you. But you cut all those folks off just like you cut us off."

Betty tried to pull her sisters over into her arms, but she couldn't hold them tightly enough to ease the moaning and crying they had all fallen into. So, she reached down and pulled Mudear's body closer and nestled the dead woman's head in the soft silk of her royal blue skirt.

Then, their loud mourning took another step and their wails became keens, high-pitched and wounded sounding like animals. Their teardrops fell on Mudear's face, her breasts, her arms, her stomach, her thighs like the sprinkle of baptismal water, but it brought no healing relief for the girls.

"The Lovejoy women are having a hard time, huh?" Emily asked as all of them sat on the floor rocking each other with Mudear's stiff body lying across their laps, their faces streaked with makeup and tears.

Betty looked at Emily, then at all the Lovejoy women stretched out on the floor, and said, "Um-huh."

"Mudear, too?" Emily asked.

Betty looked down at Mudear's head and noticed for the first time nappy little balls of gray hair at the nape of her neck. The silvery pepper pods stood out in stark relief against the brown skin of her neck.

"Mudear, too, Em-Em," Betty replied.

And they all reached down to touch Mudear again: Betty her face, Annie Ruth her tight-looking breasts, Emily her bare legs and feet. Without consulting each other Betty began.

"Mudear, you remember that pink flowered bed jacket that disappeared a long time ago, your favorite bed jacket you swore someone snuck in the house and stole. I tore it up and burned it in the backyard."

Emily then took her turn.

"When I was nine or ten, Mudear, I used to pray that you would die so we would get a new mama."

Annie Ruth was last.

"When I first moved to L.A., I told people there that you *already were* dead."

They were silent again.

"She's so little," Annie Ruth said to her sisters in surprise. "Damn, does a person have to die, have to be in a casket before you can really see what size they are?"

Betty reached over and tried to smooth down her mother's stiff hair. "She used to say, 'I'm not selfish. People just think that because I'm short.' I think it was something that she used to say when she was a girl, flirting, maybe. She didn't say it much after the change, though. I hadn't thought about it in years. She just stopped saying it."

Then, they were silent again. They thought and thought, but there didn't seem to be anything else to say.

Suddenly, they realized that they could hear the faint sounds of organ music and for the first time since Mudear fell out of her coffin they thought to look around them.

There was a crowd at the door. Poppa stood at the front and looked at all the Lovejoy women sprawled on the floor of the chapel, their arms and legs and purse straps and high heels entangled.

Seeing them there together made tears come to his eyes. These girls always did belong to Mudear, he thought.

The girls looked up at their father dressed in his dark-blue Sunday suit as if they had been caught grave-robbing. He sort of raised his hand as if in greeting, then, he turned to go look for one of the Parkinson boys to help lift his wife's body back into her coffin.

But he had to practically fight his way down the hall. It seemed that half the town—the mourners from the two services across the hall, the staff of the mortuary, the florist from next door delivering arrangements, the organists, even one of the ministers who had just preached a funeral—was standing behind him trying to look over his shoulder for a peek at the Lovejoy women, together for the last time.

CHAPTER 33

I cannot believe how many people there are jammed into this little memorial room for my services this morning! There must be ninety-five, a hundred people in here. I'm not surprised at some of these folks here. Even though Carrie and I stopped speaking a year or so ago—now what did I say to her that made her so mad? I can't recall—I figured she'd be here. And the folks from Betty's shops, I expected. But look at Effie over there, the big heifer, sitting up there with her whole family. She never did like me. I think she's even fatter than she used to be. I'm in so much better shape than these big-assed, no-exercising women I used to know in East Mulberry. And look at Agnes. Good God, hasn't she got old and ugly. Now, who is that woman with the black and white polka-dot dress on? I don't think I recognize her.

Lord, people will come out when they think they gon' see a show. Bet they thought it was gonna be an open casket. They shoulda come yesterday if they really wanted to see something: my dead body dressed in this ugly navy blue dress sprawled out in the middle of the floor with my girls standing over me acting crazy.

My girls do look nice today, though, don't they? That's a beautiful black wool suit Emily has on even though she ought to know better than to be wearing slacks to a funeral. And that designer knit skirt is pulling mighty tight 'cross Annie Ruth's butt and stomach under that long georgette jacket. But they all look right nice. I always did like Betty in that black silk suit with the long wide skirt. And that cream-colored blouse with all those baby pearl buttons down the front is just the right touch.

Nobody can't say I didn't teach my girls how to dress. And how to carry themselves. Ain't got to say one time to any of 'em to pull up their chins and look to the stars today. Lots of women woulda been too ashamed after the way they behaved yesterday in this funeral home to show their faces around here.

I'm glad the girls or somebody had the good sense to take a pair of shears from the shed out back and cut some of my flowers to put around this place for my memorial services. That big vase of delphiniums is striking. I wonder which of the girls arranged it. But who let those funeral home floral arrangements in here? I hate those things. There's a broken wheel with white and yellow carnations. Corny. Must be from Carrie. And I guess they can't have a funeral without one or two of those bleeding hearts. Red and white carnations. Don't these florists know 'bout nothing but carnations? Well, there's a spray of white roses at least, but they don't have any scent. Uh, store-bought refrigerated roses. That bunch of poppies and larkspur and all kinds of wildflowers from the front of the house by itself put all these others to shame. Now, what's that one supposed to be? It looks like a sheet of lavender chrysanthemums edged in golden ones. What is it? A book? A closed book? A closed book? Is that supposed to be funny? Well, at least there's nothing that says "Rest in Peace." I wonder if they even use that anymore written on banners draped across a floral arrangement. "R. I. P." or "We Loved Her but Jesus Loved Her Better."

Look at Annie Ruth sitting there with her hand resting on her stomach.

Does she really think she or any of my girls are ever gonna be "free" of me? Especially now that she's gonna have a girl of her own?

Right, like I'm gonna let her bring up that child without me hovering over. Especially now that I got all eternity with nothing to do unless somebody hand me a garden fork or a remote control sometime soon.

Humph, those girls don't know me at all. Or themselves! Now they think they free women 'cause they think they got me told. Humph, getting mad is just the first step.

What's old Ernest getting up for? Don't tell me he gon' give my eulogy! He don't know nothing about public speaking. Hell, he don't know nothing 'bout me!

Well, that wasn't bad. "Esther Lovejoy's life spoke for itself." Well, that ain't bad at all. "Esther Lovejoy's life spoke for itself." And he had enough sense to get up, stand up tall, say his piece, and sit his butt back down.

Now, here come that little Parkinson boy. He think so much of the Lovejoy women, I better watch out he don't sneak his hand up in this casket. Oh, he has an announcement. "Will the family and mourners please proceed to the cars."

What? That's it? They're not gonna read something from the Bible? Like "Where your treasure is buried, so is your heart." Or "The humble shall be exalted when the exalted are humbled." Not even "Jesus wept"?

Ain't nobody gonna stand and sing a heartbreaking solo like "Take My Hand, Precious Lord"? No music?

Well, I guess it is more dignified this way. Actually, I kinda liked it.